CW00386478

Crit

CJ Wood

Other books by CJ Wood in this series are available in paperback, eBook or Kindle Unlimited online at Amazon UK:

County Lines (Part 1.)

There comes a time to batten down the hatches and choose those you trust very carefully. Jason Hamilton's criminal drug dealing operation has made him a successful, powerful, wealthy man. As the head of a Manchester Organised Crime Group, he is ruthless, violent and feared by his enemies and associates alike. An unexpected sequence of events leads to betrayal, suspicion and paranoia within his firm. Cracks began to appear—internal feuds fuelled by jealousy, revenge and paranoia of police informants. To make matters worse, the Drugs Squad is also taking an interest in his activities. He has always kept his friends close, but his enemies closer ... now he's not sure which is which... events start to spiral out of control. Can Hamilton turn this around, or is it the beginning of his demise?

Crossed Lines (Part 2.)

The criminal code is there for a reason… cross the line at your peril.
'Crossed Lines' is the sequel to 'County Lines', the page-turning crime-fiction drama by CJ Wood.

Following his failed attempt to murder a rogue associate, Jason Hamilton wound up incarcerated in Strangeways, HMP Manchester. But doing time is just an occupational hazard for Hamilton. He has the reputation and tenacity to cope well inside. Also, he isn't planning on staying long …

Driven by revenge against the undercover cop who nicked him, Hamilton has to decide whether he can trust his organised crime group associates and bent solicitor Frank Burton or whether he needs to take matters into his own hands.

Meanwhile, DI Andrea Statham is determined to crack two murder cases, and all the clues lead back to Hamilton. Now she's watching and waiting for his next move?

But will Hamilton's next move be the last line he crosses … or will he succeed?

Disclaimer

This book is a complete work of fiction. Names, characters, places, businesses, events and other content are the product of the author's imagination. Any resemblance to actual persons, living or deceased, is coincidental.

For Lucy & Chloe

1

Detective Inspector Andrea Statham suddenly realised her mind had wandered elsewhere and re-focused her attention back to the moment, resuming eye contact with the Detective Constable sitting opposite her. It was 2:00 a.m., six hours into her twelve-hour night shift. She was senior detective duty cover for the annual political party conference, being hosted at a hotel in Manchester. Struggling to stay awake, she fought the temptation to close her eyes and sleep.

Detective Constable Bob Levy wasn't making things any easier for her either. He was briefing Andrea in his trademark monotone delivery, chapter and verse. A couple of sentences would have sufficed. Bob informed her that a conference delegate had reported the theft of her security pass whilst she had been out drinking in the city. The theft of a security pass, a minor problem, was laboured with far too much detail. Andrea's eyes strayed to the CCTV screens whilst Bob's words formed a distant hum. Brevity wasn't one of his strong points. 'Just cancel the identity card and ensure the circulation list is updated by security staff,' Andrea suggested when Bob eventually paused for breath.

In her earlier years in the Force, Andrea used to relish the night shifts. Those dark hours were prime time for the more serious criminal offences. Catching thieves, burglars in the act and other serious crimes was the real essence of policing back then, a thrill that defined what the job was all about. She used to get by effortlessly with just a few hours of sleep the following day. But not anymore, and being more health-conscious these days made her feel more uneasy about night shifts. She was aware of scientific research findings that suggested working nights could reduce life expectancy and negatively affect the body's circadian rhythm.

Earlier in the day, she had politely declined an email invitation from the Deputy Chief Constable to start her shift early to meet and greet the visiting politicians and other dignitaries. The Prime Minister's visit to the Command Centre was an event she had been more than happy to miss. Andrea gave mutual back-slapping meetings between the Force hierarchy and politicians a wide berth at all costs; it wasn't her cup of tea.

It was the last day of the Party Conference in Manchester. Andrea looked forward to completing her Conference Command Centre duties as Investigative lead and resuming her usual work with the Serious Crime Division.

*

Detective Sergeant Pete Higgs was also in Manchester city centre that night, at his favourite casino. An independent establishment tucked away off the beaten track. He liked the contrast of the place, compared with the upmarket casinos in the city centre frequented by the well-heeled and in-crowds.

The casino was shabby and slightly worn around the edges, looking at it through rose-tinted glasses, creating an unpretentious feel. The dim overhead lighting pulled together an intimate ambience, casting a warm glow over the tables and slot machines.

Head slumped, face down, resting on the backs of his hands at the roulette table. Pete had taken solace here following things going belly-up at the blackjack and poker tables earlier, taking financial hits he couldn't afford.

He suddenly felt a stranger's hand take a firm grip on his upper arm. Instinctively, in his drunken state, he lashed out to free his arm, but the imposter's grip tightened. He was in no fit state to launch a counter-attack. The cacophony of noise helped to bring him around from his drunken stupor, the clatter of chips, the winning jingles and coins cascading from the slot machines, laughter and excited chatter.

'Time for a break, Sir. Come on, stand up,' ordered the black-clad security guard. The croupier and other players at the table paused the game momentarily, looking on uncomfortably at the events unfolding before them, avoiding eye contact with the drunk.

'Get your hands off me. I'm leaving anyway,' Pete slurred. He knew he'd had too much to drink and felt vulnerable while struggling to get to his feet. The grip on his arm tightened as the security guard led him across the gaming floor towards the exit. Pete felt the urge to resist, but it took all of his effort to stand up and stay upright, let alone fight back. He leaned on the security guard for support as he escorted him away from the table.

Pete reached out and tried to grab the rail of the bar as they passed. Drinkers appeared to clock the danger, stepping aside and turning their backs on him to avoid getting dragged into the fracas. The bartenders continued serving drinks without flinching at the events unfolding before them; they'd seen it all before. 'Just one more drink before I go,' Pete pleaded, 'I'll be no trouble; I just want a drink. I'm a regular here; the owner is a personal friend of mine.'

'Like you've not had enough already, no chance,' the security guard said, catching his colleague's eye with a knowing look and smile.

Pete suddenly took stock of the situation and experienced a surge of energy. He swung a punch at the security guard. His fist connected with the security guard's jaw, a decent effort. The security guard let go of Pete's arm, trying to maintain his balance and composure as he staggered back. His colleague stepped forward with purpose and punched Pete hard in the face, sending him crashing backwards into a collision with a woman playing the nearby slot machine. The woman had no time to react and fell to the floor, her plastic cup of coins spilling everywhere. Pete landed on top of her before rolling over to make a pathetic attempt at finding his feet. Blood was spilling from his nose and lip.

The security guards roughly dragged him to his feet and unceremoniously frog-marched him towards the door. This time they weren't taking any chances, restraining him with arm locks. 'I'll have your fucking jobs for that; you don't know who you're dealing with here,' Pete shouted.

The middle-aged woman in the glittery party dress was helped to her feet by her concerned friend, who was struggling to manoeuvre in her high heels, whilst a member of staff began gathering up her scattered coins. She looked shocked and immediately took her phone and made a call, 'Police, please,' she said before the member of staff had the chance to intervene and cajole her from reporting the matter. The police visiting the casino didn't go down well with management. Staff were encouraged to resolve any incidents in-house.

On reaching the privacy of the fire exit corridor, the door automatically swung closed behind them; the corridor was cold, damp, and deserted. There were no witnesses here. The security guard, with a sore jaw, pushed Pete to the floor. 'Right, it's payback time, you bastard.' He kicked

Pete in the ribs and was lining up a second when his colleague intervened, pulling him back.

'Leave it, he's one of Wayne Davies's men.'

'No, he's a cop,' he replied, taking another forceful kick into Pete's abdomen, breathing heavily with the exertion. Pete groaned, curling into a protective ball to deflect further blows.

'That's enough. We don't want to piss off Wayne Davies. Let's get him outside; he's not worth it. I'm sure I heard the old girl phoning the cops; we need to be quick and get him out of here.' They scooped Pete up and dragged him to the door.

The security guy pushed the fire exit bar with his free arm, and the door swung open, banging into the exterior wall with a clatter. Pete was ejected with a forceful shove and shivered as the cold air instantly enveloped him. He stumbled precariously across the pavement, reaching out for a signpost to steady him.

'Where's my jacket?' Pete demanded defiantly as the security guard dusted himself down.

'You weren't wearing a jacket, you prick. And don't bother coming back, you're barred.'

'Watch your mouth dickhead. You've not heard the last of this,' Pete retorted as the door slammed shut behind him, leaving him suddenly alone on the pavement. The alleyway was dark, but for the intermittent light cast from the vintage-looking neon sign flashing above the casino door.

He stumbled a few yards, using the wall for support, and felt a rush of panic. He patted his pocket, a sudden alarm gripping him. The feeling was instantly replaced by relief as he felt the reassuring presence of his wallet, still safely tucked away. Losing his warrant card and credit cards was the last thing he needed.

He remained slumped against the wall, seeking its support, while he concentrated on taking deep breaths to steady himself. His dark blue shirt concealed the blood flowing from his mouth and nose. He wiped his face gingerly with his forearm.

The frigid air was sharp and cutting, but he knew that sobering up would require much more than a bit of fresh air. A group of revellers strolled past him, huddling together to shield themselves from the cold. They barely glanced at the drunken guy struggling to stay on his feet. A sight which was not out of the ordinary at this time of night.

He looked to his left and watched with horror as a police van approached and parked near the casino reception. The last thing he needed now was to be arrested; Andrea Statham would love to hear that news, proving her right that Pete was a liability to the Force. He watched as the two young uniformed police officers entered the casino. Taking his chance, he staggered away to make himself scarce.

Pete found a doorway and allowed himself to slide down the wall and take up a crouching position. He closed his eyes and tried to sleep, but it was too cold. He took out his mobile phone; he needed help, somewhere to stay again.

The security guards made their way back into the casino, laughing and making light of the incident. 'VIP guest, he knows the owner, you know.'

'Maybe we should have laid out the red carpet before booting him out, eh?'

One continued to the security room to ensure there was no footage of the incident on the hard drive by the time the police arrived whilst nursing his injured jaw. It always seemed to be the case after such incidents that there were faults with the casino security camera systems.

The other guard approached the group of staff, tending to the woman in the party dress and supported the manager in persuading her not to pursue the matter with the police. She finally agreed, having accepted complimentary drinks and slot machine tokens as a goodwill gesture.

*

DI Statham inhaled hard on her cigarette; the glow of the burning tobacco momentarily lit up her face in the darkness of the dingy 'smoker's corner'. She savoured the nicotine hit whilst surveying the murky shadows of the police headquarters car park, soaking up the tranquillity of the twilight hours but fighting guilt for being weak-willed and succumbing to smoking during the night shifts, breaking her year of abstinence.

The ringtone of her mobile phone broke her moment of peace and guilty pleasure. Andrea's heart sank when she saw the caller's identity on the screen; she considered declining the call for a moment but knew she would only delay the inevitable conversation.

'Christ, Pete, do you know what time it is?'

'Andrea, I'm sorry to wake you up. I need a lift from town. Can I kip on your sofa? I don't like asking, but I'm desperate. I've nowhere to go.' Pete's voice was slurred. Andrea regretted answering the call. Her patience with Pete of late was running thin. His behaviour was erratic. Andrea suspected he was getting too close to Wayne Davies's organised crime gang members to the extent that she now questioned his credibility and allegiance to the job.

'I can't, Pete; I'm at work. It's too busy for me to get away,' she responded, thankful for the legitimate excuse.

'Besides, it wouldn't look good if you stayed at my place. What would Rachel make of it? I reckon she'd go ballistic. And I'm not getting dragged into your divorce proceedings as the other woman, especially when I'm not the other woman. You need to get a grip and sort yourself out. I'll transfer you thirty quid to get a taxi to one of your mates.' She knew Pete had been sofa surfing since the split with his wife and guessed he'd find somewhere tonight.

'I'm not after your money. It's good to know who your true mates are, though. Leave it with me; I wouldn't want to put you out.'

Andrea felt a guilty relief when he hung up on her. He was no longer the trusted colleague he had once been since the Jason Hamilton case. His conduct during the investigation and subsequent hostage-taking incident had raised Andrea's suspicions that he was up to no good. She had tried to help him with hand-outs for old times' sake. But he wasn't helping himself; he was in self-destruct mode. She stubbed her cigarette on the wall-mounted tin box and threw the empty packet into the bin. She was back on the patches; no more smoking.

*

Pete Higgs stumbled to his feet and staggered to the nearby taxi rank. He closed the door of the black cab behind him and fell back in the welcoming, comfortable leather seat, soothed by the instant intense warmth inside the vehicle.

The driver looked over his shoulder at him wearily, like he'd been here before, 'If you throw up, there's a cleaning charge. Money up-front, pal, or we're going nowhere.' Pete rummaged in his trouser pocket and handed the driver his last twenty through the gap in the clear plastic security screen.

'That's all I've got. There's more than enough there. So don't be trying it on, I know what you dodgy fuckers are like.' Pete gave his destination, leaned back and gazed out of the window as the taxi driver set off, shaking his head.

A scruffy-looking bearded guy was sitting, leaning against a shop front, a takeaway container on the pavement beside him containing a few donated coins. The guy's dire circumstances resonated with a realistic fear of doom in Pete's mind; he felt a shiver as he turned away.

The illuminated shop fronts and signs flashed by before being replaced by tall modern glass-fronted apartment and office block buildings. Topped by the red glow of aviation obstruction lighting, brightly contrasted against the dark sky.

The taxi stopped in a queue of red tail lights at a junction. Pete watched as revellers wrapped up in their own stories made their way along the pavement in groups dressed obliviously to the cold. The darkness once again prevailed over the electric glow and vibrancy of the city until they reached the Victorian railway arches. Pete glanced into the dim-lit tunnel of one of the railway arches; the working girls were out in their numbers, plying for trade to the drivers of cars passing slowly through the tunnel. A moment of temptation was washed away with the realisation that he had no cash left.

'Wake up, mate. We're here,' The driver announced, sounding keen to get rid of his drunken fare. Pete awoke and leant forward, almost losing his balance, falling into the street. He stumbled the short distance to the front door of the red brick building and let himself in, tripping on the doorstep. He slowly ascended the stairs, maintaining a tight grip on the handrail for support. Once inside, he crashed out on the familiar red leather Chesterfield sofa. These days he couldn't afford to be too fussy about where he got his head down.

2

'Christ, Pete, it smells rancid in here. Worse, in fact,' Frank Burton bellowed on entering his office the following morning.

DS Pete Higgs slowly woke up and watched bleary-eyed as Frank Burton struggled to open the decrepit wooden sash window. Although Pete struggled to tolerate the interruption of his sleep, he was thankful that Frank appeared to be in a good mood and wasn't angry with him for dossing down in his office again. Pete still felt pissed; his mouth was bone dry. 'Sorry, Frank, I had somewhere else lined up, but a so-called mate let me down at the last minute. He got lucky and disappeared with a woman. I'll make us some coffee,' Pete croaked, getting up from the sofa and wincing at the pain emanating from his ribs, which rekindled flashbacks of him getting kicked out of the casino.

Frank lit a cigarette and watched Pete slowly lift himself from the sofa.

'I've asked Wayne to sort you out with some temporary accommodation. It'll be better than sleeping in my office. You can't go on like this, Pete.'

'That would be great, Frank, as long as it's not in some shit-hole housing estate.' Pete was well aware of the usual standard of housing stock the gang used for drug dealing, predominantly in no-go areas. But the cold reality was something he had to swallow, a bitter pill in a life of hard knocks. Ever since Rachel, his wife, had shown him the door, Pete found himself at the mercy of Frank and a handful of other associates for somewhere to get his head down. She'd had enough of his behaviour from drug-taking, drinking and gambling, and Pete couldn't blame her. He accepted she was right. Rachel and the kids came first, and they deserved better. To Pete's shame, he accepted he had let them down massively.

'Far from it, Pete,' Frank intoned with a sly smile, 'he's built up an impressive property portfolio since taking over the business from Jason. He'll probably call in a favour or two in return, though.'

Pete didn't feel the need to acknowledge Frank's last comment. Nor take issue with Frank's sly smile. He had reluctantly accepted his precarious relationship with Wayne Davies's organised crime group and knew it didn't come without expectations. But, unfortunately for him, he'd crossed the line, and they now had dirt on him in the form of his criminal activity. He couldn't afford any slip-ups, especially with DI Andrea Statham watching him like a hawk, increasingly suspicious of his conduct.

'Are you not supposed to be at work today?' Frank inquired, sitting down at his desk.

Pete sensed he'd overstayed his welcome. 'I'm going to work a late shift. The gaffer knows about my marriage break-up; he's giving me slack with flexible duties and extra overtime to help with my debts. Pete blew into his coffee and looked towards Frank; no compassion was forthcoming.

'I'm guessing you hit the casino again last night?' Frank asked knowingly after exhaling smoke towards the window. 'Did you get into a spot of bother, too?' Frank continued while scrutinizing Pete's face, 'It looks like you picked the wrong fight.'

'I need help, Frank; I'm going to contact the welfare department at work and get some counselling or something sorted out,' Pete said despondently, looking towards the floor.

'It wouldn't be such a problem if you had the occasional win, but you're always too pissed to play,' Frank said before taking a long drag of his cigarette. He placed the cigarette in the ashtray and shuffled his papers, fully focused on reading a court brief in preparation for a case the following day.

Pete laughed, conscious that he was overstaying his welcome. 'I'll have a wash and be on my way; I can see you're busy, pal.' He knocked back the remainder of his coffee.

Frank looked up from reading his legal papers. 'Extremely busy Peter, one of Wayne's boys, has just been charged with dealing; the police seized all his cash and his drugs stash. The police must have received a tip-off; their timing was too good to be a coincidence. I will need you to run some intelligence checks for me and maybe, get rid of some evidence. This guy is central to the operation; Wayne wants to keep him out of prison.'

Pete felt a wave of paranoia. Does Frank think I'm the grass? He closed the washroom door and looked at his reflection in the mirror. The black bags under his eyes looked ugly, and his face looked puffy. His nose cleaned up well, but the cut on his lip looked a mess. He felt engulfed by dread on hearing Frank's last request. What a shambles, he lamented. There's no quick fix; I'll have to go with it. I've done okay up to now, he affirmed to himself. Pete splashed more water onto his face, confident that he could handle Wayne Davies and his boys. He needed to keep his nerve and keep going; feeling sorry for himself wasn't an option, although a little more compassion from Frank would have been appreciated.

'Right, I'm out of here, Frank. Thanks for letting me kip on your sofa,' Pete said as he approached the office door.

'Before you go, I've just spoken to Wayne. He's sorted a place for you to move into; here's the address. Meet him there at three o'clock today.' Frank slid a piece of paper across the desk.

Pete picked it up and noted the address, 'Not bad, that can't have been cheap.'

'Wayne looks after his boys, Pete.' Frank said, looking up from his papers.

'I know, but the pound of flesh he'll expect in return concerns me.'

'Beggars can't be choosers, Pete. You need to sort yourself out; don't become a liability. Wayne won't tolerate it.'

Pete stopped in his tracks and swung around, 'Liability, what the hell is that supposed to mean, Frank?' he snapped instinctively. 'You'd have been fucked without me helping you out lately.'

'As I said, Peter, sort yourself out. Maybe start with ditching the alcohol for a while and staying away from casinos, perhaps refraining from getting involved in bar brawls, too. We don't carry passengers,' Frank said without lifting his gaze from the document he was reading.

Pete shook his head in disbelief, 'Christ, Frank, kick a man whilst he's down, why don't you.' Slamming the door behind him, Pete stomped off down the stairs, seething. Although he knew Frank was talking sense. Pete didn't want to hear it spelt out like that. Walking to his car, mulling over his current predicament, wasn't easy. He was used to being in control. By the time he reached his car, he had cooled down and was beginning to regret kicking off with Frank, a bad move. He grabbed his phone and scrolled through the contacts.

'What now, Pete? What part of, I'm busy, don't you understand?' Frank asked.

Pete bit his lip and held back from what he really wanted to say, 'Sorry, Frank, just an apology for my outburst. I know you've got my back and appreciate it.'

'Apology accepted; can I get back to my work now?' Frank hung up.

'You arrogant bastard, fuck off,' Pete said aloud, then checked his phone in a panic, fearing Frank was still on the line. You won't speak to me like that once I've finished using you, Pete brooded; Frank was just a means to an end for him, to be discarded at the earliest opportunity.

Later the same day, Pete arrived at the apartment earlier than anticipated and parked up, waiting for Wayne to arrive. He kicked himself for not using his time more wisely. He should have called for some food. Or perhaps it was better he hadn't; Pete was self-conscious of the weight he was piling on because of all the junk food and takeaways he was eating. He looked at his watch for the third time in twenty minutes. It was twenty past three. He felt anxious, his fingers drumming on the steering wheel; he doubted that Wayne would show up and was about to leave and address his hunger pangs and rumbling stomach when a black SUV crawled ominously into the car park and stopped near the entrance door of the apartment building. Pete watched as Wayne Davies stepped out of the car and walked to the door, not showing any acknowledgement of Pete's presence. Davies walked with a confident swagger: his slim athletic physique and designer clothes gave the image of a successful businessman, which rankled Pete whenever they met.

'Do you want this place or not?' Wayne shouted over his shoulder as he reached the door, sorting out a bunch of keys, not even looking towards Pete.

Don't rise to it. Keep calm, Pete affirmed to himself, resisting the urge to retort. Instead, he walked over and followed Wayne into the building. He struggled to keep up as Wayne leapt the stairs two at a time to the second floor. 'You're not even out of breath,' Pete said, as they reached the door of number six, whilst trying hard to suppress his laboured deep breathing. Wayne looked back at him disdainfully. 'Maybe losing some weight would help you.' Pete immediately regretted trying to engage Wayne in friendly small talk.

They entered the flat, a typical new build, with light grey walls and slate-coloured laminate flooring. No previous occupants, Pete guessed as he looked around at the new fixtures and fittings.

'Frank tells me your wife has thrown you out,' Wayne gloated, 'Finally seen sense as she?'

'For the record, I left. Anyway, thanks for sorting me out with this place,' Pete said, changing the subject. Listening to Wayne talking about his family unsettled him; it made him feel vulnerable. He needed to keep the two worlds well apart.

'No need to thank me. It's a favour for Frank, not you. It's never sat well with me, working with a bent cop. We should have ditched you back into the sewer with the other rats long ago.'

Try as he might, Pete couldn't hold back from Wayne's latest poke at him, 'That's rich, coming from you… a fucking small-time drug dealer.' Pete's body tensed as the words came out.

'Don't push your luck, fat boy, you bent bastard,' Wayne snarled, stepping forward, going toe to toe with Pete,

'You're living on borrowed time as it is.' Wayne sniffed in an exaggerated manner. 'I think you should try the shower. Your personal hygiene is fucking horrendous.' Wayne threw the door keys onto the floor by Pete's feet and headed for the door. Pete bent down to pick them up. He didn't see any point in continuing a row with Wayne, not just yet, anyway. He felt humiliated and downtrodden after Wayne's last remark and walked over to the kitchen, relieved to find a washing machine.

3

DI Andrea Statham felt a knot of guilt in her stomach as she strode away from the inconspicuous grey office block nestled in the heart of the anonymous business park on the outskirts of Manchester. The sun felt warm on her face as it peeked through the clouds, casting mottled shadows on the pavement, instantly cheering her mood, albeit the threat of rain remained likely.

Meeting with Detective Superintendent Samuel at the Counter Corruption Unit had a way of unsettling her. Making a referral in relation to her suspicions about DS Higgs, to the CCU had not been easy. But with every step she took, a reassuring sense of clarity washed over her, convincing her that she had done the right thing.

Through his actions, Pete Higgs left her with no choice. She was convinced that it was only a matter of time before Pete's unscrupulous behaviour caught the keen eye of the force hierarchy. She felt she had perhaps expedited the inevitable, aiming for the least amount of fallout – damage limitation.

She drove the short distance to meet Detective Sergeant Lee McCann at their favourite café, a quaint premises with washed wood interiors. They served quality coffee and cakes, located off the beaten track, hidden away from unwanted attention. Lee's obsession with cloak-and-dagger secrecy amused her; no doubt remnants of behavioural habits picked up from his days as an undercover officer.

The rich scent of ground coffee greeted her. 'I've got you a cappuccino,' Lee announced as Andrea chose a seat in a private cosy corner.

Sighing, Andrea said, 'I'm ready for it, thanks, Lee. I've not re-adjusted from the night shifts yet; I'm convinced they are not good for your health, especially as you get older.' Andrea took a sip of coffee and relaxed back into her chair.

'Have you done the dirty deed?' Lee asked mischievously with a smirk.

'I have,' she began, her tone sober, 'but the Corruption Unit has bigger fish to fry; limited resources and other investigations mean they do not have the capacity to take the job on. Superintendent Samuel said it's not a priority, but they will keep a watching brief for developments. I was surprised at his decision; someone with Pete's knowledge and experience could do the force a lot of damage.'

Lee paused, swirling his coffee thoughtfully. 'Well, you've done your bit. You've informed Samuel of your suspicions; the ball's in his court now. Look, I've known Pete for a while now; sure, he has always sailed close to the wind. Call it what you will; old-fashioned coppering or bordering on noble cause corruption. I'd be surprised if he's gone corrupt. I can't see him being in anybody's pocket. He's probably playing them along for the intelligence he gets in return. He's always been his own man and done things his way, and he tends to get the results, too.'

Andrea's brow knitted in frustration; She considered her suspicions to be more than just circumstantial. She wondered why Lee didn't see it. Was his judgement impaired by the opinion that Pete saved his life at the hostage siege? 'I wish you were right, Lee, but that doesn't convince me. I think Pete turned up at your apartment to help Jason Hamilton escape. Saving you was just... a convenient cover for him.'

'Maybe so; I can't rule that out yet. But Pete put himself at risk to rescue me; that was no act, I can tell you. Hamilton was genuinely shocked and angry to see him and gave him a proper kicking. I could see real fear in Pete's eyes. I was in no doubt that Hamilton's intention was to kill me. At one point, I thought he would kill Pete as well; if they were acting in cahoots, they hid it well. Surrounded by the cops, Hamilton had run out of options; he was like a cornered animal. Whatever Pete Higgs said to him worked, it saved my life.'

'Well, maybe Pete entered the building to help Hamilton escape, and rescuing you was a collateral benefit?'

'I'm not too sure. There's no doubt he's a maverick, but corrupt? I can't see it. I understand your concerns, but it's a big accusation. I'll keep an open mind for now; I owe it to him.'

Their conversation lapsed into an uneasy silence, each immersed in their thoughts. Andrea knew that Lee's opinion was blurred because he genuinely believed Pete Higgs had been his saviour. Maybe he held Pete in high regard, some sort of saviour syndrome? Or was he just playing his cards close to his chest for now?

Her voice firm, Andrea broke the silence, 'If the Counter Corruption Unit hasn't got the staff to take on the investigation, we will undertake our own discreet enquiries in the meantime.' She watched carefully for Lee's reaction. 'We can't just stand by and do nothing; that's not what we signed up to do.'

'Well, he's texted me, suggesting we should go out for a pint, so maybe if I get a bit closer, I will get an insight into what he's up to,' Lee replied. It was the response Andrea had wanted to hear; although she felt somewhat troubled at Lee's favourable position on Pete Higgs, she trusted that, in time, Lee would reach the correct conclusion. He was a bright guy and shrewd operator, qualities which attracted her to him. Andrea was in a good place with their relationship; they shared great chemistry, and she loved spending time with him.

'Shall I come too, Lee?' Andrea asked playfully.

'I'd love you to. I don't think Pete would feel the same though,' Lee laughed.

'He probably won't give much away. Especially as he knows we're seeing each other. Just tread carefully; remember it's a social drink, not an operational deployment.'

'Yes, Ma'am, you're the boss,' Lee mocked in response to Andrea stating the obvious.

'Just don't forget it,' Andrea said with a wink.

4

DS Pete Higgs closed the flat door behind him and took a moment to appreciate the quietness of his own space. The flat was clean and tidy, everything in its place. He slid his keys onto the kitchen worktop, grabbed a beer from the freshly stocked fridge and made his way to the living room. He fell back onto the sofa, taking his first gulp from the bottle; it tasted good. The comfort of the sofa helped relax him; this was top-quality furniture. No expense spared; he could get used to this. It had been an exhaustive long shift, cooped up in the back of an uncomfortably hot van on a surveillance operation. He felt drained of energy. It was good to be back somewhere he could call home, in his own space, a welcome change to sofa surfing and condescending lectures from Frank Burton.

Suddenly the subtle vibration of his mobile phone pulled him away from his reprieve. Pete's first instinct was to ignore it, thinking, I'm not answering that. I'm not on-call if the suspect is on the move; someone else can sort it. The thought of spending another minute in the van didn't bear thinking about. He glanced at the display, and a wave of relief washed over him as he realised it wasn't a call from the office.

'Bloody hell, Lee, long time no see. How are you doing, pal?' Pete said, genuinely pleased to receive the call.

'Not bad, mate, I can't complain. I got your text; a beer or two sounds like a great idea. You're right; it's been far too long.'

'What's the excuse? Has Andrea ditched you?' Pete said, letting out a laugh. 'I've heard you two have been getting quite close recently. Will you need to run it by Andrea first to get a pass out?'

'Piss off, mate; we've just been out a few times. A few drinks. Just casual, you know the score. It's early days yet. Anyway, why do you ask, are you jealous?' Lee mocked. 'No longer the golden boy, eh?'

'No-strings? It can't be bad; it's all right for some. I'm persona non grata; she's got a serious downer on me. She sees me as an embarrassment since I split up with Rachel and hit the bottle and tables. But I'm getting back on track; I've got a new flat and kicked the gambling into touch.'

Pete suddenly froze and fell silent; having thought he could hear the sound of movement from the spare bedroom. He could hear Lee asking if he was still there in the background, but he didn't respond. He held his breath and strained to hear, trying to discern the origin of the sound. This time, he was sure; he could hear footsteps in the spare bedroom.

He raised the phone back to his ear, 'Got to go, Lee. I'll call you back.' he whispered. Pete felt a sudden rush of adrenaline, his senses heightened, and he was no longer tired. The feeling of fatigue was replaced by the surge of adrenaline pumping through his veins. He was looking for a makeshift weapon; the empty bottle was the best option in the little time he had to prepare himself. The noise of someone moving around the bedroom continued, getting louder.

Just as he got to his feet, the door opened, and the intruder appeared, wearing a grubby T-shirt and boxer shorts, scratching his head.

Pete no longer felt threatened. He recognised the intruder straight away. 'What the hell are you doing in here?' Pete demanded, a rush of relief making his voice waver. Ryan Young hadn't changed much since Pete had last seen him;

maybe he was looking leaner and now sporting a tanned complexion.

Ryan yawned, placing his hands down the front of his boxers and looking unapologetically at Pete. 'I was getting some Z's until you woke me up. Wayne told me you wouldn't be back here until later. Have you got another beer? I'm gasping, I was well away.' Ryan asked.

'I thought you were living in Spain? Anyway, more to the point, how did you get into my flat?

'Your flat?' Ryan sniggered, 'Don't you mean Wayne's flat? I've got a key, too; I doss down here whenever I want. Maybe Wayne wants me to keep an eye on you?' The smirk on Ryan's face irked Pete.

'You need to hand over the key and do one. I don't need a flatmate, especially one of Jason Hamilton's sidekicks.'

'I can't say I'm so happy about sharing with a bent cop, but it's a needs must for both of us, I guess.' Ryan helped himself to one of Pete's beers from the kitchen. As he walked back to the bedroom, he paused, tossing a barbed comment over his shoulder, 'From what I've heard, you can't afford to be too choosey. You've got yourself into a bit of a mess, haven't you? You need to give alcoholics anonymous a call, you pisshead. From what I've been hearing, taking a beating and getting slung out of casinos isn't a good image. Be a good lad and keep the noise down.' Ryan closed the door behind him, ending the conversation.

Pete was about to go after him to remonstrate but thought better of it and returned to the comfort of the sofa, shaking his head. He needed time to collect his thoughts. Ryan still had the cocky edge and swagger he had displayed at the police station when Pete last saw him and reluctantly cancelled his bail due to lack of evidence of drug dealing. Ryan had also declined Pete's invitation to give evidence against Jason Hamilton on that occasion, relating to the allegation that Hamilton arranged a hitman to kill Ryan, which had, in turn, led to Ryan fleeing to Spain.

Pete lay outstretched on the sofa mulling things over. Why was Ryan back from Spain? Was he now back in the fold following Hamilton's disappearance? Pete understood that Ryan had gone to Spain to keep his head down and avoid further attempts by Jason Hamilton and his crew to kill him.

Whatever the case, the two of them living together wasn't happening. Pete decided he needed to speak to Frank to get things sorted.

The blueish glow from the television bathed the room, illuminating Pete's face. He opened his eyes and looked across the room, realising he'd fallen asleep watching some vacuous TV programme. He was lying on his side, neck twisted at an acute angle against the armrest. He adjusted his position and winced as a pain shot along his neck as he sat up.

He wasn't surprised to see Ryan Young in the armchair opposite but hadn't bargained on seeing Wayne Davies sitting in the other chair. He wondered how long he'd been asleep, but more importantly, how long they'd been sitting in the same room.

Wayne was staring at him with a look of intimidation. 'Look at this, Ryan… Plods finest at your service,' Wayne said, smirking. 'Good of you to wake up and join us.' With a sarcastic toast, he took a swig from his can. 'I need to discuss an errand or two that requires your attention,' Wayne said before taking another drink from his can.

'What time is it?' Pete asked, to neither of them in particular, nonchalantly ignoring the request and trying to mask his unease.

'Just gone nine. You've had a few hours of sleep,' Ryan chimed in before Wayne could respond. 'I'll get you a beer; you look like you need one.' Ryan walked over to the kitchen. Pete noticed that Ryan's tone was friendlier than Wayne's cold detachment.

'You need to start earning your keep; you're not living here rent-free. I want you to stay away from the casino, too. Knocking old ladies over when you're pissed out of your skull isn't the way our firm operates; you're drawing too much attention to yourself for the wrong reasons, which isn't good for business,' Wayne stated, disdainfully, eyeing Pete over the top of his beer.

Ryan handed Pete a beer and returned to his seat. Pete took a long drink and struggled to make himself comfortable due to the pain in his neck. He looked over towards Wayne, who was still staring at him. Pete was in no doubt as to where he stood with Wayne, and he recognised the potential threat. He returned Wayne's stare to show he wasn't intimidated. Pete knew a charm offensive would be wasted on Wayne. Ryan was more likely to be of use as an ally.

'So, where's Hamilton these days?' Pete asked, looking towards Ryan rather than Wayne whilst rubbing his neck, attempting to take control of the conversation and breaking the uncomfortable silence.

Wayne looked over to Ryan, then back to Pete and said, 'None of your business; you are asking too many questions lately for my liking. Do you think we should pat him down, Ryan? The fucker is probably wearing a wire.'

The noise of the intercom buzzing interrupted the conversation. 'Pizza's here,' Ryan said, jumping up and making his way to the door. The silence returned between Wayne and Pete; the tension simmered. Ryan returned and placed the open pizza boxes on the coffee table, 'Tuck in, boys,' he said enthusiastically. Pete didn't hold back and stretched over, taking a piece of the nearest pizza. He sensed that Ryan was trying to be diplomatic to improve the atmosphere but not getting very far. 'This is good,' Pete said, eating the pizza; he noticed Wayne hadn't taken a piece. No doubt because his body was a temple.

'It's from Italiano, next door to The Crown, it's always good food from there,' Ryan said, selecting a second piece.

As the beers flowed, an easier football conversation followed in its wake. Ryan was easy company, but Wayne didn't let his menacing edge drop. It worked. Pete felt uneasy in his presence, although he tried hard not to show it. He didn't fancy his chances against Wayne and worked at avoiding a physical confrontation.

Ryan picked up his phone and read a text from Wayne, '*I've slipped him a Micky Finn.*' He smirked and winked at Wayne. Pete clocked the interaction and felt uneasy, wondering what they were up to; he had an uneasy feeling and needed some space, as far away from Wayne as possible.

'The pizza and beer have finished me off, fellas. I need a kip,' Pete announced, placing his empty can on the table, about to stand up.

'Not yet, we need to talk business,' Wayne instructed, 'I have a package that I want you to deliver for me.' Before Pete could protest, the intercom buzzed once again. Ryan answered the door, and three women entered the flat, following Ryan into the kitchen area. The strong smell of floral perfume wafted over to them, a welcome addition. Wayne continued talking over the noise of excited chatter and laughter spilling into the room. 'The boys will deliver the package to you here. Don't fuck up.' Wayne walked over and joined in the chatter with the women at the breakfast bar.

'There's some prosecco in the fridge, girls; get stuck in,' Ryan offered, casting a lustful eye over the newcomers, helping themselves to drinks.

Pete saw his chance and got to his feet whilst rubbing his neck. 'I'll leave you to it. I feel knackered.' He glanced towards the kitchen and realised no one was listening to him. The three attractive women caught his eye; their party dresses didn't leave much to his imagination. He felt a sudden urge to change his mind and get another beer. But he was experiencing waves of drowsiness and felt dizzy. He suddenly felt out of sorts. He couldn't understand why; he'd only had six or seven beers. Maybe it was the fatigue caused by a tough day or the stress of dealing with Wayne.

'Lightweight,' Wayne muttered whilst watching Pete leave the room. Ryan started to smirk at Wayne's comment.

Pete turned about; it was the female company more than Wayne's sly dig that changed his mind. 'Pass me a beer, Ryan.' Pete took the beer and joined the others leaning on the breakfast bar for support; he was now experiencing hot sweats and feelings of disorientation.

5

Pete Higgs had suffered more than his fair share of severe hangovers over the last few years. But none of them compared with this one. He was caught in a duel between the nauseating gripes in his stomach and the relentless pounding in his head. As he attempted to stand, the room lurched violently, sending him crashing to the floor, his head narrowly missing a collision with the edge of the coffee table.

Attempting to regain some composure, he managed to drag himself back onto the sofa. The world tilted and spun around him, and the sickly aroma of perfume blending with the stench of stale cigarettes threatened to tip his nausea over the edge.

An icy chill raked over his body; he began to shiver. I need to get dressed; where are my clothes? Why the hell am I naked? Fragments of memories started forming but dissipating just as quickly, His mind was in overdrive, trying to fill in the gaps, drinking with Wayne and Ryan, and partying with some women. His mind was racing at speed to establish the facts but failing miserably. He looked towards the kitchen and saw the stacked empty pizza boxes; he remembered eating pizza. Perfume? Empty prosecco glasses? Who were the women? He felt confused and struggled to think straight, let alone remember the details of the night before. He curled up into the fetal position on the sofa. A slumber consumed Pete, pulling him down into its dark depths.

He awoke several hours later; the room was enveloped in darkness. Reaching for his phone, its pale glow provided just enough illumination to paint the room in shades of blue. Drenched in sweat, he rose, feeling marginally better but still thirsting like he'd been cast away in the desert for days. After a cold shower and the task of clearing the remnants of last night's black hole, he felt like he was crawling back to his usual self. The uneasy sensation of dread and anxiety still gnawed at him, though; why had he once again let himself spiral out of control?

Pete glanced around the spare bedroom, relieved not to see Ryan asleep on the bed. He was satisfied that no one else was in the flat with him. He couldn't cope with anyone from the firm right now.

While scanning the rooms, Pete noticed an unfamiliar black holdall on the floor, tucked sneakily under the edge of the bed. He pulled the zip back quickly and revealed four handguns; two Baikal IZH-79s and two Glocks. Pete recognised the pistols, the Baikals being distinctive compact weapons; the go-to choice for gangland criminals; cheap, reliable and accurate. Small enough to fit into the palm of a hand and lightweight, only weighing about two pounds. Perfect for concealment. The pistols, which originated from the Russian Urals, had flooded into the UK underworld weapons market during the early Millennium.

Pete suspected the shrink-wrapped accompaniments were ammunition and silencers. Panicking slightly at the discovery, the thought of being nabbed by the police in possession of these weapons didn't bear thinking about. He used a bed sheet to clean any trace of DNA from the zip puller and pushed the holdall back under the bed. Questions whirled in Pete's mind: Why were these guns here? What was their purpose? He recalled Wayne tasking him with a delivery; No chance gun running was a step too far, he decided. But the haze of the previous night's excess weighed on him, making it hard to delve deeper into the situation.

Pete returned to the sofa seeking his phone. He had decided this was no ordinary hangover; it was time to establish what had happened the night before. He was feeling stupid and guilty for having let his guard down. He scrolled his contacts and punched Wayne's number.

'I was wondering when you would appear from under your stone. Have you recovered from your blowout?' Wayne asked, sneering.

'What did you spike me with, you fucker?'

'Steady on, piss head; making accusations like that could get you into deep trouble. Don't worry; we didn't violate you, sweetheart,' Wayne mocked with a sinister tone.

Pete was irritable and struggling to tolerate Wayne's jibes. He rubbed his temple with his free hand. 'What's your game, Wayne? What is it you are trying to achieve here? Why are you constantly fucking with me?'

'Calm down. It was just a bit of fun. Like you enjoying sex with the underage girl last night, you fucking nonce.' Wayne's tone was menacing and followed up with silence.

Pete felt a knot in the pit of his stomach, and fear enveloped him with the realisation that Wayne had set him up. Something about the girl rang true in his subconscious, incomplete recollections of a naked woman sitting astride on him swirled around in his mind, but he still struggled to process the memory blanks.

Wayne continued, 'You've gone quiet, Peter. I've got photos to remind you if you don't believe me. Not the kind of shit you'd want your family or bosses at work to see.' His voice was quiet with a sinister edge.

'You're blagging me; she wasn't underage.' Pete tried hard to remember the women at the flat. No way were they underage; confused recollections were dripping back into his memory from the bedroom, two naked women this time, but he struggled to recall the whole picture. Ruminations started to spiral out of control; what if she made an allegation of rape? What if she has DNA evidence? Waking up naked took on a more sinister connotation now. Pete took a seat on the sofa. Dreading to discover the reality of the night before. He felt sick; a chemical-tasting reflux hit the back of his throat.

'I've also got photos of you posing with our pistols, cowboy. You loved them, especially the Glocks, and wanted to keep them. I struggled to get them back from you. But don't worry; the photos are just an insurance policy. If you behave yourself, they won't see the light of day, or as we say these days, the internet.' The phone went dead. Pete's head was in meltdown; he placed his head in his hands.

Pete immediately pressed redial, not really expecting Wayne to answer.

'What now? I'm busy,' Wayne answered casually. Almost like a different person from the one he'd just spoken to.

'If you want me to stay onside with you, you're going about things the wrong way. I've got nothing to lose; if I go down, you're coming with me. Which prick brought the pistols to the flat? Get them moved, or I will ditch them in the river Irwell,' Pete said in a futile attempt to regain credibility and some measure of control.

Wayne sniggered, 'Okay, tough guy. You're in enough trouble already; you'll do nothing of the sort. I'm giving the instructions here. Look after them until I tell you where to take them.'

'I'm not getting involved in gun running, no fuckin' chance,' Pete spat out.

'From where I'm sitting, it doesn't look like you have a choice in the matter. You'll do as you're told.' For a second time, Wayne terminated the call.

6

'You look like shit, mate. Have you been out on a bender again? Lee McCann quipped as he ambled over to Pete Higgs. His gaze shifted to the full English breakfast that Pete Higgs was tucking into, 'But that looks good; I'm tempted to order one.'

Pete looked up, munching enthusiastically, 'Cheers, mate, good to see you too. Nothing an all-day breakfast can't sort out,' Pete retorted between bites and continued to eat his breakfast. He was still suffering the effects of the Rohypnol or whatever other chemical it was that they spiked him with, which had numbed his ability to fire a witty comeback. His thoughts incessantly replayed the events of the night before, attempting to bridge the gaps yet ultimately falling short.

Lee returned from the bar with two pints and sat opposite Pete. 'Andrea is concerned about you, mate. She told me you turned into a late-night caller, pissed out of your head the other night, asking to kip at her house. What's happening, mate? I thought you were getting your act together.'

Pete cringed at the memory, irritated that Andrea had shared this embarrassing account with Lee; he'd tried to repress the memory of that night deep into his subconscious. 'I had a relapse, Lee. I was out of it. I'd been at the casino on the free drinks, drinking on an empty stomach. I've not been there since; this recovery is a slow process, it's not easy, but I'm getting there.' Pete thought about adding that he'd not touched a drop since, either. But the half-empty pint in front of him told another story. 'I'm thinking of going to one of these support groups: Gamblers

Anonymous, or something like that,' Pete said, pushing his empty plate away and wiping his lips with a napkin, 'Look mate, I'm not looking for sympathy, but the separation with Rachel hit me hard, and I went off the rails, but I'm getting myself sorted now, it was a one-off.' Pete got the vibes that Lee wasn't convinced, but in fairness, neither was he.

'That's good news, mate. Keep focused. I know it can't be easy for you. I'm always here if you need me. I've heard good things about the twelve-step programme for addictions, but you've got to be committed, mate. Give it a go.' Lee took a drink before continuing. 'How's life on the surveillance unit going? Are you still enjoying it?'

Pete leaned back in his chair, 'It pays the wages and the gaffer; Dave Ferguson is a top bloke. I can't complain.'

'And you? What investigations have you got on; anything juicy?' Pete asked, his eyes showing a flicker of curiosity. Thankful to change the conversation from his own troubles.

'Funnily enough, we managed to arrest one of Wayne Davies's gang, Declan Marsh, for possession of crack cocaine and committing a nasty assault. It looks like a drug deal went tits-up. I'm hoping to charge him with grievous bodily harm with intent. He wouldn't talk about Hamilton or Davies; he made no comment throughout the interviews. It's like Hamilton has disappeared off the face of the earth. There is no intelligence forthcoming, nothing.'

A wave of paranoia and panic hit Pete. A cold sweat washed over him. He feared that Lee was digging for information to incriminate him. Did Lee know more than he was letting on about his activities? Lee was a wily and shrewd detective; Pete knew he had to box-clever and be careful what he said. He suddenly felt the urgent need for a time-out to ease the pressure. 'I need a piss, mate,' Pete said, leaving the table.

Lee filled the void of Pete's absence by glancing around the pub at the regular punters, the type of blokes who looked like they had probably been waiting outside for the doors to open this morning, craving their first pint of the day. This pub served as their sanctuary, offering affordable beer and food without the frills but exceptional value for money.

Pete returned to the table, having composed himself. He'd concocted a cover story, just in case his fears of Lee digging were justified. 'I've not heard anything about Hamilton, except he fled to Spain in a hurry. It's spooky that you mention him, though. Ryan Young is back from Spain; living near me. I sometimes see him in the boozer. I can press him for information if you like. He's not an informant yet, but I'm working on turning him. Pete became conscious of his anxious non-verbal behaviour, leaning forward and talking faster than usual. He sat back, relaxing into his chair, pleased with how he had manipulated the truth into a more plausible and benign story. If Pete had seen them together, it was now explained away.

Lee looked surprised. 'Weird, I thought he would have given you a wide birth. If his associates saw him with you, there's only one conclusion they would draw…grass. But I suppose he feels safer in Manchester if Hamilton has gone. I read an intelligence log that implied Hamilton had been murdered by a rival gang, maybe even a Colombian cartel.'

'I think Young's showboating, maybe gloating. We never managed to charge him with any offences, did we? He probably thinks he's untouchable. Which is music to my ears; he's there for the taking if he becomes too complacent. I've read the same intelligence reports about Hamilton; it sounds plausible to me.'

'Well, see what information you can get from him,' Lee suggested. Pete felt smug. He'd covered all the bases with his cover story and felt safe again. He was in no doubt that he could run rings around Lee and extract whatever he needed from him. Lee continued, 'Talking of Hamilton; I feared he would kill me when he took me hostage. It was brave of you to get me out of there. You saved my life, pal.' Lee paused as if he was unsure of whether to ask his next question, 'You're not suffering from post-traumatic stress disorder, are you, mate? That was a horrific ordeal we endured there. I mean, it would explain the excessive gambling and drinking.' Lee purposely didn't mention the drug taking, maintaining the charade that he was unaware of Pete's drug habit.

'No, I don't think so. I just did what any decent mate would have done. The negotiators weren't going to talk you out of there. I just gave Hamilton an option, but how he evaded the armed police cordon and got away after I set him up is beyond me. I thought he'd get arrested as soon as he stepped outside the building. Pete knew he'd sounded convincing, content that Lee had been totally taken in with the skewed version of events. He liked the PTSD idea, tucking it away in a recess of his brain; if things came on top for him at a later date, it was a defence he and Frank Burton could explore.

'I'll always owe you for getting me out of there. Don't forget, I'm here for you if you need help, Pete. My phone is always on,' Lee said.

'Shame Andrea doesn't see things the same way.' Pete said, hoping Lee would take the bait to convince her otherwise.

Lee's phone vibrated with a soft chime, pulling him momentarily from their conversation. It was a message from Andrea. '*How about dinner at my place tonight? Craving some Italian.*' A small smile played on Lee's lips as he quickly typed back, '*Sounds perfect.*' Turning back to Pete, Lee quipped, 'Your turn to buy, mate. Fancy another one?'

Pete raised an eyebrow, a playful smirk forming. 'Priceless – I saved your life, and now I'm the one buying the beers?' They both laughed as Pete headed to the bar shaking his head in mock disbelief, satisfied that he had Lee in the palm of his hand.

7

Leaving Pete propping up the bar, deep in conversation with a punter who'd just bought him a pint. Lee jumped into his taxi and headed to Andrea Statham's house. Whilst the taxi sped along the dark lanes under the orange glow of the street lights, he mulled over his conversation with Pete. He understood where Andrea was coming from; Pete's account of recruiting Ryan Young as an informant didn't add up. Something wasn't right, and he felt like he was onto something.

On arrival, he kicked his shoes off in the hallway. The welcoming aroma from the kitchen pulled him in that direction. 'Smells good. Have you got the caterers in?' He teased.

Andrea chuckled, her eyes glowing with fondness. 'Watch it! I slaved over that lasagne. Made from scratch, thank you very much.' She handed Lee a glass filled generously with Merlot. Holding her gaze in his direction, she smiled, noticing how he appeared to be much more at home and relaxed when he was at her place these days.

Settling down at the kitchen table, Andrea served some appetizers: olives, slices of rustic bread, and a tray of delicious dips. 'The main course will be ready soon,' she informed him, popping an olive into her mouth.

'Have I missed anything at work whilst I've been off?' Lee asked before dipping some bread.

'Not really. The victim, O'Leary, has been released from hospital. He was treated for minor head injuries and a stab wound to his abdomen. O'Leary declined to make a formal complaint concerning the assault. He told us to contact his solicitor if we wanted to speak again. I guess that's the last we'll see of him. The medics said he was lucky not to have received more serious injuries; he took a nasty beating.'

'Who's his solicitor?'

'He failed to mention that, funnily enough,' Andrea said before taking a sip of wine.

'The injuries are the least of his worries; they also stole his stash of crack, and somebody higher up the chain won't be happy with him. It will probably result in another kicking or a debt he'll end up paying off for the rest of his life.'

'Let's see what we get back from forensics; if his prints or DNA are on the packaging, we might be able to pressure him to give evidence against Marsh as an alternative to being charged himself.'

'He won't give evidence against a gang member like Declan Marsh, especially if the Crown Prosecution Service can only charge Marsh with grievous bodily harm and possessing class A drugs with intent to supply. Do we know which gang O'Leary is affiliated to? Lee said, sitting forward, hoping to establish some investigative links.

'Yes, it's a Warrington gang. We think O'Leary had visited Manchester to pick up a shipment of drugs, to sell in Warrington. But evidentially, we need more evidence to prove he had possession of the drugs when Marsh robbed him. At this stage, O'Leary is a victim of assault; we have no concrete evidence of him having had possession of the drugs.

'I guess Declan Marsh double-crossed him; O'Leary probably bought the drugs from Wayne Davies's gang with Declan Marsh waiting nearby to assault him and steal the drugs back.

They continued talking shop whilst enjoying the lasagne. After dining, they walked through to the lounge and opened another bottle of wine. Andrea, now more than a little tipsy, noticed with appreciation that Lee opted for the sofa rather than the distant armchair. The proximity hinted at the growing intimacy between them.

'How was your meeting with Pete?' Andrea probed, seeking insights into Lee's earlier engagement.

Lee shrugged. 'He's Pete. When I left him, he was deep in conversation with a regular at the bar. He claims he's on the path to getting his act together. Less gambling and cutting back on alcohol. I'll believe it when I see it. He even mentioned a new flat—so you won't get those late-night distress calls anymore.'

Andrea quirked a brow and poked Lee in the ribs, 'Really? Where's this new flat?'

'He didn't say, but it's near the Northern Quarter. He spends a lot of his time in the boozers there. Talking of which, guess who he's been drinking with? No other than Ryan Young,' Lee said with mock shock and horror.

'Seriously,' Andrea exclaimed, sitting up, attentive.

'Yep, he was very casual about socialising with Young. It was almost as if the significance of his integrity, fraternising with a criminal, didn't register with him. He offered to press Young for information about the gang for us. The best bit was that he thinks he can get Young to come across as an informant. I can't see that happening.'

'I smell a rat,' Andrea said, sounding unconvinced.

'Don't overlook the fact that he decided to tell me about Young. If he was in cahoots with the gang, as you suspect, he wouldn't have mentioned it, would he?' Lee tested, quietly pleased that Andrea's reaction mirrored his own.

'Pete's smarter than that; he told you for a reason. It's probably a cover story to cover his tracks and explain his association with Young.'

'Pass me the tele control; that's enough job talk for now. If you want to continue, you will need to pay me overtime, boss,' Lee said, laughing.

Andrea handed him the control and cuddled up, resting her head on his chest. 'What are we watching?'

'What do you fancy?' Lee said, scrolling through the latest movie releases.

8

Frank Burton's observant eyes traced Pete Higgs as he settled onto the plush red Chesterfield. The changes in Pete since his last night out at the casino were evident, both in his demeanour and his appearance. There was a distinct clarity in Pete's eyes and an absence of that perpetual haggard look that had recently swamped him.

'You're looking well, Pete. That health kick is obviously paying off,' Frank commented, a hint of genuine surprise in his voice.

Pete couldn't help but smile faintly, running a hand over the sofa's smooth leather. 'Not having to get my head down here, there, and everywhere helps, although you can't knock the comfort of this sofa, though. My new bed is a dream; it's obviously top of the range.' His nostrils flared subtly, picking up the aroma of freshly brewed coffee. 'Do you fancy a coffee, Frank?'

Frank waved the offer away, extending one hand to show off his already half-drunk cup. 'I've already got one, Pete, help yourself.'

Pete pushed his chair back, preparing to stand. As he made his way to pour himself a coffee, Frank's voice carried a heavier tone, catching Pete mid-action. 'By the way, Wayne asked me to sort out your debt at the casino. Those threatening calls you've been getting recently should stop now.'

Frank then flicked a lighter, illuminating the end of a cigarette. Smoke curled upwards, and he exhaled slowly, watching Pete intently. Pete's reaction would be telling.

'I appreciate that, Frank, thank you. But I'm not sure who I should fear most, though: the heavies from the casino or Wayne Davies,' Pete said wearily, sitting back down, almost spilling coffee from the overfilled cup as he settled onto the sofa.

'Whether you like the term or not, you're already in Wayne's pocket. You're one of us; maybe you'd be better just accepting it rather than fighting it. Wayne's probably the best friend you've got right now, after me.' Frank raised his eyebrows and studied Pete before stubbing his cigarette on the smoked glass ashtray. Although it irked Pete to accept it, Frank had a point. He felt relaxed by the way Frank made situations and decisions seem simple. Maybe Frank was right; Pete knew life would be easier if he acquiesced more to Wayne and accepted his new position in the pecking order rather than getting pissed off and rowing with him.

The office door swung open, and Wayne Davies entered the room with a swagger and purpose as if on cue. Pete watched him enter and reluctantly accepted that he had something fetching about him; Wayne had a similar appearance and demeanour to the former special forces guys Pete had watched on reality television the night before. He certainly didn't present as a drug-dealing gangland boss.

Without seeking permission or extending the courtesy of offering to others, Wayne poured himself a coffee and took a seat. He took a deep sip and motioned towards the plush seating area, 'Come over and join us on the comfy seats, Frank,' his voice more command than an invitation. Frank frowned and slowly abandoned his desk, settling beside Pete on the sofa. With an air of casual menace, Wayne began, 'How's life in the flat?'

Pete wondered how such a simple question could make him feel like this was the start of an intimidating interrogation. 'It's been okay for a week or so. I've not had any more uninvited guests or visitors spiking me with rohypnol or whatever it was that you used.' Pete couldn't help himself. He always had to kick back. His new resolution had lasted no longer than five minutes. It was no wonder he had always learned the hard way over the years. Frank's advice had gone out of the window at the first time of asking.

'Well, that's gratitude for you,' Wayne's smirk grew wider as he observed Pete's discomfort. 'See what I mean, Frank? He deserves fuck all from us.'

'Come on, gents, play nicely; let's get down to business. We need to cut this in-fighting it doesn't help us to focus on the matters at hand,' Frank mediated; he smiled, though it didn't reach his eyes, betraying a hint of his own unease.

Seizing control, Wayne leaned forward, his predatory gaze fixed on Pete, 'Good idea, Frank, down to business. The photographs from the party at your flat will never see the light of day, provided you behave yourself. I must keep you on your toes until I'm satisfied you are not a threat to the firm. You understand that, don't you?' Wayne's tone was menacing.

'Okay, let's get on with it,' Pete said nonchalantly, having heard it all before, refraining from poking Wayne back.

'One of my lads is looking at a prison sentence, Declan Marsh. The trouble is, I need him on the outside. And that's where you come in; you need to sort it for me.'

'What the hell can I do?' Pete asked, looking puzzled, causing Frank to shift uncomfortably in his seat.

Wayne responded with a patronising tone, 'You're the top detective. You shouldn't need to ask me. Get rid of some evidence, intimidate some witnesses, or even put some pressure on your mate, DI Andrea Statham. Whatever it takes.

Pete's eyes sought out Frank's, trying to find a semblance of solidarity or understanding in them, but Frank avoided eye contact and gazed at the leaden Manchester sky through the window, conveying a reluctance to intervene. Or maybe he didn't have an issue with the request.

'You'd better give it some thought, Sherlock. And by the way, there will be a package at the flat when you return. Keep it safe until I tell you where to take it. Right, that's you dismissed,' Wayne pointed towards the door.

As Wayne was about to stand up, Frank gesticulated for him to remain seated; Wayne immediately acquiesced, easing back into the seat. 'I need a word, Wayne.' Pete observed the nuance of the power-play and wondered who was actually pulling the strings in the firm; maybe it wasn't Wayne.

Pete felt ruffled but was trying hard not to show it; his default instinct was always to put Wayne in his place. Instead, he looked at Frank and shook his head wearily. Frank smiled sympathetically, 'Thanks for coming, Pete. Keep me updated with your plans for Declan Marsh,' Frank said, almost paternalistically.

Pete could feel the heat rising in his cheeks, but he forced it down, refusing to let Wayne see just how much he had got under his skin. Pete stood up to leave. He couldn't resist the urge to have the last word. He turned about and levelled a direct gaze at Wayne. 'No worries, Wayne, I'll keep Declan Marsh out of prison. But remember, respect and trust aren't a one-way street. You need to work with me or let me walk away. It won't work for either of us otherwise. Pete walked to the door, anticipating Wayne's reply, but it never came. Pete left the building feeling confident that he had stood his corner well.

A short while later, Pete arrived back at his flat. He felt out of breath at the top of the stairs and berated himself for letting his fitness level slip this much. Not for the first time recently, he committed to eating healthier and getting fit. He walked inside and looked around, relieved that Ryan wasn't in residence. He clocked that the holdall containing the pistols was still there. Just as he was about to conclude there was no new package, he saw a black holdall down by the side of the sofa.

He grabbed a pair of marigold gloves from the cupboard under the sink and placed the bag on the coffee table. He took out a supermarket carrier bag and looked inside; three clear plastic bags containing wraps of heroin and crack cocaine, bagged up and ready for distribution.

Pete was just considering skimming some cocaine from the bags to make a few quid on the side for himself when he heard the door open. Ryan walked in, looked at Pete and started laughing. 'You fucking weirdo, marigolds. Thank fuck I walked in before you got started! I wouldn't have wanted to have caught you in the act, you fucking deviant.'

Pete placed the bag of drugs back into the holdall and peeled off the gloves. 'Sorry to disappoint you, Ryan, there's nothing deviant going on here. I'm just forensically aware, unlike you fucking amateurs. Anyway, Wayne told me there'd be a bag dropped here; this must be it. Do you know where he wants me to take it?' Pete asked, letting the piss-taking about marigolds slide.

Ryan leaned against the door frame, the smirk still evident on his face. 'You'll get a text. Wayne will let you know.'

'What about the pistols too? Surely, you must have a better safe house than this?' Pete said, glancing at the unwanted bag.

'Think about it. Who's going to suspect good old DS Pete Higgs of the yard to be storing guns and drugs in his flat,' Ryan laughed cynically, 'I bet you wish you weren't involved in all this shit now. But it's too late; you're one of us.' Ryan went to his bedroom room, still laughing. His comments grated on Pete's nerves; it was bravado, an attempt to assert himself. Pete suspected Ryan was the weak link in the gang. He wasn't a significant threat, just an irritant.

Pete walked over and opened the bedroom door. 'But I'm not one of you, am I? Wayne makes that abundantly clear at every opportunity. If he wants the best out of me, he needs to accept me and show me some fucking respect,' Pete shouted before slamming the bedroom door closed.

A moment later, Pete could hear the rhythmic thuds of fists against the punch bag and Ryan hissing and grunting with each punch from the bedroom. Pete sneered to himself whilst imagining the feeble efforts of the wannabe. Pete felt tempted to go in and show him how it was done.

9

The buzzing of Pete Higgs's mobile phone broke the stifling silence of his dimly lit flat. The instruction was brief and to the point, as usual, lacking deference. He picked up the holdall and left the flat. He felt an uncomfortable churning feeling in his stomach. Every time he found himself embroiled in some assignment for the firm, there was this niggling thought at the back of his mind: Was this a setup? Setting him up to get lifted by the police. He tried to dismiss the fear rationally by concluding that Wayne would have nothing to gain besides feeding his perverse personal grudge and relishing Pete's life unravelling.

Pete walked to the car, putting the dark thoughts to one side. The cold Manchester air bit into him as he walked across the car park, each step echoing a rising apprehension within him. He opened the boot of his car and placed the holdall inside, subconsciously scanning the vicinity for any threats, dodgy-looking vans or groups of males sitting in cars. These days, he always felt a nagging feeling that he was being watched by either the police or rival gangs.

He was about to slide into the driver's seat when the roar of an engine sliced through the quiet car park. High-beam headlights pierced the darkness, blinding him momentarily. A vehicle was charging right at him, its intention unclear. Panic surged, urging him to flee, but he rooted himself to the spot, heart pounding, teeth clenched. He grabbed the wheel nut wrench from the boot, holding it by his side, just in case. Was this a strike by the cops, or worse, a member of a rival gang moving in on him to steal the drugs? The uncertainty, the danger of Manchester's underbelly, was all too real, and Pete had placed himself in the thick of it.

The car screeched to a stop only a few yards from him. Pete's stare was focused as he watched Lee McCann step out of the driver's door. Pete's eyes then darted around the car, relieved to discover that Lee was alone. Lee's grin, a familiar combination of mischief and warmth, brought a momentary sigh of relief to Pete. He casually threw the wheel nut brace back into the boot.

'I was just on my way home and saw you, at least, I thought it was you, but I wasn't sure. So, this is where you're slumming it. A location like this couldn't have been cheap.'

The instant confusion and shock of Lee suddenly arriving dissipated quickly. Pete was conscious of the need to compose himself. 'Jesus, mate, I wondered who you were. Don't do that to me. I thought I was about to get turned over by the local scrotes.'

Lee gave him a quizzical look, 'Nice location, mate. Which one's yours?' Lee pushed.

'Number seven, mate,' Pete informed him reluctantly, knowing it would appear suspicious if he were evasive.

'Have you got time for a quick pint?' Lee asked, 'I could use one. It's been a busy day.'

Pete glanced at his wristwatch, feeling the weight of the contents of the holdall pressing on his conscience. 'Sorry mate, another time, eh? I'm heading to Rachel's to drop off some presents for the kids, I'm already at the last minute. I'll text you when I'm free.' Pete looked at his watch again; he needed to get a move on. 'I can't be late, or she'll kick off. She takes any opportunity to have a go at me these days.'

Chuckling, Lee replied, 'No need for any drama on my account. We'll grab a beer another time. Drop me a text when you're free.'

Pete nodded, relief evident on his face. 'Definitely, mate. See you later.' As he got into his car and drove off, he couldn't help but feel that it hadn't been just a chance meeting, as portrayed by Lee. Was Lee keeping tabs on him? Could he still trust him? Pete's ruminations kicked into overdrive. He looked around, trying to locate Lee's vehicle; it was lost in the early evening traffic. Pete cursed; he didn't have the time for any worthwhile anti-surveillance driving; he'd just have to be vigilant. Maybe he's not so fucking gullible, Pete mused.

Pete stopped at the pre-arranged location and looked at the time on the dashboard display. He was a few minutes late. He drummed his fingers on the steering wheel whilst looking across the road at the kebab shop, its lights illuminating the litter-strewn pavement outside. Pete watched a skeletal-looking employee carving the donner meat, the sleeves on his sauce-stained oversized white jacket rolled up to his forearms. Pete suddenly felt the pangs of hunger; he couldn't remember the last time he'd eaten.

A gang of hoodies were hanging out by the bus stop, doing their best to look intimidating. One of the gang jumped up and grabbed the roof's edge before swinging back and forth. Another hoodie tried to grab the swinging legs but wasn't quick enough; getting swiftly kicked in the head for his troubles, he retreated to a safe distance to the apparent amusement of the others.

Pete purposely didn't look in their direction for too long and busied himself, flicking through radio channels.

Suddenly, the inside of his car was illuminated by headlights from behind; he adjusted the rear-view mirror to shield his eyes from the intense glare. A car had stopped behind him with the headlights still blazing. He pulled the peak of his baseball cap further down. A shadowy figure dressed in dark clothing approached from the car to his driver's door. Pete opened the door a few inches before the woman blocked it with her knee. 'Stay in the car, you tool. Pass me the bag,' she instructed.

Staring her down, wanting to level things up, Pete noticed she was hardly more than school-age. She looked like life had been harsh on her. Thin and scrawny, most likely a user herself, dealing drugs to pay for her own drug habit. 'It's in the boot; I'll release the lid.' Pete pulled the catch and watched through the mirror as the boot flicked open momentarily before being slammed shut by the teenager, the thud echoing throughout the vehicle. She got back into the passenger seat of her waiting car; the handover was complete in less than a minute.

Two inquisitive hoodies from the bus stop drifted slowly over to her. Pete pulled his car forward slowly and mentally noted the registration number of the girl's car. The car accelerated past Pete's car with no lights on, driven by a male, his face hidden under a baseball cap, disappearing into the housing estate. The hoodies migrated back over to the bus stop.

Later that evening, back at the flat, Ryan was sprawled out on the sofa watching a football match on television. He wore grey sweats, the same ones he wore the day before and probably the day before that. Pete's nose wrinkled in distaste at the sight of Ryan's grubby socks abandoned on the floor as he entered the flat.

Ryan tilted his head back, but not far enough to make eye contact with Pete. 'Great timing, mate; grab me a can from the fridge, will you?'

'Another one of my cans?' Pete asked, not attempting to hide his irritation. Pete grabbed two cans and passed one to Ryan before taking a seat. He wasn't in the mood to watch football. He took a long drink and sat back, looking over at Ryan. 'I did the drop-off. Who is the gobby bitch with an attitude who collected it?'

'She's just a street dealer for the locals; the driver was the main man. Why do you ask? Do you fancy shagging her? Or did she give you a hard time?' Ryan laughed, sitting up. 'She was here at your party. Do you not remember her? You couldn't keep your hands off her before you decided to fuck her.'

Pete felt a swell of anger and an urge to punch Ryan in the face but kept his control. He wanted to give the impression that Ryan's goading didn't faze him. 'Don't forget, Ryan, what goes around comes around.' Pete stepped forward, his face inches away from Ryan's face. 'So, you'd better be careful.' Pete stepped back and sat on the sofa, surprised that Ryan remained silent.

'I thought she looked familiar,' Pete said nonchalantly, 'So where are these photos? Do they actually exist?' Pete said. Ryan ignored him and continued watching the football.

Changing tack, Pete asked, 'I've not seen you do much. What's your role these days?'

'I'm hands-off, me,' Ryan replied, looking at Pete, 'What's it got to do with you anyway?'

'I'm curious, that's all. We are both low in the pecking order. You've already received the wrath of Hamilton and Davies. Maybe it would be mutually beneficial to have each other's backs. Wayne is behaving a bit unpredictable these days.' Pete thought he detected a brief flicker of mutual understanding in Ryan's eyes for a split second, so he paused and left his words hanging.

'Yeah, right. Like you give a shit about me,' Ryan replied, sounding disinterested, not taking his eyes away from the television.

Pete felt smug; he guessed he had unsettled Ryan and planted doubt regarding his safety and standing within the firm. Just like Pete, he would benefit from forming an alliance. 'Can you sort me out with some coke?' Pete asked, testing the mood music.

'There's some in the bottom of my wardrobe. Lift the wooden base; it's underneath. Don't take the piss, just a couple of lines.'

'Nice one,' Pete said, sensing an air of submission, leaving Ryan to contemplate his proposal.

10

DS Lee McCann sat transfixed in his dimly lit office, eyes glued to the pale glow of his computer screen. So far, he hadn't found any intelligence about the car he saw parked up behind DS Pete Higgs near the kebab shop the night before.

From his concealed vantage point, he hadn't been able to get a clear glimpse of the young woman in the car, but he was sure it wasn't Pete's wife. It didn't look like two divorcees passing over their children's belongings either. Nor was it a likely place for Pete and Rachel to meet; it was a notorious crime area that even the locals feared and tried to avoid at night.

Lee was frustrated that he couldn't establish who used the car or the woman's identity. But it was another investigative lead, which he could monitor for now. The incident had also convinced him that there was no doubt Pete Higgs was involved in criminality; there was no rational explanation for the handover other than an illicit deal going down.

Pete wasn't treading the thin line to catch the bad guys; he'd crossed the line and implicated himself in drug dealing. Lee switched off the computer and finished writing his notes. He felt downcast about Pete's predicament; he was once a solid detective. But marital problems, money worries, and addictions didn't justify corruption or criminality. The force welfare department was there to help staff experiencing such difficulties. Maybe misguided, but Pete had made the wrong decisions. There was no sympathy forthcoming from Lee, Pete had made his own bed, and now he would get what was coming to him in the form of justice.

Lee had no time for corrupt officers; it was non-negotiable, totally unacceptable. The damage caused to the lives of individuals and the reputation of the police was unforgivable. Lee called the intelligence bureau and arranged for a covert tag to be placed on the intelligence system so that he would receive any intelligence or sightings of the vehicle.

It was time for his morning meeting with the boss. He walked through the banks of desks in the open-plan office. Most desks were unoccupied; the detectives were out on enquiries or grabbing a fry-up for breakfast to set them up for the day.

Lee gently tapped on the open door as he walked in and sat at the round meeting table. Andrea looked up from her computer, 'Morning Lee, give me a minute; I'll just finish writing this email.' Lee opened his case book and read through his notes on the Declan Marsh case.

Andrea joined him at the table. 'Any update on Declan Marsh's victim?'

Lee took a deep breath, 'Nothing; he's keeping his head down; he's totally disappeared off our radar. It's obvious he doesn't want to talk to us.'

'We'll just keep looking; I'm sure we'll find him.'

'Or he'll get locked up sooner or later. We still have Declan Marsh bang to rights on the possession with intent to supply charge, so he's looking at a few years inside. But without O'Leary's evidence, he will walk away from the assault charges.'

'How is the investigation progressing time-wise?'

'We're up to speed; just waiting on the forensic analysis of the drugs at the forensic labs. I've chased them up, but they've got a huge backlog. I'll give them another call.' Lee scribbled a reminder for himself in his casebook. 'I saw Pete Higgs last night on my way home,' Lee said.

'How is he?' Andrea asked, sitting forward in her chair.

'Funny you ask, he seemed on edge. He looked ruffled and relieved when he realised it was me pulling up alongside him and not some gangland enforcer.'

'We need to keep a good watch on the intelligence database for Wayne Davies's firm. We might just get a lead on what Pete's up to.'

Lee scribbled more notes in his casebook. He wasn't about to tell the boss about his 'chance encounter' with Pete Higgs outside the kebab shop. She didn't need to know just yet. The exchange he saw take place was insufficient evidentially. And the car was long gone from the scene by the time he got back to his car. Lee also suspected that other colleagues might have questioned the legitimacy of his presence there.

Lee's experience and knowledge in 'the job' had developed him into a shrewd investigator. He knew some things were better kept under wraps for the time being.

'Pete Higgs has invited me out for a beer tonight. Do you fancy coming?'

'I'm out with the girls; it's our cinema night,' Andrea smiled with relief.

She stood up and returned to her computer, indicating the meeting was over, 'I've got a raft of emails to get through. Close the door, will you, Lee.' Lee returned to his desk to further research the intelligence database; Ryan Young was next on his list.

*

DS Pete Higgs was also busy researching the intelligence database, too. He'd just returned from a site visit to familiarise himself with the layout of a building of interest to him. It was a task he needed to get right. The building was a reasonably modern build on a drab out-of-town business park. It was one of many private companies undertaking forensic science work for the police. Pete preferred the good old days of the Forensic Science Service before private companies entered the market with profits in mind.

Pete left his office and walked down the stairs to the car park. As always, it was full of vehicles abandoned in any available space. He walked over to the memorial garden and sat on a bench. The lunchtime sun felt good on his face; it made him feel good. Life was slowly getting better, and his confidence was returning. He'd stayed away from the casino, albeit he still indulged in online bets. And he was making inroads to a better understanding and working relationship with Wayne and Ryan. He intended to continue his course of action until he'd made enough cash to disappear into the sunset.

He selected Wayne from the contacts on his burner phone and looked around to ensure no one was nearby in earshot.

'Have you got the info?' Wayne Davies asked, getting straight to the point.

'Yes, it will be a straightforward job. Double glass doors secure the main entrance. A cheap roller shutter covers it out of hours. Inside, there is an open-plan reception area. The secure storage room is behind the reception desk; the door is signed, staff only.

'That's enough. I don't need any more details,' Wayne interrupted, 'What about the dealer who Declan Marsh turned over? Will he be making a formal complaint to the police?'

'No, I had words with him. He won't cause you any issues. I think the intimidation had the desired effect. We won't be seeing him any time soon.'

'Are you sure he's not under witness protection?'

'One hundred per cent. O'Leary hasn't made a statement nor cooperated in the slightest. I will be the first to know if he resurfaces, and you'll be the second. Pete said, satisfied with his actions.

'I'll be in touch.' Wayne's phone went dead.

Pete slipped his phone into the inside pocket of his jacket and strolled back to the office in time for the afternoon staff debrief.

11

It was late in the afternoon; DI Dave Ferguson had stood down the surveillance operations for the day and given the teams an early finish. It was recognition for their commitment during a particularly demanding week of working excessive hours to get the job done. He'd asked Pete to hang back; the empty office provided the opportunity to catch up. Dave had invited Pete to his office for a 'welfare chat', a tick box exercise for some supervisors, but not Dave Ferguson.

Pete entered the DI's office and sat beside the rubber plant on one of the old, comfy lounge chairs. How the neglected old plant still thrived was a mystery; it had been on its last legs for as long as Pete could remember. The office hadn't changed much over the years, an untouched time capsule. It was a welcome relic of the past, only lacking a blue haze of cigarette smoke to complete the picture. It reminded Pete of the good old days.

Rumours had been circulating for years that the building was being sold to developers or knocked down, yet neither had materialised. The occupants appeared to be on borrowed time, dreading a relocation to one of the new soulless private finance-funded buildings.

'How about a sneaky whisky?' Dave suggested with a conspiratorial grin.

'Why not? It's Friday,' Pete replied, amused at the irony of having a whiskey in a welfare interview, albeit it was an informal meeting. He held Dave in high regard; he was a remnant of the traditional leadership style. With more than three decades under his belt, Dave could have hung up his boots years ago. Yet, he was a creature of habit and wasn't ready to step away from the job.

Dave poured two whiskies and slid one over to Pete, 'So, how're things at home, Pete? Are you both making an effort to work things through?'

'Getting better; I've managed to stay away from the casinos. Rachel is now speaking to me again, so I might even be allowed to see the kids sometime soon.' Pete kept it short; he needed to give just enough information to justify his welfare concessions, but not too much. He felt comfortable talking to Dave and knew that Dave was genuinely concerned; he wasn't just completing a requirement on behalf of the Human Resources Department.

'Is that it?' Dave gently probed.

'Yeah, one day at a time, as they say. I've settled in at the new flat, and I've joined a gambling addiction group which is helping.' The last bit wasn't true, but Pete sensed it would be music to Dave's ears. It was what he probably wanted to hear.

'Good man, it sounds like you're getting back on track, Pete. I'm always here if you need me. Unfortunately, you aren't the first detective to experience these problems, and you certainly won't be the last. Dave took a glug of his whiskey and continued, 'Andrea's worried about you, too, Pete.'

'I appreciate what you're doing for me, Dave; the time off and flexibility with the shifts. It makes things a lot easier to deal with,' Pete replied, letting the mention of Andrea slip. 'I'm slowly getting back on top of things; it's just a matter of time now.'

Dave finished the last drops from his glass and rose from his desk, 'I'm off, and I'll catch up with you next week. We've got tickets to The Halle at The Bridgewater Hall tonight. I can't be late; Mrs Ferguson would give me a right earful.' He paused, hand on the doorknob, and looked back, 'Remember, you can always ring me if you need a chat.'

'Thank you, I appreciate it. Have a good weekend, boss,' Pete followed him out of the office but continued down the corridor into the main detective's office. He quickly scanned the desks and identified a computer one of the team hadn't logged off from. Pete sat and began some 'anonymous' research whilst finishing his whiskey. The next hour passed quickly, and Pete's work was completed once he was thoroughly updated on the latest intelligence relevant to the OCG and Declan Marsh in particular.

He left the computer switched on and made his way down the steep, winding Victorian staircase and out of the rear door into the station yard. The place was deserted; it was no longer an operational parading station for Uniform, CID and traffic officers bustling with activity. No surveillance operations were planned for the weekend either, so surveillance teams were working the on-call system.

He exited via a secure side entrance onto the street and hurried along the litter-strewn pavement towards the Metro Link station. Most of the shop premises he passed were boarded with metal sheets, plastered with fliers for music gigs, long since abandoned. The only surviving shops were takeaways, off licences and bookies. The charity shops didn't even fancy their chances here. Unemployment in the area was high, and the crime rate was rising too. Pete couldn't help but believe the police were losing the streets in places like this.

He reached the foot of the stairs at the Metrolink station and heard the distant rumble and metal-on-metal noise of an approaching tram. He climbed the stairs at a sprint, needing to catch his breath at the top. His timing was perfect; the tram breaks screeched as it came to a stop, and the hydraulics hissed as the doors slid open. The carriage was empty, but for a few passengers keeping their heads down, avoiding eye contact with fellow passengers. Pete sat next to the window, looking forward to a few beers and hooking up with Lee McCann. He needed to get as much information out of Lee as possible before Andrea convinced Lee that he was up to no good. Pete relied on Lee's loyalty and naivety from having saved him from Jason Hamilton but knew it had a sell-by date. Pete feared that Lee also had an ulterior motive in reporting back to Andrea Statham, so he had to be sure he fed him good-quality misinformation to keep them off his case.

Pete left the tram at St. Peter's Square station. He headed for Oxford Street, alongside the early evening drinkers mixing with the straggling commuters heading home.

He reached the pub and squeezed through a group of rowdy lads having a smoke outside at the pub door. Inside the bar area, his eyes slowly adjusted to the darker environment as he approached the bar. Pete recognised the barman; the guy had worked behind the bar for years and was part of the place's charm, friendly and engaging. He reminded Pete of the mild-mannered saloon bartender character in the old Western movies, respectful and meticulous in his actions, fearing any trouble from the drunken gunslingers. Pete took his pint and found a seat next to the window, watching the pedestrians walking by while drinking his beer.

The place was buzzing with customers engaged in enthusiastic chatter and laughter; the dark ambience of the lounge area hid the tired and worn furnishings.

Lee suddenly appeared before the table, 'You look like you were miles away, Pete; I'll get them in.' Lee walked over to the bar, disappearing into the crowd of punters. Pete realised Lee must have entered through the side door, which would explain why he had not seen him approach. Pete had let his guard down; he'd not had time to prepare his game face.

Lee returned and placed the drinks on the table. 'I asked Andrea if she fancied a pint, but she's already got plans,' Lee said before taking a generous swig, 'That's nice; I was ready for that.'

'Very diplomatically put, Lee,' Pete guessed that Lee had come straight from the office. He looked smart in his dark blue suit and open-neck white shirt. 'It would have been good to catch up with her. I must apologise in person now as I've got my act together. I take it she is still pissed off with me?' Pete asked, doing his best to sound sincere; a social drink with Andrea did not appeal to him.

'No, I don't think so, pal. I think she's happy you're sorting yourself out and no longer phoning her in the middle of the night!' They both laughed and mirrored each other by taking a drink.

Pete sensed Lee didn't want to talk about Andrea and suspected it was because they were in a relationship. Pete wasn't jealous; he'd always been pals with Andrea but nothing more. They had always been close, but nothing had ever developed romantically or physically, for that matter. But, now, as far as Pete was concerned, she was persona non grata; the bitch had nailed her colours to the mast.

Pete was there for Andrea during a difficult time when her ex-partner turned up out of the blue from London with hopes of rekindling their relationship. He had left the Metropolitan Police under a cloud and sought somewhere to live and lick his wounds rather than a genuine attempt at reconciliation. Andrea was no fool when it came to him and wasn't taken in by any of it. He didn't linger for long before returning to London.

'You're miles away again; are you sure you're okay, mate?' Lee asked.

70

'Yeah, I was reminiscing about Andrea; I need to get things back on track. I've let her down.' Pete said, hoping Lee would report his remorse to her and maybe buy him some slack from her relentless witch hunt.

'Give her time; she'll come round sooner or later,' Lee said, not believing his own words for a moment but wanting Pete to feel at ease enough to talk openly.

'I like it here; it's one of the best pubs in the city,' Pete said, taking in the surroundings. It was now standing room only, and it was difficult for them to hear each other speak over the clinking of glasses, constant hum of lively chatter and sporadic raucous laughter.

'I've been to quite a few retirement parties here over the years,' Lee chuckled at the memories. 'Do you remember Ted's retirement party here?'

'I do, yes, the poor sod. As soon as his pension date was within reach, his wife decided to leave him, along with her half of the money,' Pete said, shaking his head. 'Poor Ted didn't even see it coming.'

'Yes, but he didn't hang about; he'd had quite a few drinks and was chatting up a few of the women one after the other. So, one of the lads took the microphone from the DJ and made an announcement, 'Ladies, Ted appears to be working his way around the room in search of a new romance but failing miserably. To save him time, if anyone at the far end of the room is interested in dating Ted, please raise your hand.' They both laughed at the recollection.

'Poor, Ted, I recall there were no takers,' Pete said before taking a drink.

'Wonder what he's up to now?' Lee mused.

'Still working through his list, I guess!' Pete laughed.

'I thought you may have bumped into him at the football; he's a massive United fan,' Lee said.

'I've not been for a while; it's just Match of the Day for me these days.'

'How's things with Rachel? Any thawing of the ice?' Lee asked.

'No, just the same.' Pete's abrupt reply indicated it was not a subject up for discussion.

'Have you seen Ryan Young lately?' Lee asked, ditching the small talk for the important stuff.

'Yeah, he's in the local sometimes. I've had a few beers with him; he's opening up slowly. Did you know he had a fling with Kirsty Hamilton?'

'No way, I didn't think he had it in him. Christ, he's either brave or stupid. Jason Hamilton would kill him if he found out. Listen, Pete, get into him. I need to know what they are up to; an inside source would be perfect. How close are you getting to him talking?' Lee said, leaning closer.

'I'm doing okay; you know the score; you can't rush these things.' Pete realised he had probably sounded evasive. He felt uneasy, even paranoid. Was Lee onto him? Did Lee suspect he was now part of the OCG? Or was he just trying to get evidence on Ryan Young? He glanced down at Lee's almost empty glass. 'I'll nip to the gents and get the beers in on my way back.'

In the gents, Pete selected a cubical and did a couple of lines of coke. He took a deep breath and sniffed hard before concealing the white powder bag into his jacket's lining. He checked in the mirror for signs of powder under his nose before returning to the table, via the bar, with the beers. His mood had lifted; he felt good; he felt like he could deal with anything Lee presented to him now.

'We can take Davies's gang down, Pete; Ryan is our way in. Have you got any leads on him at all?' Lee pressed.

Lee wasn't letting go. Pete felt wary; where was this new sudden interest coming from? Pete felt the need to dampen

72

his enthusiasm. 'How's your Declan Marsh investigation going?' He asked, digging for information himself.

'Still waiting on the forensic examination results; apart from that, we haven't got much more. That's why I need you to get into Ryan Young's ribs; he'd be an invaluable informant. A good result would help you to re-focus, too, mate.'

'I know, Lee, you've mentioned that once or twice already; funnily enough,' Pete laughed, 'take a chill pill. I get it.'

After a few more beers, Lee decided it was time for him to leave; he felt tired, and the lager was going straight to his head. Pete was enjoying the coke and beer too much and decided to stay for a few more, heading back to the bar.

12

Pete Higgs swayed on unsteady feet, stumbling through the crowd of drinkers. The last thing he needed was to knock over a pint and find himself in the middle of a row or a fight. Reaching the safe haven of the bar as a steadying support, Pete clumsily perched onto his bar stool. The punter he had been talking to earlier had taken the opportunity to slip away.

Pete caught the eye of the barman and ordered another double whiskey. He was self-conscious about slurring his words and tried desperately to sound coherent. Pulling a twenty out of his trouser pocket, he was oblivious to the other crumpled twenty-pound note that fell to the floor.

Pete felt his phone vibrating against his leg. The call had ended by the time he'd finished fumbling to grab it. A missed call from Ryan Young appeared on the display. Pete was thinking about returning the call when an incoming text alert pinged, '*Where r u?*'

Pete slowly texted back, '*Deansgate out on the lash.*'

'*Be outside the library in ten c u there, don't be late*' appeared almost instantaneously. Pete was on a roll; he welcomed the company of Ryan for a few more beers. He hadn't noticed the barman serving him but suddenly became aware of the whiskey and his change on the bar. Pete necked the whiskey and slid clumsily from the bar stool. Slowly, he made his way to meet Ryan.

Pete took several deep breaths; the cool, fresh air felt good. He walked the short distance along Deansgate to the neo-gothic-styled library building. He took a moment to appreciate its beautiful architecture. Usually, in the fast pace of life, he would drive by without giving it a second glance.

He leaned back onto the black cast iron fencing and watched a young couple walk across the pedestrian road crossing in his direction. They took him back in time, thinking about when he and Rachel had first met and enjoyed carefree nights out in the city. He reminisced and wished he could turn the clock back to those happy days. He believed it was still possible; a friend at work had suggested to him that reconciliation was always possible until one of you **was** six feet under—quite the philosophical perspective.

A sleek black sports coupé suddenly swerved from the other side of the road and skidded to an abrupt stop in front of him. The music's bass line was pounding loudly, even louder, when the driver's window lowered. 'Oi, Pete! Get in!' shouted Ryan Young, whilst drumming the steering wheel.

Pete heaved himself up from where he'd been slumped against the cold iron fencing, ambling around the car's front whilst steadying himself with a hand on the bonnet. His gaze shifted to Ryan; Pete had faith that Ryan would join him in his audacious plan to steal Wayne's wealth, a daring scheme that would fund Pete's dream of starting a new luxurious life overseas.

He opened the front passenger door and eased into the black leather seat, which smelt new. A warm, red glow illuminated from the dashboard. He became aware that there was another person in the back seat. Pete couldn't be bothered looking around to discover who it was or attempt any conversation–the music's blaring volume was far too loud for that. He looked over to Ryan, who appeared to be in a trance-like state, nodding in time to the music.

'Strap yourself in, in case I turn this baby over,' Ryan shouted over the music blasting out from the quality sound system.

Ryan accelerated away from the pavement erratically, swerving back onto the opposite lane. The driver of a passing car blasted his horn, having been forced to slam the brakes to avoid a collision. Ryan yelled, 'Fuck you,' to the amusement of the guy in the back as they made their way out of town. The sudden motion pushed Pete back into his seat, causing him to instinctively snatch the seatbelt and fasten the buckle.

The acceleration continued, getting faster; Pete began to feel anxious and looked over to Ryan, 'What's the fucking rush? Slow down, you knob-head! You'll fucking kill us.'

Ryan responded with laughter and pressed heavier on the accelerator pedal. 'This handles like a dream. I want one.' Pete heard more laughter from the guy in the back. Pete's happy, drunken mood was dissipating fast. The high speed of the car and loud music combined created a surreal, unwanted adrenalin-pumping experience.

'For fucks sake!' Pete shouted as the car shot through a red light at the Portland Street junction. He braced himself, ready for the impact of an oncoming vehicle. Relieved that he'd survived, he reached for the media centre and turned the volume of the music down. Ryan slowed the car as if the volume setting controlled his right foot.

'That's better. What are you trying to do? Bait the cops to chase us?' Pete asked, wishing he was still sitting at the bar in the pub.

'Calm down, plod. The cops wouldn't be able to keep up with us in this anyway; that's why I nicked this one.' As if to prove his point, Ryan suddenly accelerated harshly. Pete began to feel nauseous as the buildings flashed by, becoming a blur of bright lights.

'Where are we going?' Pete asked, hoping Ryan would slow down to answer his question.

'To the forensics company,' Ryan shouted loudly, to be heard above the music.

'No way, stop the car; I'm getting out. I've provided you with the layout of the building. I don't need to be there when you go in.' The possibility of being chased by the police while being carried in a stolen car suddenly paled into insignificance after the latest disclosure. Pete was seriously regretting getting into the car. He couldn't risk compromising himself.

'No can do, I'm afraid. Wayne wants you to take part to make sure we don't fuck up. And to give you the chance to demonstrate your commitment to us.' Ryan replied as he accelerated onto the motorway slip road and headed into the third lane.

13

Pete felt relieved when the car unexpectedly swerved into a parking area and stopped. He couldn't believe they weren't either dead or being pursued by the police interceptor patrols. Ryan had been driving like a prick. They got out, and Pete followed Ryan and his accomplice to the boot of the vehicle. 'I shouldn't be here,' Pete protested, 'I'll probably be a liability; I've never done anything like this in my life.' However, his genuine concern for not taking part was the risk of getting arrested and the consequences that came with that. No reprieve was forthcoming.

Even though he was finding the events to be a sobering experience, Pete tried once again, 'I'm too pissed, I'll slow you down. Would I not be of more use as a lookout?'

'Stop moaning, for fucks sake and put these on,' Ryan said, tossing a black boiler suit and a black woollen balaclava to the floor in front of Pete. Ryan's mate laughed as he had at every wisecrack Ryan made during the journey. His hyena-sounding high-pitched giggle irritated Pete, making him feel even angrier. Pete glared at the hyena, who was buttoning up his boiler suit, but the hyena didn't return the stare. He was gangly tall with a wiry build. Probably a flunky at the bottom of the firm's food chain rather than a peer of Ryan's. Pete slipped into the boiler suit and pulled the balaclava over his head, keen to hide his identity from any security cameras rather than in compliance with Ryan's order.

'Right, get back into the car,' shouted Ryan excitedly. As the doors were being slammed shut, Ryan set off. He stopped the car just before the junction of the Hawthorn hedged parking area and the business park central through road.

A stationary car parked over to the right flashed its headlights from the darkness of a layby. 'It's showtime,' Ryan shouted. Hyena laughed dutifully on cue. Ryan accelerated away, causing the wheels to spin. Pete detested the acrid smell of burning rubber engulfing them; it made him feel like being sick. He held the door handle tightly and looked into the wing mirror at the other car as it pulled out and followed them.

Pete watched Ryan, who appeared to be hyperactive; he was clearly on a big high. Pete desperately didn't want to be with them but reluctantly accepted it was too late to escape from this mayhem.

Pete recognised the building of Trenchant Forensic Services in the headlights ahead of them. Having visited many times to discuss the strength of forensic evidence with the scientists. Without warning, Ryan accelerated and mounted the pavement with a metallic bang; the car bounced onto the manicured lawn, narrowly missing a mature oak tree, wheels spinning as they fought to get traction on the slippery surface. Pete felt like everything was happening before him in slow motion.

He knew their plan but was overwhelmed with panic. The car headed straight towards the building. Pete covered his face with his arms for protection from the impending collision. The vehicle crashed through the reception glass doors and window. Pete's head hit the car roof as the impact threw him out of his seat. He felt nauseated by the crunching sound of the car smashing through the window frame and the breeze-block wall of the storage room. Pete shot forward, enveloped in the inflated airbag. His ears were buzzing, and he was struggling to catch his breath.

He got out of the car, feeling dazed and disorientated. Following on behind the others, his trance-like state was broken by Ryan pushing a holdall into his chest and shouting, 'Fill that up.' They frantically started emptying as many packages as they could from the metal industrial storage shelving. 'Don't worry about anything that's obviously not drugs, clothing, shoes, stuff like that can be left behind,' Ryan shouted, whilst swiping the plastic exhibit bags from the shelf using his arm. 'Any shooters will be useful, so grab them, too,' he added as an afterthought.

Pete found two plastic containers marked 'controlled drug samples' with a bio-hazard warning taped across them; he emptied the contents into his bag. A strong smell of petrol suddenly wafted across the room from behind them; Pete guessed it was leaking from the crashed car until he saw a fourth accomplice dowsing the place in petrol.

Between them, they had emptied the shelves in no time. Pete bent down and zipped up his bag; he'd filled it, and nothing more would fit inside.

Ryan ran carrying a bag over his shoulder. 'I can't see any more packages here. Is there anywhere else we need to look, Pete?'

Pete looked around for a split second, but his priority was getting as far away as possible before security guards or the police showed up. 'No, that's the only storage area,' he said, purposely failing to mention anything currently being processed in the laboratories.

'Well, if we've left anything behind, it will be destroyed in the fire,' Ryan said.

Pete picked up his holdall and slung it over his shoulder to help manage the weight. 'I don't think we've missed anything,' he said, looking around in dismay at the carnage.

'Time to go,' Ryan shouted, like a man possessed. Pete stayed close to Hyena as they fled the building through the wreckage of the reception.

A sudden whoosh of hot air and a fireball engulfed them as they ran. Pete was struggling to stay upright, slipping on the shards of glass and other debris underfoot. Relieved to have made it to the getaway car, he dropped the holdall and patted himself down to ensure he was not on fire. 'They're fireproof, you clown,' shouted Ryan, 'Get the bag in the boot and get into the car.' Pete complied, suddenly becoming aware of the wailing security alarm.

The new driver was the last to get in. Pete was sitting in the back next to the Hyena, and Ryan was the front passenger. 'I've burnt my fucking arm,' Ryan mumbled as the driver raced from the building. No sympathy was forthcoming from any of the others. Pete's eyes darted around, expecting to see blue flashing lights heading their way at any moment. The fire had taken hold of the building, creating a bright beacon against the dark sky for the cops to be drawn towards.

The car was driven across the business park, taking junctions at ridiculous speeds. Pete clung onto the headrest in front of him as he and Hyena struggled against gravity, being thrown about in the back seat.

The car screeched to a sudden halt. 'Get out, throw your boiler suits back into the car,' Ryan instructed. Pete climbed out of the back, relieved that the adrenaline-rush journey was over; his ears were still ringing. He tossed the balaclava and boiler suit onto the back seat.

The fourth man pushed him out of the way and began dowsing petrol everywhere, this time inside the car. Pete picked up his holdall and quickly made up some distance, sprinting to catch up with the others as they disappeared into the darkness along a cinder track that led into the surrounding woodland.

The surrounding area lit up momentarily as the fire took hold of the car. Pete struggled to keep up with the others, jogging along the woodland pathway, gasping for breath and trying to ignore the burning pain in his lungs.

They continued over a canal bridge and into an even denser wooded area. Pete begrudgingly admired their criminal expertise. Within minutes, they were far away from the crime scene and off the beaten track, hidden from the attention of any approaching police patrols.

Just as Pete felt like his lungs were about to explode, a clearing appeared ahead of them, where a parked car had been left earlier for them. Pete dropped the holdall unceremoniously and leaned forward, placing his hands on his knees for support, fearing he was about to throw up, whilst gasping for breath.

Ryan grabbed Pete's holdall and threw it into the car boot. 'Get in the car,' Ryan yelled at him while running towards the front passenger seat.

The fourth man entered the driver's seat, 'I'll drop you two first, Ryan.' His delivery was calm and measured. Ryan didn't answer; he was gingerly attending to his injured arm. Pete looked at Hyena; he still didn't return a look but maintained a vacant stare ahead of him. Pete guessed that he wasn't the brightest button in the box. He didn't recognise him as a gang member but was determined to remember his face for future reference. The fourth man didn't acknowledge Pete either; Pete guessed he was from the upper echelons of the gang, probably one of Wayne's trusted lieutenants, calm and professional in his approach. He looked like a seasoned gangster, not to be messed with. And Pete had no intention of doing that.

14

DS Lee McCann had not slept well; he'd awoken at two o'clock and not managed to drop off again. His mind was ruminating over his conversation with DS Pete Higgs and wouldn't settle. Eventually, he gave up trying to sleep and got up at five o'clock, deciding to use the time wisely and run to work; the exercise would also help to clear his head.

His mind returned to the day Jason Hamilton attacked him outside his flat as he walked towards the communal parking bays. Which happened every time he left the apartment. He knew he should buy a new place to live but never had time to look for somewhere new. He glanced over to the bushes by the car parking spaces, to the exact spot where he initially saw Hamilton. His mind flashed back to the moment of Jason Hamilton, standing, staring back at him, cold hatred in his dark eyes; the shock of seeing Hamilton outside his home and then the realisation that he was about to be attacked still lingered vividly. His emotions were still raw, the threat still real.

Breaking into a run, he shook away the thoughts and built up a decent pace, heading to the cinder trail pathway, which led through the country park. Lee loved running early in the morning; the fresh air was invigorating, and the smell of the damp earth and vegetation was soothing. The exercise also calmed his mind from figuring out why Pete Higgs was getting involved in stuff he shouldn't be and how Lee could obtain the evidence against him.

A mile after leaving the nature oasis, Lee was breathing in the car fumes of suburbia. The volume of cars commuting to the city centre was building up already. The police station came into view. It was a modern, characterless building, but for the retro blue lamp and corporate logo affixed to the side of the building. He found a burst of energy and upped his speed for the final stretch.

The changing rooms were empty; he placed his rucksack on the bench and headed for the shower. He enjoyed the sense of achievement and feel-good endorphins released during the run. The power shower was relaxing: he gradually decreased the heat to cold. He'd read that cold water promoted muscle recovery but wasn't brave enough to step into a cold shower from the off.

Once dressed, Lee went to the kitchen and made a coffee. The office was slowly coming to life. Several detectives were already sitting at their computers, starting work early to beat the congestion on the M60. Lee noticed DI Andrea Statham was at her desk; he made his way over to her office.

Andrea was engrossed, reading an incident log on her computer and didn't acknowledge Lee. He was just about to say he'd return later when she looked up at him.

'Morning, Lee. Have a seat.' It was more of an instruction than an invitation. Lee sat down and took a sip of coffee. He noticed Andrea didn't have a coffee and felt guilty for not making her one while she finished reading.

Lee wished he'd returned to his desk rather than wait: he also had work to get on with whilst Andrea was busy. Although he was intrigued to know what had grabbed her attention, he suspected the team had been allocated a new crime investigation from an overnight incident and would need to be briefed.

'They're taking the piss big time now,' Andrea announced, breaking away from her computer, 'the cheeky bastards have ram-raided the forensic science labs and torched the place.'

'I'll get onto them and find out if we've lost the Declan Marsh drugs in the fire,' Lee said, not holding out much hope.

'No need; the forensic submissions branch is coordinating the situation and will update us asap.'

'Has any CCTV footage been recovered?' Lee asked, growing intrigued about who dared to carry out such an attack.

'I'm not sure yet; the local CID is dealing with it. If they have destroyed our evidence and the victim, O'Leary, won't cooperate, we will struggle to get a conviction,' Andrea said, sounding deflated.

Lee said what they were both thinking. 'I'm putting my money on Wayne Davies's firm being behind this.'

'It's one of at least three labs we use locally. It's no coincidence that they picked this one.'

'Surely, Higgsy wouldn't stoop that low. Would he? To tell them which lab was undertaking the examination of the drugs,' Lee asked.

'It depends on how desperate he is, I suppose. Nothing would surprise me; he's a lost cause,' Andrea said.

'I'll have a drive over to the CID office and see how their investigation is going. Catch you later.' Lee left the office and headed to his car.

*

Later that day, DS Pete Higgs had finished his shift and collapsed onto the sofa with one purpose: to vegetate in front of the television. He was tired; the beers at the pub on the way home had made him feel sleepy.

He'd only intended to have a couple of pints, but the new arrival at the surveillance unit, DC Steve Comstive, had wanted to empty Pete's brains of everything he knew about the team and how the unit operated. He seemed very keen and eager to make a good impression. Pete had lost count of how many beers they had drank but was pretty sure it fell within the definition of binge drinking.

Pete took another drink of Chablis and continued to follow the travels of a former politician across Europe by train only because there was nothing else he fancied watching.

The clicking of a key opening the front door, followed by chatter, brought him back from his drunken stupor to the present. Ryan entered the lounge, followed by Wayne.

'For fucks sake, what do you two want now?' Pete groaned.

'Not you piss-pot; I thought you were easing off the booze, you drunken bum. I told you, Ryan, he's a fucking liability,' Wayne responded, shaking his head and placing a black holdall by the sofa.

Ryan got a beer and sat down, smiling at Pete's discomfort. Wayne remained standing; he looked at Pete with disdain. Pete ignored him. He felt too pissed to engage in a row. Instead, he looked at Ryan and noticed the bandage on his right arm.

'How's your arm? Have you had it checked over?' Pete asked Ryan, changing the subject from Wayne's predictable sly digs at him. So much for building mutual respect between them, Pete mused. Wayne was as antagonistic as ever.

'He nearly became a human fireball; he had one job, one job!' Wayne interrupted, mocking Ryan. Ryan didn't bite; he took a long gulp of lager and replied, 'My arm is fine. We pulled the job, didn't we? Even bent bastard Pete got stuck in. And we blagged a shed load of cocaine and methamphetamine as a bonus.'

'Credit where credit's due, you did okay. Even you plod, you bent bastard,' Wayne acknowledged.

'Give it a rest, Wayne. I've heard it all before. You're becoming tedious now. I've ensured O'Leary won't give evidence, and I got the drugs back for you last night. So now the cops won't be able to charge Declan Marsh, and you're still on my case. Anyway, is it wise for you two to visit here so often? Pete asked, irritated more by the intrusion than the risk of being seen with them.

'Good point, you can move out if you want; I'm sure Frank wouldn't mind you dossing in his office again,' Wayne sneered.

'What's in the holdall?' Pete asked, wanting to change the subject again.

'A few Glocks and some ammunition. You will take them to the Irish boys tomorrow, so you'd better sober up. I can't afford any fuck ups on this deal. These boys will want loads more if they like the merchandise.'

Wayne helped himself to a beer and took the remaining chair, immediately scrolling on his phone.

Ryan had switched the channels and was now engrossed in watching a fly-on-the-wall documentary about police firearms teams.

Pete's anxiety was swelling, darkening his mood like storm clouds; if it weren't for the calming effect of the beer, he'd be struggling to keep it together.

The ram-raid was a step too far; he had always been confident that he could explain away the drugs. He felt like he was losing control again. He'd gone through a mental checklist of how they had covered their tracks the night before and was satisfied the cops would not find any evidence to connect them. But, as Pete knew very well from experience, it wasn't unheard of to have not located a CCTV camera or a nosey security guard. His only defence would be one of duress, that Wayne had threatened to harm his family if he didn't comply.

He sat up and looked into the black holdall, immediately recognising the Glocks. He noticed Wayne had looked up from his phone and was watching him closely. Pete feigned not to have seen the attention he was receiving. He took hold of one of the pistols and looked for the magazine; it wasn't there. Next, Pete slid back the working parts to check the chamber; there was no ammunition in the spout either. Probably for the best, he thought; the temptation to slot Wayne may have been too hard to resist.

15

The specialist video evidence-gathering detective produced a working copy of the DVD and was setting up the viewing station as DI Andrea Statham and DS Lee McCann entered the room; Andrea took in the surroundings. It was her first visit since the state-of-the-art refurbishment. CCTV evidence was now paramount to the success of major criminal investigations; it needed to be right. The place exuded an air of sophistication, meticulously designed with dark soundproof panelling covering the walls, casting a subdued ambience courtesy of the soft lighting. Banks of television monitors lined the room, casting an almost surveillance-like atmosphere. The smell of newly installed electrical gadgets hung in the air, adding to the room's technical intrigue. Andrea took a seat and pulled her jacket tighter in response to the cool air being pumped out by the air conditioning system.

The geeky-looking detective pressed play, and the footage commenced. They were fully focused, watching the early draft compilation. It was still a work in progress; further trawls to locate CCTV cameras along possible routes taken by the ram-raid team were still progressing.

The operator rewound the compilation footage, 'I'll rerun it for you,' he said. Andrea pulled her chair closer to the screen, and they began watching the footage from the start again. With each viewing, Lee knew there was an increased chance of spotting more vital details not identified in previous viewings. He had not been surprised that the gang wore boiler suits and balaclavas, and he suspected they had probably destroyed the clothing shortly afterwards.

The internal footage downloaded from the cloud file showed three figures decamping from the car and filling bags with any forensic evidence packages they could lay their hands on. The picture quality of the footage was poor because of a cloud of dust and other debris from the impact of the car collision. But the images were more explicit on external cameras when the offenders reappeared outside with the fourth man from the second car until the smoke from the fire began to billow from out of the building, obstructing the view.

Lee knew that obtaining high-quality identification evidence from this footage was probably a non-starter. The imagery wasn't the best, and the offenders had concealed their faces with balaclavas. But that didn't deter his enthusiasm; he had made an observation that gave him hope. It was a long shot, but at present, the best opportunity to glean some evidence. He had a good feeling; he felt he was onto something.

'Would you excuse us for a few minutes, mate? Lee asked the detective operating the equipment. 'I need to speak to Andrea about some sensitive evidence.'

'Of course, give me a shout if you need me. I'll be in the main office,' the detective replied before leaving the room.

Andrea gave Lee a quizzical look and asked, 'What sensitive evidence?'

Lee sat forward on the edge of his chair and rewound the footage to the start. 'Focus on the offender who gets out of the front passenger seat,' Lee said before pressing play. He wanted Andrea to have the opportunity to discover what he had for herself without influencing her observation.

Andrea didn't ask why but watched the footage once again.

'Does anything catch your eye about him?'

'Replay it,' Andrea said, leaning forward. Again, she watched closely, focusing on the front seat passenger.

'My god, I know what you're thinking. Is that Pete Higgs?' Andrea asked, pointing at one of the offenders with her pen.

'Bingo,' Pete exclaimed. 'That's what I thought; his build and movements are consistent. He also appears more hesitant than the others, which would be understandable. What nails it for me is how he gets in and out of the car. I think it's him,' Lee said, unable to hide his satisfaction.

'We'll need to get some footage of Pete as a control sample to compare the two and get them analysed forensically by an expert. We could be onto something here, Lee,' Andrea said.

'I think we are; it's got to be him. For both of us to suspect it, that's no coincidence.'

'You absolute moron, Higgsy, you've done it this time; we're onto you,' Andrea beamed.

They watched the footage again before leaving the unit, optimistic about their discovery.

Whilst walking to the car, Andrea took a phone call. She held the car keys in Lee's direction, gesturing for him to drive. Lee took the keys whilst trying to eavesdrop on her conversation. He was thwarted when Andrea didn't join him immediately in the car; she remained standing by the passenger door, continuing the conversation. Lee started the car engine, hoping it would prompt her to get in before finishing the call.

Call finished, Andrea took a seat, and Lee left the car park, purposefully taking a route including Wilmslow Road and their favourite kebab shop.

'Well, I wasn't expecting that. The ram raiders didn't manage to destroy our drug samples in the fire.' Andrea smiled.

'Result!' Lee replied enthusiastically, 'today's is just getting better by the minute. Remind me to buy a lottery ticket on the way home.'

'Most of the drugs were stolen or went up in smoke, but luckily for us, the samples being used for forensic analysis were being processed in the labs. We've got the quick response of the fire brigade to thank for that.

'Basics, poor security, that's privatisation for you. Forensic contracts are tendered to the most competitive bidder. I doubt top-grade security is a necessity.'

Andrea didn't continue the conversation. She knew the privatisation of the Forensic Science Service was a bugbear for Lee; they'd been down that road many times.

'We might as well get some lunch whilst we're passing,' Lee suggested, turning the car into a side street off Wilmslow Road. He parked alongside an industrial-sized bin on wheels, cardboard boxes and other debris stacked high, with the remainder having fallen on the floor.

'I'll just have a samosa. I'm not that hungry,' Andrea said.

They took their usual seats at the dining bar by the window overlooking the busy activity on Wilmslow Road. Andrea was slowly picking at her samosa whilst Lee set about his chicken and donner kebab on nan bread.

'Do you fancy coming over to mine tonight?' Andrea asked.

Lee gestured to his mouth, chewing a mouthful of kebab. He then took a drink and wiped his lips with a serviette. He could have been accused of buying time before giving his answer. 'I'd love to, but I've got other plans.'

'No worries, you don't need to explain. It was only for a quick drink. I would probably benefit from an early night anyway.' Andrea interjected and focused back on her food.

Lee felt awkward; he was overly conscious that he had declined Andrea's last invitation and realised he had to choose his words carefully. 'That would have been great; we've not crashed out with food and movie for a while now.'

'Don't worry about it. How's your kebab?' Andrea asked.

Lee laughed nervously, 'Steady on, hear me out,' he said, amused by Andrea's snappy reaction. 'I have an alternative plan. I want to meet up with Pete Higgs and think it would be a good idea if you came too. He's keen to get back into your good books, and I'm keen to push him for insight into what's happening with him and Ryan Young. If you two kiss and makeup, it might soften him. And we'll be able to watch him, to compare with the footage.'

'What sort of alternative plan is that? Have you ditched me for drinks with Pete Higgs? Charming, at least I know where I stand now.'

Lee was relieved at her humour. 'I'll set it up then.'

'Can't wait,' Andrea teased.

*

Pete watched as Ryan checked his mirror, slowed the car down and turned off into the layby, trying hard to avoid the water-filled potholes created by heavy goods vehicles.

'We're the only car here; we stick out like a sore thumb. It's hardly a low-key location.' Pete grumbled and slumped back in the front passenger seat. It was plain to see he didn't want to be there. Pete preferred working in the background in a more inconspicuous role rather than front-of-house, exposing his identity to every Tom, Dick and Harry.

Ryan manoeuvred the car between two parked trucks and killed the engine, ignoring Pete's belligerent behaviour. 'Come on, let's go and get a coffee from the burger van,' Ryan said as if trying to appease a child.

Pete followed Ryan, tiptoeing around the potholes. Three truck drivers stood at the van chatting to the two women behind the counter. The women were both in their twenties, chatty and confident. They appeared to be enjoying some banter with the truck drivers.

'Are you getting them in, then? Black coffee, no sugar,' Ryan said before walking off in the direction of a wooden picnic table. Pete ordered the drinks and watched as Ryan sat down at the wooden trestle table and made a call on his mobile, obviously not for Pete's ears.

The conversation at the counter didn't interest him enough to join in; he'd become bored of politics long ago. Pete switched off from their conversation and glanced at the grill; the sausages looked appealing, and the fat-spitting noises and cooking smell gave him an instant hunger pang. He considered ordering food but couldn't be bothered waiting for the women to cook it. He just wanted to get the meeting done and get away from here. He'd not managed a line this morning, leaving him feeling fatigued and cranky.

Whilst walking towards the picnic table, Pete watched Ryan talking on his phone. He was curious about how Ryan would handle the meeting. Pete was slowly warming to Ryan and hadn't yet ruled out the possibility of going into cahoots with him—Pete as the senior partner, of course.

He joined Ryan and placed the drinks on the table. Ryan tucked his phone away and gave Pete a long, hard stare. Pete stared back but said nothing.

'What's up with you this morning? Ryan asked, 'You've had one on you all morning.'

'Nothing, all is good in the hood,' Pete's answer sounded cagey. Ryan shook his head and smirked. Pete continued, 'I just think I could be of better use rather than doing stuff like this.'

'Wayne's just making sure he can trust you; he's not keen on bent cops. You know that.' Ryan's face now looked serious; the smirk had gone. He nonchalantly blew into his paper cup to cool the coffee.

'Do you trust me, Ryan?' Pete said, maintaining a locked-in stare.

'Why do you ask?'

'It would definitely be mutually advantageous to have each other's back. From talking to Frank Burton and Jason Hamilton, I know gang members are expendable. Hamilton knew you were shagging Kirsty behind his back.' Pete retained eye contact, watching for a reaction.

Ryan laughed awkwardly but didn't reply. He cast his mind back to the night in question; Hamilton was in Amsterdam. His partner Kirsty had returned to their home and disturbed intruders, who fled over the fence. She'd invited Ryan around to check the house and ensure there was no further threat. Having done so, Ryan accepted the offer of a few drinks, and one thing led to another.

Pete wasn't letting go, 'We both know he tried to kill you, and Wayne worked alongside him. You need to consider whether you can trust Wayne,'

Ryan's memory of the night dissipated, 'I'll take my chances; I've done okay up to now. I'm still here to tell the story–Hamilton's not.'

'Where is Hamilton?' Pete regretted that his question came across as too eager rather than an idle curiosity. But the way Ryan said 'Hamilton's not.' gave Pete the impression that Ryan enjoyed boasting about it and may want to elaborate.

'Are you back in cop mode?' Ryan asked defensively. Pete knew he'd asked one question too many. But the way Ryan spoke about Hamilton had a finality about it.

'No, like I said, I was just thinking whether we need to have each other's back.' Pete felt like he'd achieved his objective; Ryan had gone quiet and reflective, maybe thinking it over. Pete remained silent, hoping Ryan would start talking and opening up.

'The Irishman's here,' Ryan announced, sounding relieved to leave the conversation behind. A truck driver, the Irishman, climbed down from the cab—a big guy, six-foot-tall, overweight, shaved head, wearing a black down jacket and jeans. Tattoos creeping down his arms onto his big shovel hands. He bought a drink and approached the table with a confident swagger.

'You're in my seat,' he bellowed; this comment and his accent confirmed who he was to Ryan.

'I'm Ryan. Good to meet you.' The Irishman sat beside Pete, and the table's wooden legs sank further into the turf with his weight.

'And who the fuck is this?' He said, giving Pete an intimidating once over.

'Don't worry about him; he's a cop,' Ryan said dismissively.

'Of course he is,' the Irishman laughed, slapping Pete on his back. Pete liked the humour and laughed, too, impressed with Ryan's guile and quick wit. 'So, what have you got for me then?'

'Over here,' Ryan said, standing up. Pete and the Irishman followed Ryan to the boot of the car. The Irishman pulled on a pair of surgical gloves, then looked inside the black holdall. Pete and Ryan watched him as he silently examined the pistols with an air of expertise, hidden from view by the adjacent truck.

'They seem okay, fellas. But do you have enough?'

'Not a problem, we can supply as many as you need. The same delivery method as the crack and 'H'.'

'No, we'll collect the weaponry from you. We like to inspect it first before taking delivery.'

'Fine by me,' Ryan said.

'I'll take these samples with me. The boss will want to give them a proper once-over at the firing range. What about the machine guns?'

'They're in safe storage; moving those around is too risky. You can inspect them on the day,' Ryan replied.

'They'd better be good, you wouldn't want to fuck us about, would you?'

'You won't be disappointed; this is all quality stuff from the Gulf Wars. In fact, I guarantee you'll be back for more.'

'Is that so? I'll be in touch, boys.' The Irishman lifted the holdall from the boot and headed for his truck.

Once the Irishman was out of hearing range, Pete said, 'He's an intimidating lump, I wouldn't want to piss him off.'

'Nah, it's just the accent, and besides, nothing a 9mm wouldn't sort out.'

'Yeah, right,' Pete said, chuckling at Ryan's gangster bravado. 'Let's get out of here.'

16

Andrea and Lee strolled along the wet pavement of Deansgate; Andrea was feeling invigorated at the prospect of them having identified Pete Higgs taking part in the raid at the forensic labs.

'I'm not sure meeting up with Pete is a wise move. Further down the line, his defence might make all sorts of accusations about us contravening the Police and Criminal Evidence Act, obtaining evidence unfairly,' Andrea said.

'We'll be fine. Pete is still a colleague and a supposed friend. We won't ask any leading questions and obviously can't use anything he says as evidence because he's not under caution, but it gives us a heads-up. Besides, Pete invited me for a beer. He'd suspect something was amiss if I suddenly ghosted him,' Lee reasoned.

'Fair point. We just need to ensure we develop a water-tight case which won't be weakened by the defence muddying the waters,' Andrea said, still unsure.

'I thought we'd meet him here,' Lee said, pointing to the pub just ahead of them on his left.

'Is it not a bit too busy here?' Andrea asked, following Lee inside.

'No, there are plenty of nooks and crannies; we'll be fine. It's like hiding in plain sight.' The long bar on the pub's right-hand side stretched towards the far end. Lee continued manoeuvring around the tables and headed up the stairs on the left. He selected a table tucked away in a corner and slid onto the bench seat. Andrea chose a chair opposite him.

'This is a great place to sit, but it's a right trek to the bar,' Andrea said.

'Don't worry; it's my round anyway. The staff sometimes open the other bar through there,' Lee said, pointing to a door. 'It used to be a cinema back in the day. Apparently, it's one of the largest pubs in the country.'

'No surprises there,' Andrea said, looking around the vast lounge area as Lee went for the drinks.

Lee returned to the table a short time later, 'It's a shame we're not in the car. We could have offered Pete a lift home and studied how he got in,' Lee said with a wry smile.

'I think we'll leave the forensic work to the experts,' Andrea replied, chuckling at the thought. She leaned over conspiratorially and lowered her voice. We may have another strong lead.'

'What? Since I've been at the bar?' Lee asked, looking puzzled.

'I've just taken a call from a trusted contact who overheard an interesting conversation on the concourse at the Crown Court today,' Andrea announced, clearly pleased with her scoop.

Lee also leaned into the table, lowering his voice to a whisper, 'At Crown Court, eh? So, it's likely to be from a cop or a con?'

'You can keep guessing all you want; I'm not revealing my source to anybody. The information is always off the record and very reliable. He insists on remaining anonymous, so I need to keep it that way and not piss him off to keep it flowing.'

'So, it's someone who knows the system and the pitfalls too. A wise man,' Lee said, now struggling to hide his curiosity.

'Frank Burton was talking to a scrote on the concourse; my man recognised him as one of Wayne Davies's boys. After the conversation, when Frank Burton had left, the scroat got on his mobile phone to someone else and was talking about Ryan shifting some pistols.' He was giving it large, the wannabe gangster, thinking no one was about, totally unaware of my man standing in the shadows listening to him.

'Ryan Young?'

'Exactly what I suspected; it's got to be. We need to do some more research and get a search warrant.'

'So, agreeing to meet up with Pete Higgs could be more fortuitous than we expected. Come on down, Higgsy, let's see what you let slip to us after a few beers.'

'I'll get us another drink. I wish we had one of those apps to order at the table,' Andrea said before grabbing her handbag and heading to the bar.

Lee was scrolling through social media on his phone when he became aware of a figure approaching the table. He looked up, expecting to see Andrea with the drinks, only to find himself staring straight at Pete Higgs.

'How are you doing, Lee? Has Andrea had second thoughts about coming?' Pete asked with a grimace.

'No, she's at the bar, mate; I'm surprised you didn't pass her on your way here. I'm fine, mate, how are you?'

'Not bad, mate; I've still got a lot of shit going on, but I'm managing to get by. Andrea's not going to peck my head, is she? I could do without it, to be honest.'

'No, you're safe for now. Talk of the devil, and here she is,' Lee said, looking at Andrea as she returned to the table.

'I saw you arrive, Pete, so I got you an IPA. I hope that's still your tipple?'

'Perfect, thanks, Andrea,' Pete replied. Lee sensed Pete wasn't as relaxed and confident as usual; he looked apprehensive, and his appearance was dishevelled, too, a shadow of his former self.

'Yeah, I saw you head for the gents for a quick visit, or was it for a quick line of Charlie,' Andrea continued.

'A fucking line! What are you on about?' Pete exploded; his apprehensive disposition suddenly vanished. Lee laughed, trying to make light of the skirmish, but Andrea went for the kill with her next line.

'Calm down, Pete, and wipe the powder off your nose; that's the giveaway!' Andrea started laughing.

'That's not fucking Charlie; it's sugar from a doughnut,' Pete explained, wiping under his nose with the back of his hand.

'I'm joking; I'm just winding you up. There's nothing there, you muppet,' Andrea said endearingly, but continuing to laugh, satisfied she'd put Pete on the back foot under the cover of apparent humour and broken the ice.

'Pack it in, you two, for fucks sake. You'll get us thrown out,' Lee said, joining in with the banter. Pete started laughing and sat back. He looked uncomfortable and rattled.

'It's been a while; how are you doing?' Andrea asked; she strongly suspected he was still on the coke judging from his explosive reaction.

'Fine until you started winding me up; good job, it's you. Anyone else would have got both barrels,' he said. Andrea felt a pang of sorrow for Pete; he looked like he wasn't in a good place. But he'd not helped himself. She had tried hard to help him through his relationship breakup, but he had pushed her away.

The small talk flowed easily, mostly around Pete's divorce, drinking and gambling. Followed by reminiscing about the good old days, long before the job was fucked, a view many cops held in relation to current policing practices and bosses.

Pete headed to the bar for another round of drinks. 'Christ, Andrea, I thought you were trying to start World

War Three when you suggested he'd just done a line; it was close to the bone,' Lee said.

'You forget Lee; I know Pete well, even so, I had him rattled. If there was any doubt about him being on the coke, there isn't now.' Lee smiled and shook his head. 'At least give me some advanced warning next time.'

Pete returned with the drinks, having knocked back a confidence-boosting double whiskey at the bar. 'I'm glad you came tonight, Andrea; it's been too long. I'm sorry I've been a pain in the arse, but I'm back in control now. I've got my head around the divorce and stuff. It's not been easy,' Pete took a drink, and a pause in the conversation followed. Lee guessed that Andrea wanted him to continue talking, so he, too, remained quiet, filling the gap with a drink.

'How's work? Are you still happy at the surveillance unit?' Andrea said, letting him off the hook for now.

'Can't complain; Dave Ferguson has been good to me. He allows me some flexibility with shifts, and in return, I'm mentoring the new lads for him.'

'Sounds good, Pete. Our syndicate is getting busy again; the Superintendent has tasked us with investigating Jason Hamilton's organised crime group again. Apart from the intelligence that suggests he's been killed, there hasn't been anything else, certainly no sightings or intelligence on current activities,' Andrea said.

Lee suspected that Andrea was poking Pete for more information about Hamilton's alleged demise and kept quiet, just watching Pete's non-verbal behaviour. Pete didn't let anything leak; he'd regained his composure.

'I think the intelligence we are receiving about him is consistent and reliable; it's got to be from a gang member. I suspect Hamilton's dead. That's the word from his associates, too. I've heard talk that suggests a Columbian cartel may have assassinated him or that he'd pissed off the boys in Amsterdam,' Pete said. Lee sensed Pete felt in control, talking but not telling Andrea anything that she didn't already know.

'Lee mentioned that you were working on Ryan Young to get him grassing for you; what's he said about Hamilton?' Andrea's question was on the edge of being work-like. But she satisfied herself that they all were interested in Hamilton following the siege at Lee's flat. Lee was watching Pete closely for any adverse reaction.

'He's approached me several times in the pub, and we've had a beer. I'm just listening to what he has to say. Hopefully, he will develop some trust and start to tell me things. If he comes over as a source, that's a bonus. When he talks about Hamilton, I get the idea that Hamilton is dead. And he's certainly not fearful of him anymore, which you would have thought he would be after Hamilton tried to kill him.'

'What criminality is Young involved in these days?' Andrea said, firing questions in quick succession.

'I get the idea he's hands off these days,' Pete replied, shifting in his seat before picking up his jacket. Andrea nodded, knowing Pete knew much more than that. She sensed Pete had suddenly become uncomfortable talking about Ryan Young.

'Right, I need to get going. I'm seeing my kids tonight. I'll give you a bell if Ryan Young comes up with any interesting information. Good to see you, Andrea. Keep in touch.'

'No surprises there,' Lee said once Pete had walked out of sight. 'He was never going to incriminate himself or the others.'

'No, I guess not. Pete was cagy and on edge, like a man with lots to hide. Why the hell has he gone down that road? It's all going to end in tears for him.'

'It's usually down to money in these situations; he's probably racked up bad gambling debts. But did you see the way he stood up from his chair…it's definitely him on the video!' Lee burst out laughing, unable to keep a straight face.

'I get the feeling you're not taking this seriously,' Andrea laughed.

'Do you fancy one for the road?' Lee asked, having broken the tension of their meeting with Pete.

'No thanks, I'm meeting Sarah Lovick for a Mexican. Why don't you join us?'

'I might as well; it beats microwaving a dinner for one on my own,' Lee replied enthusiastically.

The restaurant was just a stone's throw from the pub. As they stepped inside, Andrea glanced over at Lee, 'You're in for a treat; this place is amazing. Sarah and I are regulars.'

'Sounds good to me; I'm famished,' Lee said, looking around, taking in the surroundings.

A young waitress took Andrea's name and led them to a table in one of the booths. Andrea brushed the fabric covering the bench, 'These bright colours are beautiful; I'd love a dress in something similar.'

'It's really nice,' Lee said, taking in the decor of the place; terracotta, vibrant yellows and deep blues. 'The food smells delicious.' The aroma of meats cooking in spices and chilli sauces didn't help to quell his hunger.

They both drank bottled Mexican beer whilst waiting for Sarah to arrive.

'Here she is,' Andrea said, waving Sarah over.

Sarah sat on the bench next to Andrea, facing Lee. 'You must be Lee. Nice to meet you,' she said.

'Nice to meet you too, Sarah. I'm sorry for gate-crashing your dinner. It's a great place you've discovered here.'

'I don't mind; I wondered when Andrea would introduce us,' She said, winking at Andrea.

The waitress returned and took another drink order. Andrea and Sarah ordered their usual bottle of wine. Lee decided to stay on the bottled beers.

Lee's mobile phone began to ring, 'Do you mind if I take this? It's an important call.' He left the table and headed for the foyer as Andrea and Sarah shook their heads, offering no objection to the interruption.

'Well, he's a catch,' Sarah said, watching Lee walk away. 'Well done you, you've found a keeper.'

'We get on well, and the chemistry is brilliant; I'm glad you approve,' Andrea said, whilst checking Lee out through the restaurant window.

'Do you think he's the one?'

'I hope so,' Andrea laughed.

Lee returned to the table, and the waitress took their food orders. The place was now bustling, with a vibrant, friendly atmosphere. A friendly hum of chatter filled the room. After a further drinks order, the waitress approached the table, balancing a large tray and placed the three dishes on the table. Andrea took in the aromas from the dishes and followed the other two, tucking into the food.

After indulging in their meals, the trio savoured another bottle of wine. Andrea was heartened to see that Sarah had appeared to take quite a liking to Lee; the conversation between them was flowing easily. Andrea, felt a warm satisfaction about how the evening had unfolded.

'We've booked a taxi to Andrea's. Do you want us to drop you off on the way?' Lee asked.

Sarah smiled politely, 'I'm fine, but thanks for the offer, Lee. I'm taking the train home.'

Lee stepped in to pay the bill and left a tip for the waitress. They headed out of the restaurant and said their goodbyes, agreeing they should meet again soon before heading off in opposite directions. Andrea linked Lee's arm as they strolled towards the taxi rank.

Andrea and Lee huddled together in the taxi. Andrea felt contented and emotionally fulfilled as she nestled into Lee. The anticipation of spending the future with Lee was an exciting thought. She rested her head on his shoulder and closed her eyes.

17

Ryan strolled lethargically from the kitchen carrying two of Pete's cans from the fridge, and handed one to Pete. The chill of the lager matched the frosty reception Pete had given him on his arrival. Pete felt irritated by Ryan's presence; he'd not spent any time at the flat for a week or so, and Pete was getting used to enjoying his own space.

'Wayne mentioned your conversation with him about DI Statham being back on our case,' Ryan said, opening the ring pull on the can. 'What's her problem with us? There must be other shit going on in Manchester that she could look at.'

Without shifting his gaze from the telly, Pete responded dryly, 'Keeping Wayne updated on police sniffing around him is my job.' Pete swung his legs off the sofa and sat up, facing Ryan. He opened his can and took a swig. 'You and Wayne have let your standards slip. You take unnecessary risks that attract attention from the cops, like visiting here for a start. I'm a significant asset to the firm; you should go out of your way not to be seen with me. Operational security doesn't register with you guys. Wayne risks everything by sending me out on minor tasks, which any of his boys could do, just to belittle me and get his kicks. It's all about flexing his muscles rather than getting the best use of my skill set.' Pete had enjoyed breaking the news to Wayne; it wasn't what Wayne had wanted to hear. But he would appreciate the warning and further relevant updates. Pete's usefulness and kudos were on the up, and he was ready to milk it for all he could. 'As for DI Andrea Statham, you make life easy for her. Raiding the forensic lab had your names written all over it. Was it really necessary to keep Declan Marsh from being sent down? I don't think so. I suspect that was all about Wayne's ego again. Are you seeing a pattern here?' Pete burst out into a cynical laugh, satisfied with his putdown.

'You're right; it is what he pays you for, good money, too. He's got another task for you. It might be more suited to your high-held opinion of yourself. He wants DI Andrea Statham off the case and out of our faces. He's not bothered how you do it; just get it sorted. Ryan now had Pete's full attention.

Pete's eyes narrowed; his smugness dissipated quickly, replaced by exasperation and disbelief. 'Is he on fucking drugs? How does he expect me to do that? And has he not thought it through that another cop will take her place? What the fuck is he aiming to achieve here?'

'Not my problem, just get it sorted,' Ryan laughed whilst putting his coat on, 'I'll see you in a few days, probably here,' he said with a wink.

Pete watched Ryan leave the flat, seething, guessing Ryan had enjoyed pissing on his parade. His mind was already trying to figure out what he would do.

For the rest of the evening, Pete zoned out in front of the television; he'd drunk too much wine and fallen asleep on the sofa. His mind had ruminated about how he could deliver on Wayne's latest request. Wayne's strategies developed a more unrealistic, unachievable plan with each glass of wine he necked. He'd mulled over getting on a plane and seeking bar work abroad. A drunken perspective always made this plan look like a good option.

He'd seriously considered colluding with Andrea and helping her to convict Wayne. But his involvement in criminality was too deep for the Crown Prosecution Service to do a deal. He reluctantly accepted he'd still end up doing prison time, even if he grassed. A double whammy because Wayne's boys could easily get to him inside, and being placed on the nonce wing for his own safety wasn't an option. Pete's eyes grew heavy. He dozed off on the sofa, thoughts of Statham swirling in his slumber.

Pete's eyes opened wide; his whole body jolted as if he'd received an electric shock. He rolled off the sofa and fell to the floor, landing on all fours in a failed attempt to stand up. The alcohol hadn't worn off yet. A surge of panic filled him, 'What the fuck was that?' He remained perfectly still, straining his ears. The noises continued emanating from the front door, scratching and thuds. His instinct warned him to run, but where to? He'd break his legs if he jumped from the window. It was the only door.

A deafening bang filled the room, followed by the sound of wood cracking and splintering. Pete looked up, wincing at the commotion. The front door was hanging precariously by its upper hinge, repeatedly thrust aside by each person rushing into the flat, banging into the wall and left swinging as more bodies entered the flat. Pete still felt pissed, and fear took over. Fight or flight time? Is this it? Are the bastards going to kill me? He counted at least four intruders running towards him.

A bright torchlight was shining directly into Pete's eyes. It caused a sharp stabbing pain to his already thumping headache. 'Police, lie on your front, stretch your arms and legs out. Who else is here?' From further away, Pete could hear familiar cries of 'Room clear.' He was beginning to make sense of the situation; he was overwhelmed and grateful that it wasn't Wayne's boys or a rival gang crashing through the door. But the police were still a poor alternative in the big scheme of things; he may survive, but what evidence did they have on him to come through the door? Pete's world felt like it had collapsed even further; the holdall containing the Baikal pistols was under his bed. I'm fucked, he silently conceded, regretting the day he clapped eyes on Frank Burton and his cronies.

'All right, I'm moving as fast as I can,' he shouted at the police officers, roughly manhandling him onto the floor. An officer switched the lights on; Pete screwed his eyes shut, struggling to adjust to the brightness.

The banging and shouting had stopped. Pete's fear was replaced by panic, flashbacks of him strangling Andrea Statham and images of her dead body in the foetal position in the back of his car emerged. He broke into a cold sweat and felt like screaming aloud; he was losing it.

His attention was taken by an officer explaining that he had a warrant to search for firearms. Pete let the word 'firearms' sink in, not 'murder.'

The confusion started to clear; he'd had a nightmare about killing Andrea, but it wasn't real. He feared he was experiencing psychotic delusions. Relief surged through his body. But that didn't help his current situation. It was a living nightmare.

He watched as a police officer walked towards him carrying the black holdall he'd discovered under the bed. 'Do you want to tell me what's in here before I open it?'

'I've never seen it before,' Pete replied, 'I'm just getting my head down here; it's not my flat, moving into damage limitation mode. He felt confident that his fingerprints or DNA weren't on the bag. But a nagging thought was pecking at his brain; what jail time could he expect for being in possession of firearms? Pete suspected the police had received a tip-off. They knew what they were looking for, and brought the bag to him, hoping he would incriminate himself by showing a knowledge of the contents.

Pete watched, cringing as the officer unzipped the bag; his movements appeared to be in slow motion. Pete had previously thought his life was at rock bottom; he'd been wrong. He'd just landed there now.

The officer looked puzzled. 'Sarge, have you got a minute?' He nodded towards the bedroom. The officer took the bag to the bedroom, followed by the sergeant.' Pete was intrigued. Why had they not arrested him? He was puzzled.

The tactical aid unit sergeant returned to the lounge. He knelt beside Pete, 'I don't know what you're playing at Higgsy, but be careful who you fuck with. You're pissing a lot of people off, from what I hear. Here's a copy of the warrant.' He dropped the occupants' copy of the warrant on the floor by Pete's head and got to his feet.

The search team followed the sergeant out of the flat. Pete was dumbfounded as to why they hadn't arrested him. He glanced over the warrant; evidence recovered – nil. Why had they not seized the pistols? The signature at the foot of the page was familiar, leaving him seething. The warrant had been sworn out before the Magistrates by DI Andrea Statham. Well, if she wanted to play hardball, bring it on. Pete stumbled to his feet; he needed a glass of water.

18

'That front door looks like a right mess; they've taken it clean off the hinges. You'd better get it mended,' Ryan said as he sauntered into the flat.

'Not my problem. Maybe you should speak to the landlord if you're bothered about it,' Pete replied. He suspected Wayne would have a justified claim against the police because the search had been negative, but couldn't be bothered sharing the thought with Ryan.

'I thought the police rang the doorbell these days, Ryan said. He picked up the copy of the warrant from the breakfast bar and scanned through it. 'This has Andrea Statham's signature on it, fucking priceless; she must be the laughing stock of the station. Can you imagine her face when they told her they found water pistols!' Ryan said, laughing, delight evident in his voice.

Pete looked up from the breakfast bar, munching on toast. 'You're reading too much into it. Nobody will give it a second thought,' Pete lied, putting Ryan's opinion down, knowing banter would have been flying around the nick.

Pete had managed a few more hours of kip after the police had left. A line of coke put him back on his feet again when he awoke.

'What did the cops do when they realised the bag was full of water pistols?' Ryan quizzed, smirking and enjoying Pete's discomfort.

'The cops couldn't give a toss; it was just another house search, one of many for the Tactical Aid Team. They still get paid.' Pete wouldn't give Ryan the satisfaction of telling him the details. He certainly wasn't going to mention the fear he experienced when the prospect of doing prison time hit him. Nor the humiliation of being slung onto the floor whilst fellow police officers searched his flat.

Ryan snatched the last piece of toast from Pete's plate. Pete flew out of his seat and launched his full weight at Ryan, grabbing him by the throat with both hands and running him backwards until he banged into the wall, dropping the toast on the floor.

Pete got up close to Ryan's face. 'I've just about fucking had it with you pricks. Things need to change around here. I am not taking shit anymore from you, now fuck off.' The shock and fear on Ryan's face surprised Pete. There was no retaliation, just submission. Pete pushed him away and returned to his seat to calm down. Ryan walked into the lounge area whilst rubbing the back of his head and sat down.

It was fucking naïve of Wayne to set me up just for kicks; how much of this shit do I need to take from him? The cops will discover that this flat belongs to him, probably leading to enquiries into his finances. He's poked a hornet's nest and brought unwanted police attention to us all,' Pete said.

'Wayne didn't set it up.' It was Pete's turn to look shocked. 'After you told him we were back under investigation, he switched the pistols for water pistols just as a precaution in case they raided the flat.' Ryan spoke quietly. 'You need to find out how they knew about the pistols and who tipped them off. He'll be satisfied you're not the grass; if you'd told them about the pistols, they wouldn't have raided the place whilst you were present.

Ryan's words hung in Pete's mind. If Wayne hadn't tipped them off, who had? Had he let something slip whilst having beers with Statham? No, he wouldn't have, but Lee knew where he lived. Pete suddenly became aware that

Ryan was still talking, 'Don't you need to be getting on your way?' Pete asked, interrupting him.

'I do, but so do you. You need to get a grip of Andrea Statham.'

Ryan left, and the flat was quiet and peaceful once again. Pete needed to gather his thoughts. His boss, DI Dave Ferguson, had summoned him to a meeting. But before heading to the station, he had a call to make.

'Morning, Frank. I guess you have heard about last night's events?'

'Indeed, I have Peter; the water pistol gag was a bad idea. Instead of playing games with the police, Wayne should have emptied the flat of incriminating evidence. It will probably make them more determined to investigate him now. Once you told him that Andrea Statham was on his case again, he wanted to find out how much she knew about us; we assumed the flat was under her radar, but it appears not.' Pete didn't elaborate that he had given Lee the flat's details, albeit through being under pressure at the time.

'I suspect Wayne is enjoying watching me squirm. But he may end up paying a high price for his amusement. I know he doesn't like me much, but he needs to focus on the bigger picture.'

'Point taken, Peter. I'll monitor the situation closely. I like him to have a good length of rope; it boosts his confidence and makes him more effective. But be reassured, I'll reign in him if it becomes necessary.' Frank's tone indicated to Pete that the conversation was over.

'Before I go, I must ensure we're on the same song sheet. If the cops contact you, you allowed me to stay at the flat as a favour when Rachel kicked me out. I am unaware of

Wayne's involvement with the property and assumed it was yours. Keep the alibi simple.'

'Of course, Peter, always the best way forward. Have a good day.' Frank ended the call.

*

Pete closed the door and took a seat opposite DI Dave Ferguson. Pete was looking for mood music clues. He sensed Dave was feeling a little uneasy. There was no bottle of whiskey or coffee on offer on this occasion. The silence continued, becoming uncomfortable, but both detectives prolonged it, not wanting to be the first to speak.

'What the hell's going on, Pete?' Dave broke the silence with genuine sincerity.

'You tell me. Andrea Statham's name was on the warrant. Pete went for the middle ground, not wanting to wind his boss up but not telling him anything, either.

Dave looked down towards the desktop and shook his head. 'Well, for starters, what are you doing living in an apartment owned by one of our most notorious organised crime gangs?' Dave spat out, glaring at Pete. Pete could now hear the mood music loud and clear. Dave Ferguson wasn't happy. Pete knew that was bad news; Dave was no mug, and he didn't lose his temper easily.

'Well, that's not right. Frank Burton, a solicitor, owns the flat,' Pete said, working hard to look incredulous and wounded, 'How do you know they own the flat, boss? Have they set Frank up as the middleman to get to me? Shit, are they setting me up here? I thought I could trust Frank Burton. I've known him for years' Pete progressed into victim status in an attempt to deflect any further onslaught. He stood up, pacing the room.

'Pete, it's me you're talking to, don't play games with me. Give me some respect, please. If you've dug yourself into a

hole, I can help to get you out with damage limitation.'
Dave wasn't softening; Pete knew he had his work cut out.

'Boss, I've got nothing to hide. Wayne Davies and his
boys have set me up because I've been getting under their
skin. I've been on their case for a while and rattled them.
What's Andrea said to you?' Pete asked to break the
intensity.

'What was with the bag of water pistols?' Dave wasn't for
sharing the warrant's intelligence case and sidestepped the
question.

'Not a clue, it's been there since I moved in; I just
assumed it was Frank's stuff.' Pete looked at the floor,
shaking his head slowly, 'I know I've pissed Andrea off, but
she won't listen to me; surely you can see through this
charade, boss?'

'That will be all for now, Pete,' Dave said matter of factly.
Dave had been a top thief-taker in his day and a respected
career detective ever since. He was the go-to guy for
command when a sensitive or critical issue arose. Pete
sensed Dave was disappointed at Pete's reluctance to open
up. His answers had not fooled Dave, and he was now
probably on Pete's case along with Andrea.

'One other thing, Pete, until we get this sorted out, you're
restricted to office duties. I want you to quality assess this
year's surveillance authority applications. The surveillance
commissioners are visiting soon to inspect them; they must
be flawless.'

Pete got up and strolled towards the door.

'One last thing, Pete. It would be wise to find somewhere
else to live.

Pete didn't stop; he left the office, closing the door behind
him.

19

Pete slumped at his computer; he felt besieged and vulnerable. He knew he had to take action; he had to come out fighting. He was giving lip service to the punishment task before him, his quality assessment of the surveillance authority documents on his screen, whilst his primary focus was on considering his options. He was satisfied with successfully bringing Ryan to heal. Ryan had rolled over like a submissive puppy dog.

His main threat was Wayne Davies, the friction between them was palpable, and that hadn't changed. But DI Andrea Statham was still on his case, which was worse; they had a history together, had worked well together, had watched out for each other and trusted each other in the past; it felt like a betrayal. He couldn't even rule out that Dave Ferguson was also on his case now.

Whatever he and Andrea did have going between them didn't mean much to her now. Pete assumed she must have some knowledge of his activities, but if that was the case, why hadn't she had a word with him at the outset or had him arrested?

Her decision to execute a search warrant at his flat wouldn't have been easy. Therefore, it was apparent that she was hunting him down; she'd nailed her colours to the mast. But how much did she know? Who tipped her off? Pete was determined to find out. Her actions were an explicit declaration of hostility. He accepted this and accepted there was no way back for them.

Pete was in no doubt about the two main threats, but confident he could deal with them, he needed allies more than ever; Frank Burton would always take whatever course of action was best for Frank Burton. But Pete knew he could tap into that if he created a shared common purpose between them.

He was confident he could manipulate Ryan Young. Pete suspected there was still some tension between Wayne Davies and Ryan dating back to when Jason Hamilton attempted to have Ryan killed. Pete was starting to feel more positive; he knew he could still trust and depend on DS Lee McCann to some extent. But Pete had to tread carefully; Lee and Andrea were now an item. Pete's head spun with the ruminations; he rested his elbows on the desk and rubbed his temples.

'I'm sticking the kettle on. Do you want a coffee, Pete? DC Steve Comstive asked, looking at Pete's computer screen, 'You look like you could use one.'

'Cheers, Steve, grab some custard creams, too. Let's push the boat out.' Pete had warmed to Steve and continued to help him settle into his new role at the office. Steve was ambitious and asked Pete many questions about the surveillance unit's operating procedures and tactics. But Pete didn't mind being mithered because Steve was now a regular drinking buddy. Steve continued walking towards the kitchen with his scribbled list of drinks. An open offer of coffee to everyone in the office always resulted in receiving a considerable shipping order of drinks. But that was better than taking the flak for being caught out, making a sneaky Jack brew on the quiet.

Pete returned to his thoughts; he needed to speak with Lee McCann. Lee's reaction to the execution of the warrant at his flat would be interesting, an opportunity to find out more about it.

Steve returned to the room, working his way through the office, distributing drinks to his colleagues from a tray almost overflowing with spilt drinks whilst being subjected to critical banter about the poor standard of the cups of tea being too weak or too strong.

'Here you go, Pete. I can't mess up a black coffee, can I? Steve sat next to Pete and slid a packet of custard creams in his direction, 'Do you need any help assessing the authority documents? I've not submitted one yet, so I'll probably learn the ropes from helping you. I guess there's a lot to get my head around.

'Yes, cheers, Steve. I'll show you the ropes. I've just read through a quality application. Print that one off and use it as your baseline standard.' Pete welcomed the offer and trusted Steve to do a good job; he pushed his chair to the side and selected a biscuit to dunk into his coffee. Steve quickly settled before the computer screen and scrolled through the document.

Pete focused on the custard creams, taking another couple of biscuits from the pack. 'I need to nip out on an errand. Can you cover me if the boss asks where I am?'

'Of course, Pete, no worries. Where are you going?' Steve asked.

'I'm meeting Lee McCann. I'll be back soon.' Pete knocked back the last dregs of his coffee and slipped his jacket on, 'See you later.'

Steve finished reading the document and pressed print. Looking across the open tabs on the header bar, he selected the Intelligence System page and began reading the intelligence logs that Pete had been reading earlier, also printing a copy of those, too. Surprised that Pete had been sloppy enough to leave them open. The content of the logs would indicate what Pete was taking an interest in.

Pete entered the toilets and kicked each of the cubicle doors open. Satisfied no one was about, he cleaned up a few lines of coke. Feeling better after the hit, he checked himself over in the mirror and got on his way. Whilst walking across the car park, with a spring in his step, he telephoned DS Lee McCann and ascertained that DI Andrea Statham was out of the office, at meetings all day. He felt reassured when Lee didn't take the option to fob him off with an excuse to avoid him. Pete got into his car and upped the volume. Eighties music lifted his spirits. He looked into the rearview mirror and wiped under his nose with the back of his hand. He had a plan; things were looking good.

Pete entered the Major Incident Team office carrying two coffees in a cardboard holder while balancing a bag of Danish pastries he had picked up on his way. Most of the banks of workstation desks were empty. Detectives, looking busy, with their heads down, occupied a few isolated desks. Their lack of interaction created a momentary wave of paranoia; were they avoiding eye contact with him? Had they heard about the search warrant? Or just busy? Pete greeted the ones he passed by but continued walking towards DI Andrea Statham's office, not waiting for a reply or engaging in small talk.

He caught Lee's eyes as Lee stood up from behind his desk and nodded his head towards the Detective Inspector's office. Lee nodded in acknowledgement and followed Pete to Andrea's office.

Pete walked by the round meeting table and sat at Andrea's desk just as Lee entered the room, closing the door behind him.

Pete pushed a coffee, then a pastry towards Lee, 'I come bearing gifts,' Pete beamed on a charm offensive.

Lee took the coffee and wheeled a chair from the meeting table, turning it around to sit opposite Pete at the desk. Pete had calculated that a delay in starting a conversation would allow him to assess Lee's mood and maybe encourage Lee to speak first. But Lee tucked into the pastry. Pete looked around the office whilst eating. The place felt strange; it was no longer a familiar, friendly meeting place but now the lair of the enemy, his nemesis.

'Cheers, Pete, that was delicious. I prefer the custard filling; much better than jam. Lee screwed up the paper bag into a ball, launched it into the bin, and took a drink of coffee.

'Me too, Pete said between bites, prolonging proceedings.'

'I'll get us some napkins from the kitchen,' Lee announced, leaving the office. Pete suspected that Lee was buying time to delay the inevitable conversation; the search warrant at his flat. Lee probably wouldn't have realised that he had given Pete the perfect opportunity to execute his plan.

Pete felt a rush of blood, adrenaline-fuelled; he knew this was the best opportunity he would probably get.

He knew he had to act fast. Lee or someone else could enter at any time. He slipped his hand into the lining of his jacket and retrieved a folded handkerchief. His fear of Lee returning to the office too soon was foremost in his mind; his hand trembled. His professional persona kept him focused and rational; he knew how long it should take Lee. Then again, a detective could take the opportunity to speak and delay Lee's return increasing the margin of safety.

Pete opened the top drawer of the desk. He shook the folded handkerchief carefully. The clear plastic snap bag of white powder dropped effortlessly from the unfolding cloth; into the open make-up bag. It fell perfectly, nestled between lipsticks and mascara pencils. Pete glanced down quickly, not wanting to take his eyes off the doorway for too long. The snap bag looked right, like it belonged there and had been placed there by DI Andrea Statham. Pete felt confident. He slowly pushed the drawer closed and looked up as Lee returned with some kitchen roll, content that he hadn't seen anything.

'Don't use your hanky, Pete. I've got these,' Lee said, wiping the flaky pastry off the desk into his cupped hand.

'I wasn't going to,' Pete said, chuffed at the perfect timing. He put the handkerchief to his nose and tried his best to clear his nasal passages genuinely. 'That's better; there's an awful virus doing the rounds.' Pete paused, then continued, 'Lee, I understand if you don't want to get involved, but what the fuck was Andrea thinking of, executing a firearms warrant at my flat?' Pete had decided to go for the direct, no-nonsense option. It was time to focus on the elephant in the room, to catch Lee on the hop.

'It's the nature of the beast, Pete, you know that. The way you operate, treading a thin line, getting close to the likes of Ryan Young. It's going to generate talk, and in this case, intelligence.' Lee's answer was calm and collected; he didn't appear fazed, almost like he'd been waiting for it. Pete wasn't surprised at the cool response; he had naively hoped for a defensive reply, attempting to mitigate his boss's actions, something which Pete could have probed further.

'She must have known I lived there. That's why she didn't allocate any of her team to attend the search. She maintained impartiality. Why didn't she speak to me beforehand, Lee?'

'Come off it, Pete. We're dealing with possession of firearms intelligence, not a bloody speeding ticket.' Pete was getting frustrated; Lee wasn't giving anything away; he was a seasoned operative.

'What has she said to you? What was the intelligence case, for fucks sake?' Pete asked in a raised voice. All part

122

of his plan to set up his next move. He was conscious that he was starting to sound desperate.

'Nothing, mate, you know how these things work. It's a 'need-to-know' scenario. And I know better than to ask,' Lee answered quietly and calmly, irritating Pete all the more.

Pete swept his arm out and slapped the desktop in frustration. He caught the cardboard coffee cup, and the contents spilt across the desk. Lee reacted quickly and jolted his chair backwards away from the desk to avoid getting soaked in coffee.

'Oh, bollocks,' Pete shouted, a little too enthusiastically than he had intended. 'She must have some tissues in here,' Pete said, opening the top drawer. He looked inside and feigned surprise and bewilderment; he stopped in his tracks and visibly calmed down. He was purposefully creating a silence between the two of them.

'I take it that's a no,' Lee said, looking puzzled at Pete's response; Lee retrieved the napkins from the bin and started mopping up the spilt coffee. Pete remained silent, doing his best to look taken aback. 'What's up with you?' Lee asked, his eyebrows furrowed.

'Nothing, mate,' Pete replied, trying to appear indecisive and troubled.

'Are you okay, Pete? What's the matter with you?' Lee looked perplexed. Pete suspected his performance had had the desired effect.

'Look in the drawer, Lee; I never suspected Andrea of using coke.'

'What?' Lee asked, making his way to the drawer. Pete pushed his chair back to give Lee access.

'There must be a legitimate reason; it must be evidence. There's no way Andrea uses that shit.'

'Then where's the exhibit label, and why is it not in the property store? Basic procedures that Andrea wouldn't get wrong,' Pete said, getting up and walking towards the office door.

'We both know that Andrea doesn't use coke. So what? She forgot to book it in,' Lee said, gesturing bewilderment with his arms.

Pete paused at the door and looked back. 'Well, you should know more than anyone; you're in a relationship with her,' Pete said, hoping to draw a reaction. But Lee remained silent. He closed the drawer, 'How do you want to handle this, Pete?'

'I've not seen anything. I'm not getting involved. It's up to you what you do from here. I'm not lowering myself to Andrea's level and grassing on a mucker, even if she has tried taking my legs from under me. I'll leave it with you, pal.' Pete said, walking away.

He returned to his car and enjoyed a feeling of achievement before setting off. He was on a high; he had executed his plan to perfection. No doubt Lee suspected that Pete had planted the coke, but he couldn't prove it, and in the meantime, it muddied the waters.

DS Lee McCann stood at the office window, ensuring the vertical blinds provided sufficient cover from being seen by anyone outside. He watched as DS Pete Higgs got into his car; Pete didn't appear to be in a rush, and the vehicle remained stationary.

Lee walked around the desk for the second time and studied the clear plastic bag containing white powder in Andrea's drawer. He was confident it was cocaine. But that would only be confirmed for sure by forensic analysis. He took a seat in Andrea's chair to consider his next move.

Lee had learned long ago never to jump to conclusions or assume anything and always kept an open mind until the evidence was clear. But he was pretty sure on this occasion that DI Andrea Statham had no involvement with the white powder, not from a criminal perspective. He had an excellent professional working relationship and a social one too.

Lee returned to the window. Pete had gone. He regretted leaving Pete alone in the office; it had provided the perfect opportunity for him to plant the drugs. If Pete had done so, as Lee suspected, he certainly had the motive to want to stitch Andrea up. Pete had the means, too; his maverick behaviour often involved policing methods sailing close to the wind in his pursuit of justice. Albeit, planting drugs in a colleague's desk drawer was a totally new ball game.

But did Pete really think that Lee wouldn't suspect he'd done it? Or was he not bothered? Without evidence against him, Pete knew he was untouchable.

Either it was an act of desperation by Pete, or he just wanted to create a distraction for Andrea Statham.

His enthusiasm and commitment to the task at hand had always impressed Lee. Others suspected acts of noble cause corruption. Lee considered getting rid of the cocaine, only for a moment before ruling it out. Pete obviously knew of its existence; Lee couldn't risk Pete getting some dirt on him for not dealing with it in the appropriate manner.

He took photographs of the bag using his phone, then forensically recovered the make-up case wearing rubber latex protective gloves. He would have preferred another detective to witness these actions, but he didn't want to involve others in the knowledge loop at this stage; this was definitely a need-to-know situation. It was plainly clear that this was a set-up; Andrea had nothing to fear by him taking his chosen course of action.

Andrea noticed her phone vibrating and seized the opportunity to leave the management meeting. The agenda items had been discussed and concluded. 'Any other business was now morphing into the 'point scoring to impress the boss' phase. Andrea preferred to let her actions do the talking.

'You're a lifesaver, Lee; good timing. How are you doing?'

Lee sensed she was genuinely pleased to hear from him, not just the excuse to leave the meeting. 'I need to speak to you about Pete Higgs.'

'What the hell's he done now?' Lee sensed deflation in Andrea's tone and felt sorry for her; he suspected she wished the DS Pete Higgs saga had never arisen or involved her. But he couldn't spare her involvement in this latest drama.

'It's probably best to meet up rather than discuss it on the phone. Shall I come around to your place later? We could get a takeaway?'

I'm not looking forward to talking about Pete Higgs, but I fancy a takeaway. See you at about seven o'clock.'

Lee needed to maintain the integrity of the evidence and book the cocaine into the property system. He arranged to meet up with his ex-welfare officer from the covert operations unit and book the cocaine into their property system, where it would remain under the radar from prying eyes, particularly those of Pete Higgs.

He was conscious that he wasn't dealing with this strictly by procedure. He should be briefing management, the complaints and discipline department or the counter-corruption unit. But he trusted Andrea enough to speak to her before deciding on his next move. Lee was also satisfied that his emotional involvement with Andrea was not clouding his judgment.

20

DI Andrea Statham woke up earlier than usual; she felt tired. It was always the case when she had pressing issues running through her mind; fitful sleep became the norm. She was sitting in the reception area at the Counter Corruption Unit, suited and booted in a smart black two-piece trouser suit, usually reserved for court appearances; she looked professional. Detective Superintendent Samuel hadn't arrived yet, so his secretary, Alison, wearing her usual twin-set and pearls outfit, had kindly made her a coffee.

Andrea's mind began to contemplate the implications of Lee's disclosure from the night before. The effects of a couple of glasses of wine she had enjoyed before Lee's arrival cushioned the blow. After the initial feelings of betrayal and anger, she mellowed pretty quickly. No doubt, Lee's calming presence had something to do with that. Pete's behaviour was indicative of the concerns she held about him. None of Pete's irrational behaviour surprised her anymore.

Her mind veered away from DS Pete Higgs and his betrayal onto her relationship with Lee McCann. He was still asleep when Andrea awoke. His presence felt right; she felt like they were an item. Andrea had been glad he was there and didn't want to leave him.

It was reassuring to her that Lee hadn't just gone by the book and reported the incident up the chain of command. He trusted and cared for her enough to speak first. And now, she would do the right thing.

The entrance door lock clicked open, bringing her back to the moment. 'Good morning, Andrea; sorry, I didn't realise we were meeting this morning.' Mr Samuel said before removing his black three-quarter length overcoat. Andrea smelled a strong waft of quality spicy wood aftershave from his direction; she liked it, and it suited him, but she struggled to place the brand.

'We've not got a meeting scheduled, boss, but I'm hoping you're free. It's urgent. I need to inform you of something; unfortunately, the sooner, the better.' Andrea recognised the reaction on his face. She knew the feeling well of being prepared for a busy schedule and then having an unexpected problem dropped on your toes before even having had the chance to take your coat off. 'This sounds ominous,' he said and gave her a reassuring smile, 'Come through, Andrea.'

Andrea followed the superintendent through a 'strictly private' door into the main office. Mr Samuel exchanged greetings with the small team of detectives inside, and Andrea nodded an acknowledgement. Their furtive demeanour made her feel like an unwanted intruder in their clandestine world. She wasn't interested in what they were doing and didn't want to know their business. She took a seat in the Super's office.

'So, to what do I owe the pleasure of this unexpected visit?' He sounded sincere and untroubled by Andrea dropping in unannounced; she sensed there was mutual respect between the two of them. He was one of the respected senior leaders in the Force, a cool head with plenty of experience.

'Officially, I'm here to refer myself, following a small bag of cocaine being discovered in my office drawer. However, in mitigation, I also wish to put forward a working theory that it was secreted there by the person who discovered it. I obviously deny any knowledge of it whatsoever.'

'And this person is?' Samuel asked, looking intrigued.

'DS Pete Higgs.'

'Ah, the subject of your last visit here, as I recall,' Superintendent Samuel said, 'Let me sort us some drinks out, and you can continue. Of course, only if you wish to do so, you may incriminate yourself. By rights, I should serve you papers and conduct this as an interview under caution.' Andrea guessed the comment was intended to be tongue-in-cheek.

'I've nothing to hide, Sir; if I had, I wouldn't be here, I'd be busy elsewhere, destroying the evidence. Andrea smiled knowingly.

Superintendent Samuel returned with two cups of tea and chocolate biscuits on a China plate. 'I've cancelled my meetings, so you have my full attention. We won't be disturbed.'

Andrea began to outline the circumstances of the recent events. This time she felt no guilt or disloyalty towards Pete Higgs; he had made this personal by planting drugs on her. It was now a matter of self-preservation; the gloves were off.

Superintendent Samuel scribbled down the last of his notes and placed the fountain pen in its marble-based holder. 'He's behaving like a desperate man, that's for sure. I'll be surprised if the forensic people find his fingerprints or DNA on the packet, but then again, stranger things have happened, I suppose.' The Superintendent leaned back in his chair as if contemplating his next move. Andrea sensed this and remained silent, waiting to hear his response.

Samuel leaned forward, resting his forearms on the desk, interlocking his fingers, and cleared his throat. 'I'm in no doubt that you were surprised after our last meeting by my decision not to Investigate DS Pete Higgs.'

'Not really, boss, it's a sign of the times. Since the Home Secretary decimated police numbers, covering basic duties has been an uphill struggle. Resources are beyond stretched; I know that.'

'I will level with you but require you to sign a non-disclosure agreement document. We are already investigating DS Peter Higgs. But the last time you and I met was not the right time for me to disclose it to you.'

Andrea was not surprised by his disclosure; she had half suspected it all along. She was dismissed far too quickly on her last visit. Mr Samuel hadn't reacted as she imagined he would, asking probing questions to test the validity of the allegations. But now she was intrigued to discover how their investigation was progressing and what evidence they had collected.

'Our intelligence case is based primarily on two sources; an anonymous contact via the Crimestoppers telephone line and intelligence from the Garda. The circulation of intelligence is restricted due to the sensitivity. It is flagged only to our department for obvious reasons,' Samuel took a drink.

'The Garda, I was unaware of any Irish connection,' Andrea said, intrigued.

'Wayne Davies and his organised crime group have diversified in recent times since the reign of Jason Hamilton. They are still importing Class A drugs on a big scale, but now they've ventured into firearms too.'

Upon hearing the latter, Andrea felt embarrassed; she remembered her search warrant and the haul of water pistols subsequently discovered. She decided not to mention it, even though it was obvious that Mr Samuel would be aware.

Samuel continued, 'We are working with the National Crime Agency, which provides a further firewall for operational security. We are still in the evidence-gathering stage, but the operation is progressing well.'

'So why wasn't the intelligence about the firearms at the flat restricted?'

'We had to act because of the immediate risk to life they presented. We suspected they had been taken to the flat from a larger stash, maybe for a local hit. But it was too early for us to strike, and we didn't want to compromise our operation by showing our hand.'

'Fair enough, I'd have done the same. I suspected Wayne Davies was setting Pete Higgs up to be arrested, or maybe he wanted to intimidate him. That would explain the water pistols being there. The officers undertaking the search thought that Pete looked petrified and dumbfounded when they discovered water pistols.'

'You're probably right; who knows, it could have been internal conflict or power plays.' Andrea was impressed; she guessed that the involvement of the NCA would no doubt include bigger budgets for covert policing tactics: surveillance, phone taps, and possibly undercover operatives infiltrating the organised crime group. 'So, where do we go from here?' Andrea asked, relieved Mr Samuel didn't suspect her of the unlawful possession of controlled drugs.

'Before you leave, I want you to take a voluntary drug test. A negative test supports the plan of action I am about to undertake.'

'So, you're satisfied that Pete planted the drugs?'

'It certainly looks that way. A simple plan that Pete knows would be difficult to pin on him, no matter how obvious it seems. There is no limited access to your office, no CCTV, and I'm sure there will be no incriminating forensic evidence.'

'But he succeeds because it casts suspicion on me,' Andrea said, letting her anger slide for now.'

'I propose we manufacture a ruse; the Assistant Chief Constable will suspend you from duty after this meeting. Pete will believe his plan has been successful, and maybe he will get complacent going forward.'

21

Pete Higgs walked from the toilets and slowly eased into his seat at the table. He felt self-conscious about sniffing too much and wiped under his nose with the back of his hand out of habit. 'I think I've got a bout of man flu coming on,' Pete said, attempting to cover his tracks. 'I like this place; the beer is good, and the food isn't bad either, for the price.' His mood was lifting; he'd felt low and jaded since getting out of bed, but a few lines of coke had done the trick.

'You're buzzing; how many pints have you had? Or have you had a win at the tables?' Steve asked, not mentioning what he really suspected had lifted Pete's spirits.

Pete momentarily had flashbacks from the night before. He'd certainly not had a big win; as usual, he'd lost a big chunk of money in the casino. To make matters worse, it wasn't his money to lose. It was drug money he'd collected for Wayne Davies. He felt a pang of fear and anxiety over how he was going to get the money back. 'I've only had a few, but I've not eaten, mate. It's gone straight to my head. I might order a burger. Do you want anything?' Pete realised he was talking fast and began to slow his words down.

'No, I'm not hungry, mate. I'll get us another couple of beers on the app. What's this gossip you've got to tell me anyway?' Steve asked with a curious look.

Pete completed his food order on his phone and focused on suppressing his high spirits. 'Word's not out yet, so keep this to yourself. DI Andrea Statham from the Major Incident Team is in the shit. She had a stash of coke in her desk drawer, only a user's amount, but what was she thinking?' Pete said, his words racing towards the end of the sentence.

'She won't be the only cop taking coke; it's rife with youngsters joining the job these days. They've grown up with it as a social norm in pubs and clubs. 'I've never met Andrea Statham, but I've heard she's a top detective, probably one of the most experienced in the Force.'

'Don't be deceived, mate. I've worked with her a lot over the years, and she can be a snake. She's got to where she is by stepping on the toes of others. If it suits her purpose, she'll stitch anyone up without giving it a second thought. She'll probably throw someone else under the bus to take the blame for the cocaine in her desk drawer. Pete drained the remainder of his lager as the waiter placed two more pints on the table. 'She ditched me as soon as I was no longer of any use to her. Now she's got her claws into Lee. It will all end in tears for him, you'll see, mate.'

Ryan Young grabbed Pete's attention, waving at him from the entrance. 'Give me a minute, Steve; I've just got to speak to this weasel at the bar. I've told him not to meet without prior arrangement; he's hard work. Pete left the table taking his pint with him and approached Ryan, who was now standing at the bar.

'Wayne's got a job for us tonight. So don't get shit-faced. Be back at the flat for eight o'clock.'

'What is it?' Pete asked, irritated by Ryan's authoritarian tone and presence.

'I'll tell you later. Have you got Wayne's money with you?'

'No,' Pete felt his heart race and his face flush; he needed to change the subject, 'I've got DI Statham suspended, though. You can tell Wayne she'll be off his back now.' Pete felt like a big shot, having flexed his muscles and shown what results he could deliver.

'Yeah, but where's Wayne's money? You're already late with it; he won't be happy,' Ryan asked, not appearing impressed by Pete's update on the suspension.

'Long story, but it's at the nick,' Pete replied, thinking on his feet to buy some time.

'Bring it tonight; he wants it.'

'No-can-do, but tell him about Statham; I've done what he asked. He owes me. I could take my pay from his money at the nick.'

Ryan shook his head, 'You don't help yourself. It's like you've got a death wish.' then turned about and headed for the door. Pete suddenly felt sick in the pit of his stomach. He'd made a monumental fuck up and knew he would struggle to repay Wayne's money. He bought two more pints and headed back to the table.

'Who the fuck was that? He looked shady,' Steve asked, looking over towards the bar. 'What the hell did he say to you? You look worried, mate.'

'I'm not worried; he's just high maintenance, pal. You've probably heard of him. It's Ryan Young, one of Wayne Davies's minions. I'm getting bits of useful intelligence from him, but he'll just turn up out of the blue, like he did there. He's turned up at my flat a few times, unannounced, but he's no threat.' Pete took the opportunity to develop a cover story, should it be needed to cover his tracks at a later date. He picked at the chips and pushed the burger to one side. He was no longer hungry. 'He's just told me about a local dealer who's taking a delivery of smack later. I'll give the local plain clothes unit a bell; they can take out a warrant and put the door in tonight.'

Steve looked back over to the bar, but Ryan Young was gone. 'Yes, I've heard of him. He was in a dispute with

Jason Hamilton, as I remember. I heard about you rescuing Lee McCann when Hamilton took him hostage. I'm surprised you didn't get awarded the Queens Police Medal for your bravery.'

'My face doesn't fit, mate. Believe it or not, DI Statham suspected I'd done it to help Hamilton escape! Would you believe it?'

'No way, why would she think that,' Steve asked, looking puzzled.

'I told you, she's got a downer on me, probably jealous that I always get the results on investigations by sailing close to the wind. We all know you have to fight fire with fire these days.'

'Sounds about right for the bosses in this job. So how did you convince Hamilton to let Pete go?'

'Long story, for another time, mate. I'll get us another pint.'

'I'm okay, thanks, mate; I can't keep up with you!' Steve said, holding up his almost untouched glass.

Pete stood up and paused. 'Look who's here, talk of the devil,' Pete exclaimed as Lee McCann approached the table, 'You'll have a pint, won't you, Lee? This lightweight can't keep up. How are you doing, mate?'

'I'm good, mate, thanks.'

'This is Steve Comstive; he's our newbie at the office.' Lee shook hands with Steve and took a seat. 'Nice to meet you, Steve; you settling into the job, okay?'

'Loving it, Pete's showing me the ropes and pitfalls,' Steve replied.

Lee glanced back at Pete, 'I thought you'd be in here; they'll start charging you rent soon, Pete. I guess you've heard about Andrea?' Lee asked.

'Yes, we were talking about it. What was Andrea thinking? You think you know someone when in fact, you don't have a Scooby-Do about them,' Pete replied. 'I'll buy the drinks on the phone app; they'll bring them to the table,' Pete said; he didn't want to leave them alone and miss out on any interesting talk, unsure of what they'd discuss. His next line of coke would have to wait.

'I felt like shit, but I had no choice; I had to refer it up the ladder.' Lee looked down at the table and clenched his hands together.

'It sounds like you had no choice, pal,' Steve said.

'I'm not too sure; I could have destroyed it and told her to get some help, counselling or whatever.'

Pete watched and listened; he was now in no doubt that Lee was close to Andrea from observing his reaction. Pete resolved to be more cautious about what he said to Lee.

Steve changed the subject, 'I was just asking Pete how he managed to rescue you from Jason Hamilton.'

'He saved my bacon that night, didn't you, Pete?'

'I just did what any mate would have done,' Pete said, matter-of-fact, 'So how's Andrea reacted to her suspension?' Pete changed the subject back to the more pressing issue.

'I've not discussed it, mate; I'm going to hers later. She needs to brief me on a few investigations I'll be taking over in her absence. I think I'll be covering her position.'

'Can't be easy for you, Lee, what, with you two seeing each other now,' Pete said.

'Maybe not for much longer, Pete. I can't see our relationship surviving this one. I wish you hadn't found the coke now; it put me in a no-win situation,' Lee's voice tailed off with despondency.

22

Lee let himself in at Andrea's house; he thought it was maybe too early in their romance to be given a key. But he would have felt awkward refusing it; maybe Andrea would have taken his refusal the wrong way. Perhaps she intended it as a sign of her commitment to the relationship. Lee pushed that thought to the back of his mind; he definitely felt a strong connection with Andrea, but he didn't like to rush into things, especially a new relationship.

He closed the door softly and turned the thumb lock. He'd developed a habit of heightened awareness for security since Jason Hamilton unexpectedly showed up on his doorstep and took him hostage with the intention of killing him.

He kicked off his shoes, placed them on the rack under the stairs, next to Andrea's trainers, and pushed the kitchen door open. Andrea looked up at him; she was stirring something on the hob, 'I didn't hear you come in!' she said with a welcoming smile. Lee could only just about hear her voice above the din from the noisy old extractor fan.

'How old is that thing? I need to fit a new one for you,' Lee said, reaching up to turn the airflow to a lower setting. 'That's better; I can hear myself think now,' he said, making a mental note to do the job when he had more time on his hands.

His eyes lingered on Andrea; he liked how she looked sexy in her grey sweats and impulsively hugged her, followed by a kiss. They held each other briefly before she broke away to continue stirring the curry. 'Not very romantic, I know, but this will stick to the pan if I'm not careful,' she said, returning to the hob.

'I'll consider myself ditched, then,' Lee joked, making his way to the sofa, 'How did your meeting with Superintendent Samuel go?' He asked over his shoulder.

'It went as well as can be expected. Did you manage to locate Pete Higgs?'

'Yes, mission completed, Ma'am,' he said, with a mocking theatrical salute, 'he was at his local pub as usual, with a bloke called Steve, from the surveillance unit. Steve looked familiar, but I couldn't place him.' Lee said, scrolling on his mobile phone.

'How did he react to the news of my suspension?' Lee sensed that Andrea was trying to feign disinterest in what Pete said but was keen to know his reaction.

'Low key, he sat on the fence, possibly because of Steve's presence. But it's not surprising; he knows we are seeing each other. The main thing is that he believes his plan has worked.'

'It doesn't feel good, being suspended. The gossip mongers will have a field day, even if it is just a subterfuge. I'd love to be a fly on the wall at the management meetings. I bet the vultures are circling to take my job already.'

'It's undoubtedly headline news. I wonder who was the first person to say, '*Always knew she was a bad 'un,*' Lee laughed. 'I hope Samuel sticks to a strict need-to-know policy. We can't afford any slip-ups now. The fewer managers are made aware, the better; that's where the leaks usually occur, showcasing to their colleagues about being 'in-the-know'. Pete Higgs thinks I turned you in. It needs to stay that way. He still thinks he can trust me.

Andrea turned the heat low on the hob, then looked at Lee, 'Operational security won't be a problem; Samuel's been there and got the T-shirt. Would it be wise to portray that our relationship is over as a result of you grassing me up?'

'Makes sense, I suppose.' Lee replied.

'As you're not a member of the investigation team, any unsolicited comments he makes would be useful intelligence.'

'The defence probably wouldn't see it that way, they'd probably claim we used dirty tricks, but I know where you're coming from,' Lee acknowledged.

'There could be an infiltration role for me here,' Lee suggested hopefully from the sofa, 'Superintendent Samuel could seek authorisation for me to work undercover, intelligence gathering or even seeking evidence. Pete still thinks I'm taken in by his bullshit that he's just treading a thin line. I think I'd do a good job. And it makes any evidence gleaned beyond reproach to the court,' Lee said, glancing over, hoping for a favourable reaction from Andrea.

'Are you not going to be busy enough managing our team in my absence?' Andrea asked.

'I could do both easily, no problem,' Lee said enthusiastically. The thought of an unexpected undercover deployment appealed to him. He thrived on the difficult challenges undercover work presented. He knew going against a corrupt police officer wouldn't be easy.

'I get where you're coming from, but is Pete realistically going to open up to you? Anyway, I'll mention it as an option to Mr Samuel when I see him later… Right, this curry looks ready,' Andrea said, plating up the food; they retired to the table. Lee opened the wine and poured two generous glasses.

'So, are the National Crime Agency confident of gathering enough evidence on Pete Higgs?' Lee asked.

'I'll know more when I speak to them tomorrow, but as I said on the phone, Mr Samuel seems pretty confident. He wants me to be available to assist the NCA; if anyone knows how Pete Higgs ticks, it's me.'

23

Pete Higgs opened the door to his flat and heard voices from the lounge. He had expected Ryan to be there, but who was he talking to? Pete didn't have to wait long to find out. 'You're late,' Wayne Davies announced coldly from the sofa, 'You'd better not be pissed up too.'

'Good to see you, too, fellas,' Pete replied. He walked to the kitchen and poured a pint of water from the tap, which he then gulped down in one go. Leaning on the kitchen worktop, he faced Ryan and Wayne in the lounge.

'Ryan tells me you've left my money at the police station; what the fuck are you playing at?' Wayne asked, tapping the flat of his hand on his thigh.

'I had the apprentice with me; I couldn't let him see it, could I? It's safe.' Pete lied, albeit it probably was very safe, locked up in the vault at the casino.

'It's right. I saw Pete and his sidekick at the local boozer,' Ryan confirmed, receiving a glaring look from Wayne whilst giving Pete a reprieve from the hostilities.

'Did Ryan also tell you I managed to get DI Statham suspended from duty?' Pete said, soaking up the kudos of his actions; he felt upbeat, a formidable player who could get things done. 'Not only that, I've cast doubt on her credibility in Lee McCann's mind. He could be a useful asset for us.'

'I think one bent cop is more than enough. Are you listening to this shit, Ryan?' Wayne sneered. 'He's run a small errand for me and now thinks he's a made-man in the firm,' Wayne turned back towards Pete, 'I'll get Frank Burton to make a few enquiries with his police contact; I

142

can't have you double-crossing me, can I?' Pete knew he shouldn't have expected anything more from Wayne Davies. He glared back at him with contempt, knowing he would never be accepted into his circle of trust. Pete couldn't be sure, but he thought he may have received a sympathetic look from Ryan.

'I don't know what you want from me, Wayne. I've made your business stronger and shielded you from the cops. I've even put up with you fuckers drugging and blackmailing me. But you're never happy. Pay me off. I'll walk away happily.'

Wayne stared straight into Pete's eyes. For a moment, Pete expected him to name his price. How wrong he was. 'Always the fucking victim,' Wayne said, shaking his head, 'Get out of my fucking sight, you bent bastard.'

'Right, we'll get going,' Ryan said, getting up from the sofa. I'll give you a bell later, Wayne,' Ryan beckoned Pete to follow him with a nod. Pete felt relieved at the opportunity to leave without any further drama. He followed Ryan across the main parking area and onto the service road, where Ryan unlocked a white van with a key fob. The orange flashing light from the indicators lit the surrounding area with a double flash.

Ryan started the engine and pushed the gearstick into first, crunching the gearbox, 'I've not driven one of these for a long time,' Ryan laughed.

'Keep doing that, and you'll need a new gearbox,' Pete mocked to lighten his mood. The van interior was filthy, the surfaces covered in mud and cement remnants. The floor was piled with takeaway wrappers.

'You know Wayne's never going to trust you, don't you?' Ryan said whilst turning the van onto the ring road. Pete sensed empathy in his voice and wasn't surprised, for they seemed to be getting along better lately.

'What's his problem?'

'He's ex-army, so loyalty and the brotherhood are important to him. You've crossed the line as a bent copper, shit on your own, so to speak; in his eyes, you wouldn't think twice about shitting on him. That's why he's got you incriminated up to your eyeballs; it's an insurance policy. If you take us down, you're coming with us. I can't see you coping with prison time.' Ryan's last comment sounded sadistic, but he was right; Pete had no intention of going to prison.

'So, what do you suggest I do?' Pete tested the water to see how far his rapport with Ryan would stretch.

'Not my problem, pal, that's one for you to work out. You got yourself into this mess.'

'Why won't he just have done with it and pay me off, let me walk?' Pete asked as if it was a no-brainer.

'Because you're useful… for the time being. But I think you're stressing him out; he's not as laid back as he used to be. He's getting paranoid about stuff, just like Jason did towards the end. And besides, Frank Burton has the final say.'

Pete decided it was time to change the subject; he felt satisfied that Ryan was mellowing but didn't want to push it. 'Where are we going?'

'We're just going to monitor a shipment coming up the M6 from Felixstowe.'

Pete relaxed into his seat, adapting to the unpleasant stench of the van, watching the traffic go by in the outside lane. His thoughts returned to how he would get Wayne's money back. He was struggling to devise a plan and feared the consequences. In desperation, he impulsively blurted out a plea for help to Ryan, 'I need your help; I've lost Wayne's money at the casino.' As the words came out of his mouth, he experienced a feeling of disbelief that he'd said them out

144

loud. Shit or bust, could he trust Ryan? He felt lightheaded, out of his depth, like he was drowning.

'I knew you were bullshitting, fucking hell, you must have a death wish... what are you telling *me* for?' Pete couldn't detect any empathy in Ryan's voice on this occasion. Pete instantly regretted telling him not having received the reaction he was seeking, but he couldn't turn the clock back. Pete started to ramble, 'You could back me up with a cover story... we could claim we got robbed. Or you could give me some coke to sell on the side to make the money back?'

'Are you for real? Fuck off, you prick. The best thing you can do is disappear. Don't involve me!'

Pete could sense fear in Ryan's voice. He wasn't surprised. Ryan knew what the consequences were for fucking up; Jason and Wayne tried to kill him twice. The magnitude of Pete's problem was staring him in the face. He felt physically sick. 'Are you going to tell Wayne?' Pete said, instantly regretting how weak he had sounded.

'I'm keeping out of it. Don't you fucking dare involve me, or else I'll make sure you get fed to the pigs.' Ryan shook his head in disbelief, turning up the volume of the rock music. Pete sat back and closed his eyes; his best option now was to meet with Frank Burton, or was it? He just needed time to think.

Pete jolted in his seat as Ryan bumped the van off the curb and accelerated onto the motorway. 'Christ, it's like a sauna in here,' Pete said, opening the window. The music was still blaring. Ryan didn't acknowledge him.

Ryan tucked the van into the inside lane; Pete guessed they were following the truck with Polish plates ahead of them. They followed it along the M602 before turning off into Salford, passing the fashionable Media City area on the right. It was a different area now than when Pete was a uniform cop in the eighties. Back then, it was a derelict shadow of its maritime industrial past; now, it was a vibrant hub of modern glass office buildings, TV studios and trendy apartments stretching to the sky in place of the long-gone rusting dockside cranes.

The truck finally stopped at a run-down-looking industrial depot in Trafford Park and reversed into a loading bay. Ryan pulled up into a nearby layby, tucked in discreetly between two HGVs. He turned the lights off and watched as a group of men emerged from the building and began unloading the truck.

'What's the cargo?' Pete asked.

'The first shipment for the Irishman,' Ryan answered without looking away from the activity. Failing to mention that it was, in fact, a dry run.

Pete didn't bother wasting his breath by asking further questions; the rapport he had built with Ryan had subsided since his ill-thought-through disclosure.

24

'Yes, I can hear you now, boss. Can you hear me, okay?'
Andrea was getting irritated with the technology. She
preferred to meet in person, but to maintain the theatre of
being suspended, she had agreed to keep a low profile by
not attending certain police premises. Det. Supt. Samuel
appeared on her laptop screen, his gaze directed towards
her.

'Yes, I can see and hear you, too; we got there in the end.
Anyway, Good morning, Andrea. I've had an update from
the NCA this morning. They followed DS Pete Higgs and
Ryan Young last night. Those two appeared to be keeping
tabs on a heavy goods vehicle making a delivery to Trafford
Park. The destination was a storage and haulage facility.
The surveillance teams acted fast and arranged for a uniform
patrol to attend the premises under the guise of making
general enquiries in relation to sightings of suspicious males
having been seen in the area.

The uniform patrol did a great job and managed to
confirm that the delivery apparently consisted of office
furniture without appearing to show any interest in the
delivery or truck. The intelligence unit is researching the
vehicle and premises.'

'Sounds like they're planning a robbery there or
conducting a dry run for some other delivery. Higgs is
getting up to his neck in this; he's lost the plot,' Andrea
replied, 'How long can we let him continue before we get to
pull him in?' Andrea's question was rhetorical; she knew
the answer. She had to be patient; the National Crime

Agency had bigger fish to fry in this operation. To them, Pete was a small fry.

'If we suspend him now, he gets the heads up that we're onto him. DI Dave Ferguson has deployed him on non-operational duties for now. His computer activity is being monitored, and other covert tactics are progressing. But you're right; he's obviously gone bandit on us.'

'He'll insist he's cultivating informants, focusing on the bigger picture, getting to the untouchables at the top of the pile.'

'That excuse won't cut it any longer; he has no backers who trust him. He's a loose cannon, a liability. And I've no sympathy for him; he's playing with fire. Anyway, I'm meeting the operational senior investigator at three this afternoon. I'm unsure where yet; it will be off the beaten track. I want you to come too, as my deputy. I'll give you a bell when I find out the location. See you later.' The screen went blank. Andrea was thankful for the invite; she couldn't cope with the boredom of being suspended; even though it was a ruse, she wanted to be involved and play her part in the operation.

'Christ, open the window, Frank,' Wayne demanded. 'It's like being back in the CS gas chamber during my basic army training.' Frank stubbed out his cigarette on the desk ashtray and struggled to push the antiquated sash window up a few inches. Frank walked over to the cabinet and poured himself a coffee. 'Are you sure you two don't want one?' Both Wayne and Ryan declined his second offer. Frank placed his coffee down and sat facing Wayne and Ryan on the red Chesterfield sofa. He lit a cigarette and inhaled deeply.

148

'Do you have to smoke inside, Frank?' Wayne asked, obviously irritated. He had maintained his fitness and ate healthy ever since his army days.

'It helps me to focus and concentrate, Wayne, only the best service for my clients,' Frank said, smirking at his witty sarcasm.

'Good, you need to be focused, but won't coffee suffice? Ryan and the bent cop followed the truck last night, as discussed. They had only just started unloading when two cops arrived, asking questions about a spate of burglaries. No way was that a coincidence.

'So, we are under surveillance, that confirms it,' Frank said.

'I'm in no doubt; I watched from a safe distance and clocked two surveillance vans. In fairness, they were pretty good operators, very low-key,' Wayne replied.

'The question is, have they bought into it and are convinced it was a practice run?' Frank asked.

'I think so; our insider at the warehouse offered them a cup of tea. During the conversation, he slipped in some comments to make them sit up and listen,' Wayne said, pleased with the result.

'Excellent; if we run a decoy truck on the day, they will be confident of getting a result,' Frank concluded, looking at his watch.

Wayne looked at Ryan, noticing he did not have much to say. 'Anything to add, Ryan? Did Higgs have the opportunity to call the cops in?'

'No, and he didn't know it was a dry run. We've changed the plates on our van. The police surveillance teams must have linked us to the truck; we were virtually in convey with it.' Ryan said.

Wayne watched as Ryan fidgeted with the drawstring of his hoodie. He sensed that Ryan was holding something back. 'What else happened, Ryan?'

Ryan hesitated and shifted uncomfortably, 'Believe it or not, Pete Higgs confided in me that he had blown your money at the casino. It was total bollocks about it being stored at the police station,' Ryan sounded relieved, having got it off his chest.

Wayne leapt up from the leather sofa, 'No way, you're having a laugh,' he spat out, glaring at Ryan, 'What's he playing it? Is he trying to take the piss out of me? Is Higgs goading me for a reaction? He must be in self-destruct mode,' Wayne was livid, pacing the room. Ryan looked uncomfortable but relieved. Wayne looked over as Frank sparked up another cigarette and edged forward, sitting upright. 'I told you we couldn't trust him, Frank; what were you thinking? He's probably been grassing on us all along. He probably got the surveillance set up.' Wayne continued pacing back and forth across Frank's office.

'I don't think he has, we've got too much dirt on him, and he knows it,' Ryan reasoned. He was not making eye contact with Wayne.

Frank nodded in agreement, 'Pete's been getting the results for me for years. I really don't think he's double-crossing us. And like Ryan pointed out, he's going to prison too, if he grasses.'

'It doesn't matter. The cops do deals with the judge to cover shit like that. He could even be working undercover. He's probably been wearing a wire, recording everything.' Wayne snared Ryan's eyes, 'What else do you know, Ryan? If you've been fuckin' stupid, now is the time to come clean.' Jason Hamilton's decision to kill Ryan flashed across Wayne's mind. Wayne had agreed with him at the time that Ryan was a liability. Wayne felt angry with himself for bringing Ryan back into the fold. 'Are you fucking with me too, Ryan?' Wayne launched onto the sofa and grabbed Ryan by the throat, pushing his head back. Ryan struck out with his fist, connecting with the side of Wayne's head. Wayne responded with a headbutt, which appeared to stun Ryan into submission. Wayne backed off, still glaring at Ryan. 'Come on then, do you fancy your chances, tough guy?' He shouted breathlessly.

'Let's cool down and look at this rationally,' Frank suggested, positioning himself between them.

'Fuck off, Frank, you condescending twat!' Wayne snarled. Frank took a drag of his cigarette, avoiding eye contact.

'Wayne, you know I wouldn't fuck with you, for fucks sake. I've been straight with you,' Ryan said, his voice wavering.

Wayne walked over to the window; his anger slowly subsided. 'Ryan, I want him sorting. Get some of the lads together, and get rid of him. Go on, get on the phone, get on with it. Wait outside the office for me.'

Ryan looked relieved to be getting out of the way. He didn't need to be asked twice and made his way out.

Wayne looked over to Frank, shaking his head, 'What is it with this fucker? It's like he's trying to press my buttons for a reaction.'

'I can assure you, Wayne, he is not a threat. Higgs has been on my payroll for many years. The problem here is simply his gambling addiction. He's not trying to press any buttons.'

'Yeah, right, that might come back to haunt you, Frank. For fuck's sake, we don't need this hassle. I hope you're right, Frank because if he does do us over, there will be repercussions.' Wayne said, heading to the door.

25

The office felt still and quiet, the lull after the storm. Ryan had left in a hurry, followed by Wayne. Frank sat heavily at his desk; he had never seen Wayne so angry. He was in a frenzy that had escalated from nowhere on hearing the news that Pete had gambled and lost his money, totally out of character; Frank was worried. He knew of Wayne's distrust of Pete Higgs but hadn't bargained that his malevolence was so deep.

'No way, you're losing the plot; I am not getting involved.' Frank heard Ryan shout from outside his office. Frank stood and made his way towards the door to ensure he didn't miss anything.

'If we don't sort him out, he'll take all of us down. I fuckin' warned you all,' Wayne shouted louder. Frank put his ear to the door; he needed to hear every word.

'I've told you, Wayne, he's not a threat. He knows we can implicate him in criminal activity, and don't forget about the photos of him with the underaged girl. It's not worth the risk; leave him to me. I can manage him.'

'He's brainwashed you and taken you in, you gullible prick. He's probably working undercover. Wayne said, seething as he leaned on the landing windowsill, looking onto the wet slated rooftops outside.

'You're making a big mistake Wayne; calm down and think it through.' A loud thud against the door made Frank instinctively jump back; he was surprised the door didn't give way. He could hear Wayne and Ryan scuffling outside. He considered intervening to calm things down but instantly thought better of it. His role was strategy and security, certainly not brawling. Silence followed the commotion; Frank listened carefully.

'Don't fucking tell me to calm down, boy.' There was another quiet moment before Frank heard footsteps heading down the stairs. Frank waited a moment before opening the office door. He cautiously surveyed the scene outside. Thankfully they had both gone.

Frank returned to his desk, head in hands; he needed to work effectively on damage limitation. He needed to get this right, for all their sakes. It was like dealing with Jason Hamilton all over again. He felt shaken by what he had just heard. He feared Wayne was losing his usual calm and collected disposition and would do something in haste, which he would later regret.

Instinctively he picked his phone up and made the call. 'Peter, you're in deep shit. Wayne has found out that you lost his money at the casino.'

'The snake! Did Ryan tell him?'

'That's not important. This isn't a matter of schoolboy tittle-tattle. I'm doing you a big favour and giving you a heads-up. He's seeking revenge, and it won't be pleasant.'

'Frank, I was just trying to make some cash on the side. Unfortunately, I didn't pull it off. Can you not speak to him?'

'Peter, I don't think you appreciate the trouble you are in. It's too late for that; we're past the explanations stage. He's not interested. You need to hide. The flat is not safe anymore, seriously. Get some things together and disappear, sharpish; they're coming for you.' Frank ended the call with a click. He'd done what he could, at significant risk to himself. The ball was in Pete's court now. Frank stubbed out the remnants of his cigarette and gazed through the window before deciding it was probably worth one more attempt at talking Wayne down.

Maybe Wayne would calm down. He grabbed his phone. He needed to deflate the situation; he couldn't just stand by waiting. It went straight to voicemail. Frank felt anxious; he sensed the darkening skies of a shit storm approaching. Lighting a cigarette, he stood and walked to the window, considering whether to call Ryan. He decided against it; it was bad enough that he'd tipped off Pete Higgs. Ryan had made his feelings known, and undermining Wayne wasn't a wise option, especially in his current state of mind.

*

Pete stopped talking when he realised that Frank had ended the call. He re-dialled back right away. Frank's voicemail kicked in. He placed his phone on the kitchen worktop. The ringtone belted out no sooner than it had landed on the worktop. Pete grabbed it but accidentally sent it skimming across the worktop and onto the floor.

'For fucks sake,' Pete shouted, picking it up, 'Frank, we need to nip this in the bud.'

'Nip what in the bud?' replied Ryan.

'I thought it was Frank calling,' Pete's voice sounded rattled; he felt stressed.

'You need to do one; you're in deep shit. Get away from Manchester, and I'll be in touch when everything calms down.' Ryan ended the call.

Pete had known Frank long enough to know he wasn't prone to panic or overreacting. He had been the voice of reason over the years. And now a further warning from Ryan. Fear began to consume Pete. It was time to sit up and heed the warning.

Pete went to the bedroom and began throwing some clothes and a few possessions into a holdall. His fear prompted him to move quicker; he didn't want to be here any longer than he had to be.

Suspicious noises at the door grabbed Pete's attention. Had he locked it? Shit, he hadn't. He quickly looked around for a weapon. The best he could muster was a fork nestled in the remains of a chicken chow mein. He heard a stifled laugh; it was the hyena. Shit, they had arrived. They had come for him. He'd not been quick enough. He broke out in a cold sweat; his legs felt like jelly.

'Pete, where are you?' Pete recognised Hyena's voice; he sounded on edge. It wasn't looking good for him. Pete lay down on the floor at the far side of the bed. Hopefully, they'd think he was already on his toes and leave. Pete listened carefully to muffled voices whispering and people moving about the flat, searching for him. His heart was pounding. He estimated there were at least three people; he was done for.

Pete sensed someone had entered the room; the footsteps confirmed it, and they were getting closer. A figure appeared towering above him, looking down at him. The intruder was wearing a black balaclava. He looked intimidating, 'I've found the fucker; he's here.' The intruder started to laugh. Hyena, he'd recognise the irritating noise anywhere. 'Are you hungry?' asked Hyena, as two other balaclava-clad thugs joined him, 'Careful lads, he's armed with a fork. He might try to eat you!' The group laughter that followed had a cynical edge. Tension filled the room, and Pete thought about making a run for it over the bed.

The male furthest away shouted, 'Stop fucking about; hold him down.' Hyena dropped down onto Pete, his knees landing on Pete's abdomen, taking the wind out of him. He grabbed Pete's wrist and pinned it to the floor, 'Drop the fucking fork, Rambo,' he shouted. Pete felt someone else sit on his legs; the pain was instant. Panic set in, Pete tried to wriggle free, using as much force as he could muster. He guessed this was the final chance to escape. For his efforts, Pete received a hard punch in the face. The back of his head bounced off the floor; he felt dizzy. The iron-like taste of blood filled his mouth. He was aware of the third person trampling roughly over his body and crouching over his head. Pete felt completely restrained; he couldn't move, even if he wanted to fight back.

The third thug kneed Pete on the side of his head as he crouched over him. Pete watched in horror as the assailant fumbled with a brown medicine bottle and a piece of cloth. Pete felt sick with fear realising they were about to drug him, he tried to kick out with his legs, but the attacker held him tight, restricting any helpful movement. Pete felt someone's finger pinching his nose tight. His worst fears were realised; this was it. The liquid tasted sweet and sickly; he had to swallow it involuntarily. He tried coughing and spitting but had to swallow, to allow himself to breathe. One of the intruders placed a soaking wet cloth over his nose and mouth; he felt dizzy and tired. He felt like he was drowning.

The assailant tucked the cloth and bottle away into his jacket pocket. 'Stay there; make sure he doesn't move,' he instructed the others before pushing himself up and going to the spare bedroom.

Bear hugging the punch bag, he struggled with the weight, lifting it up. The rings slid off the ceiling hook, allowing the momentum of the weight to guide onto the bed.

'Fetch him here,' the assailant shouted, attaching the rope noose to the ceiling hook. The two accomplices half-carried and dragged Pete into the bedroom. 'Lift him, get his head through there,' The assailant ordered, holding the noose wide. He slid the knot down behind Pete's neck and stood back. Pete struggled to remain conscious but knew what they were doing to him. He felt weak and helpless; the drug had kicked in, and he didn't have the energy to fight back.

'Right, let him go,' the assailant ordered, watching intently. Pete's weight made the rope taut; his feet were only half a foot from the floor. Once satisfied that the rope would hold the weight, the leader grabbed a stool from the kitchen and placed it on its side, on the floor, to look like Pete had kicked it away to commit suicide.

'Right, stick the balaclavas and gloves back in the bag; we'll get rid of the clothes later. Job done, boys. Let's get out of here.'

26

Andrea ended the call and resumed scrolling through social media. She wasn't enjoying the isolation of working from home and missed the buzz and banter of the office. Lee joined her in the lounge carrying two mugs of coffee and a plate stacked high with toast.

'Morning, you have to stop feeding me toast, or I'll need to start going to the gym more often,' she complained half-heartedly, grabbing a piece. She smelled a waft of Lee's aftershave as he leaned over. It was a bold, fresh citrus smell. She watched as he devoured another piece of toast, savouring their time together.

They were getting on well, and Lee was spending much more time at her house. 'Have you got a busy day lined up?' She asked.

'Yes, we've got an office meeting at ten, and then I'm covering for you at the senior leadership meeting later.'

'You'll probably bump into Dave Ferguson there; he's just been on the phone with me. He told me that Pete Higgs didn't arrive at the office this morning and wasn't answering his mobile phone. Pete's on restricted duties, working from the office.'

'He's probably still wasted from last night, too much booze and cocaine. I'll ask Dave if he wants me to call at Pete's flat on my way to the office. You never know who I might bump into if he invites me inside; maybe Ryan Young? And it gives me a legitimate reason to drop by unannounced.'

Andrea was impressed; she loved how Lee didn't miss a trick or an opportunity to go digging for more evidence.

Lee checked his tie in the mirror and leaned over to kiss Andrea. She gave him a hug, tempted to lead him back upstairs. He was already at the last minute, so she fought the urge and watched him leave instead.

*

Frank Burton looked up cautiously from his desk as Wayne entered, closing the door quietly behind him. 'Two meetings in two days, Wayne. I'm going to start charging you by the hour, Frank joked, assessing the mood music of Wayne's reaction, hoping that Wayne had calmed down following yesterday's outburst. Frank felt pleasantly assured that Wayne's military-like, calm composure had returned. He was clean-shaven and well-presented in designer jeans and a smart casual shirt.

'We need to re-focus, Frank, to put our foot on the ball. We can't afford distractions like yesterday. The arms deal with the Irish lads is our biggest payday yet; it must be right with no fuck-ups. If this deal goes well, it will definitely lead to more business. We could clean up here.'

'Indeed, Wayne, I totally agree. Talking of yesterday, what happened?' Frank knew his question was a digression and straight to the point, but he needed to know what had gone on to assess any immediate threats created by the fallout.

'For starters, I wasn't impressed with Ryan's attitude. He needs to buck his ideas up; I'm beginning to understand why Jason washed his hands of him.' Frank listened patiently, more interested in any punishment that Pete Higgs may have suffered. Wayne sat on the leather sofa, then continued, 'We've staged a suicide at the apartment. Pete Higgs is dead; he had it coming. I didn't trust him. The firm will be better off without him.

'Well, I wasn't expecting that to happen, Wayne. Christ, was that really necessary? Would an old-fashioned beating not have sufficed?' Frank was genuinely shocked and trying to keep a poker face. He felt numb, staring blankly out of the window. He'd always had a good working relationship with Pete Higgs and didn't take the news well.

'I told you, Frank, never trust a bent cop. But none of you listened to me. Once a snake, always a snake. I think he was playing both sides.'

'We've benefited from having him onboard, but will his apparent suicide not just bring more police attention to our door? He's one of their own.'

'No, Frank, it looks like the real thing. His life has been on a downward spiral. He's been drinking too much and addicted to cocaine. He's lost his wife and kids; he's had the police kicking his door in and couldn't take anymore. Nobody will be surprised that he killed himself. All of the tell-tale warning signs were there.'

Frank felt remorseful that his warning to Pete hadn't prevented his death. On reflection, he trusted Pete and thought that he certainly didn't deserve to die. 'Well, Wayne, I've got to be honest; I question whether it was necessary. Forensic teams are no mugs; I hope your boys knew what they were doing.' Frank said before lighting a cigarette.

'Textbook operation, Frank. We've left evidence of him having taken some rohypnol to dull his senses before hanging himself,' Wayne said, full of confidence.

'Well, I suppose we will know if the police have any suspicion of foul play once his body is discovered and a post-mortem is undertaken.' Frank was surprised at the sadness he felt. He'd known Pete professionally for years and had grown to like him.

'Are you okay, Frank? You look gutted,' Wayne said with a wry smile. 'Trust me. I got it right last time when I suspected we had an informant infiltrating us. I'll be proved right again on this occasion.'

Frank exhaled smoke and considered whether Pete was playing both sides; he doubted it. Pete had never let him down during their mutual arrangement over the years; he'd always delivered.

*

Lee McCann arrived at Pete's flat and kept his finger on the buzzer for longer than usual, anticipating that Pete was probably still asleep. There was no reply, so he tried calling on his mobile, which went straight to voicemail. Lee reached into the inside pocket of his jacket whilst studying the door lock. He selected a pick and tried to unlock the door. After a few moments, he realised it wasn't happening for him and gave up.

Lee returned down the stairs and saw Pete's car was in its usual place. Something didn't feel right. He looked into the car, half expecting to find Pete asleep, but he wasn't there. The car doors were secure, and nothing looked amiss. He stood back and looked up towards the windows; nothing obvious gave him cause for concern.

Whilst walking back to his car, he called Andrea, 'I've just been to Pete's flat; no reply. There's still time for him to surface and turn up at work. Give me a bell if you hear anything. I'll let Dave Ferguson know.'

'No worries, I've just arrived for the meeting with the Detective Inspector from the National Crime Agency. Maybe they've got him under surveillance?' Andrea said.

'It will be interesting to know how much evidence they have on Pete; see if you can find out. Let me know how you get on.' After saying their goodbyes, Lee headed for the office.

27

The door buzzer continued for longer than necessary, much louder than usual, piercing the centre of Pete's head. His headache was intense. He attempted to roll onto his side, hoping to alleviate the pounding pain in his head. But he struggled to move in his semi-conscious state and failed miserably. He felt like he had been hit by a train; the whole of his body was in agony. Slowly, he opened his eyes. The blurred view gradually became focused. He recognised the pile of his clothes and the bedroom floor carpet; it was Ryan's bedroom.

The buzzer stopped. Momentarily the pain in his head eased but then resumed. He closed his eyes. The skin on his neck was burning; he moved his hand slowly up his body to stroke the soreness. Shocked to discover the feel of coarse rope around his neck, he immediately tried to loosen it. Confusion enveloped him, motivating him to get up and make some sense of what was going on. He felt cold and began to shiver.

Pete pushed himself up and sat on the floor with his back against the side of the bed. He loosened the rope further and pulled it over his head. Letting it go, it fell onto his lap. His breathing was laboured and heavy. From the rope, his eyes instinctively looked upwards and focused on the ceiling. There was a hole in the plasterboard, exposing the wooden joist, the metal hook that once held the punch bag was gone. He scanned the floor slowly and located the metal hook at the rope's end. The circumstances slowly dawned on Pete, competing against the pain. He had tried to do himself in, to end it all, and failed.

He struggled to process what had happened, piecing together the events of the night before, but he couldn't. The only other time he had experienced brain fog like this was when Wayne set him up with the underaged girl. His recollection was non-existent, a black-out.

He managed to get up and stumble slowly into the lounge, using the wall for support. The lounge was a mess, empty beer cans and bottles; he winced at the thought of how much he must have drunk the night before. His eyes were drawn to the coffee table; a notepad with a pen placed by its side was surrounded by screwed-up pieces of paper. Pete's angst manifested with the thought that he had tried writing a suicide note. He picked up the nearest ball of paper and opened it up to find nothing had been written; he checked the other balls of paper, hoping to gain some insight into what had triggered his suicide attempt. They, too, were blank.

Pete collapsed onto the sofa, too tired to think; his head felt mashed, and he couldn't think straight. Why the hell had he done that? Unfamiliar emotions began to well up. He felt overwhelmed and experienced the urge to cry but physically couldn't. The confusion and feeling of anxiety were overwhelming. He'd had enough. He curled up into the fetal position and closed his eyes.

*

Lee's management meeting had dragged on for longer than expected. It had got him wondering whether he really fancied a promotion to Inspector and unsure of whether the role was for him. He looked at his watch and realised he'd better set off if he was going to get to the restaurant on time, somewhat optimistically.

He felt tired as he approached the Italian, ten minutes late; he would have preferred to go straight home and put his feet up in front of the television. But in fairness, he couldn't have declined when Andrea invited him out for pizza; and a few beers. He knew she had been going stir-crazy at home all week and needed to get out of the house.

The restaurant was busy; all of the window tables for two were occupied. Lee glanced past the feature olive tree decorated with glowing fairy lights, the centrepiece of the restaurant, and spotted Andrea reading the menu, seated in one of the booths on the far side. As he walked over, the smell of garlic wafted from the open kitchen. The chefs and kitchen staff were busy, orders and updates flying between them. On the face of it, the kitchen looked like a scene of chaos, but the food was always excellent.

Andrea smiled warmly, 'Glad you could make it,' she teased, 'I thought you'd stood me up.'

Lee laughed, 'Well, I had nowhere else to go; you know how it is.' Andrea raised her eyebrows in mock indignation and poured Lee a glass of wine, holding her gaze into his eyes as she passed the glass. Lee didn't want to be anywhere else; he hoped she didn't either. Her company had helped to drain his tiredness away. Going straight home was no longer appealing to him.

'There's still been no news from Pete Higgs. I wonder if he has gone on his toes?' Andrea suggested. Lee had more important priorities on his mind; he took a slug of his wine and sat back in the leather seat, gazing at the candle in the waxed wine bottle. 'The more I think about him planting the drugs in my office, the angrier I get. I am obviously responsible for his stupidity, in his eyes.?

'You searched his flat… maybe it was simply revenge? It really pissed him off when he saw your signature on the warrant. He seems to have a skewed view that you should be supporting him, even covering for him.'

'Well, he can run, but he can't hide. Enough of Pete Higgs, anyway. I'm going to have the risotto. What are you having?'

Lee fancied a pizza; he didn't need to look at the menu, 'I'm going to have a Neapolitan pizza and let's have another bottle of this,' he topped up their glasses and placed the bottle upside down in the cooler.

Lee felt amused when Andrea quickly returned the conversation to Pete Higgs, only moments after wanting to move on. 'The NCA are all over Pete like a rash. I was right all along; he's been in Hamilton's pocket. Christ knows what he's been up to. I suspect they've got undercover officers infiltrating the gang. They didn't go into too much detail, but they are confident with the evidence they have on him that they can get a result at court.'

'I thought we were moving on,' Lee laughed, 'he will get his comeuppance; it's just a matter of time.

*

Pete opened his eyes; the flat was in total darkness. It took him a moment to recollect how he had ended up on the sofa. He felt rough, still, but better than before. He made his way to the kitchen, flicked the light on, and poured a pint of water; he knocked it back, then poured another and drank that in one too. His thirst seemed unquenchable. He grabbed some painkillers from the kitchen drawer and began to gag as he tried to swallow them.

He leaned against the fridge, slowly sipping his third pint of water. Something wasn't right, but he couldn't grasp what it was. What had he taken? It wasn't a run-of-the-mill hangover. He pushed himself away from the fridge and headed back to Ryan's bedroom, scanning the flat for clues; the paracetamol packet was virtually full; surely, he'd have swallowed all of those if he wanted to kill himself. He returned to the lounge and picked up the pad of paper; it didn't look familiar, and neither did the pen. He liked quality pens and always used his favourite brand, which this wasn't. It didn't stack up.

A sinister feeling emerged in his mind; he'd been drugged and strung up. Images of Frank and Ryan entered his head but dissipated just as quickly. The image of a male wearing a balaclava; and a physical struggle were on the periphery of his consciousness, but he was struggling to put the pieces together and make sense of what had gone on. He held out his arms and noticed reddening and slight bruising; he'd been in a struggle, but he hadn't tried to kill himself. He needed to get away from here.

He grabbed his mobile phone. He needed help pronto; Lee McCann's phone went straight to voicemail. His next call was answered, 'Pete, where the fuck have been?' Steve Comstive asked.

'I can't explain right now, Steve. Any chance of me getting my head down at your place for a few days? I wouldn't ask, but I need to get away from my flat, the fuckers are onto me.'

'Yes, of course, mate. Are you okay?'

'Not really, mate; I'll meet you at The Plough in half an hour.' The memory blackout was causing Pete to feel vulnerable; what the hell had happened? Whoever did this wanted him dead. He didn't need to look far; Wayne Davies was the number one suspect. No-one else was in the frame.

28

A hastily arranged meeting was about to commence in a sparse, tired meeting room at a motorway services hotel. Andrea was last to arrive and apologised to Superintendent Samuel for her lateness whilst removing her coat. She nodded to DI Dave Ferguson and the National Crime Agency boss, Mr Williams, whom she had met at a previous meeting. She didn't recognise the male and two females seated next to him at the table but guessed they were members of his team. She gave them a nod too, and took her seat.

Superintendent Samuel glanced around the room and began the meeting. 'Thank you for attending at such short notice. There has been a significant development overnight which requires our urgent attention; to decide our next course of action. Dave will bring you up to speed with the details,' Detective Superintendent Samuel's delivery was concise and to the point. Andrea was intrigued about what had happened overnight, especially as she suspected Pete Higgs to be central to the events that brought about the meeting.

DI Dave Ferguson took a drink of coffee and placed his insulated travel tumbler on the meeting table. He began with his usual experienced, calm and professional approach. 'DS Pete Higgs didn't show up for his rostered shift yesterday. All attempts to contact him, from a welfare perspective, failed.

No surveillance operation was running at the time, so we were in the dark about his whereabouts. I wasn't too concerned about his welfare due to the nature of Pete's recent erratic behaviour, his drinking, gambling and the criminal activity we suspect he is involved with. So, I decided to call Mr Williams to suggest we activate the crime agency surveillance and review the situation in twenty-four hours if no further information or sighting was forthcoming.'

Mr Williams leant forward with his elbows resting on the table. Andrea thought he looked close to retirement age and wasn't the healthiest of specimens. She noticed signs of sweat from his armpits and wondered why he'd chosen a dark blue shirt instead of white, which also would have been a better match for his tie. She thought he had a very anxious disposition. He began to speak quietly. Andrea leaned forward to ensure she could hear him. 'What I'm about to say is obviously sub-rosa,' Williams looked around the table as if to emphasise the gravitas of his point, 'We have an undercover officer deployed, portraying the role of a surveillance detective in DS Peter Higgs's team,' Williams paused and looked around the table once again. Andrea thought he was a little over dramatic, considering he was talking to experienced senior detectives. Williams continued, 'DS Peter Higgs contacted our undercover officer yesterday in a panic and asked Steve, our undercover officer if he could put him up at his house for a few days.' Andrea sat back in her chair, recognising they'd had a stroke of luck; Pete had given the undercover officer full access to him by his own volition.

Superintendent Samuel took advantage of Williams's pause and stepped in, 'The initial debriefing of the undercover officer leads us to believe that members of the organised crime group have assaulted DS Pete Higgs. He has marks on his neck which appear consistent with a ligature injury, and other bruises, which appear consistent with having been assaulted. This morning he reported sick, suffering from stress.'

'Are we aware of why they assaulted him?' Andrea asked, suspecting they may be holding some information back to protect the integrity of the undercover officer.

'No, it's highly likely that they intended to kill him. But Pete Higgs hasn't disclosed much detail. He has indicated he will not be filing a complaint to the police.'

Andrea found herself wondering what Pete had done to piss off the crime gang. He was clearly in fear of repercussions, in effect, hiding from them. 'I wouldn't put it past him to switch sides and come back to us for protection,' Andrea said.

'Maybe, I expect one way or another, things will come to a head for Higgs over the coming week. 'We may have to strike earlier than we would have preferred if his life is at risk,' Williams said. 'But we must keep focused on the bigger picture in the meantime. Our primary objective is to convict the Manchester and Belfast organised crime groups. Pete Higgs's involvement has provided us with an unexpected opportunity to convict a corrupt police officer, and we will endeavour to achieve that goal. But not at the cost of the main objective.'

Andrea listened intently; she totally agreed with what was said, but her focus remained on Pete Higgs, recognising his conviction was a minor peripheral consequence for the Crime Agency. She accepted it was down to her to get the job done. The thought of him slipping through the net at this late stage didn't bear thinking about.

A knock at the door echoed through the room, preceding the entry of a hotel employee who carried a tray laden with tea and coffee. With a nod, they set the tray down on the table before making a discreet exit.

As the detectives poured themselves cups of tea and coffee, the atmosphere turned toward the serious matter at hand. They delved into the current operational strategy, scrutinizing potential leads and weighing up various tactical options.

Eventually, the meeting drew to a close, the strategic options having been finalized and set into motion. The detectives from the National Crime Agency, eager to put plans into action, were the first to head for the door. Andrea, however, lingered behind, taking the opportunity to engage in a more informal conversation with Samuel and Ferguson.

*

Ryan arrived at Frank's office in good time for the meeting. He was anxious to find out what Wayne had done to Pete Higgs. Whatever it was, it was low-key. None of his associates would talk to Ryan about it or admit involvement, probably under Wayne's strict orders, as a consequence of Ryan not wanting to be involved. Ryan had thought of nothing else since warning Higgs to make himself scarce.

'Christ, Ryan, you're an hour early,' Frank said, looking at his watch, 'ninety minutes early, in fact. I do have other work to be getting on with, you know. I'm in court all day tomorrow.' Frank used the interruption as an opportunity to put his briefing papers down and spark up a cigarette.

'It was your idea to meet here. It was much better when we met at the builders' yard.'

'It's safer here, Ryan, you know that; lawyer and client confidentiality makes it more difficult for the police to listen to us,' Frank said dismissively.

'What has Wayne done to Higgs?' Ryan blurted out.

'We'll find out when Wayne arrives. Make yourself a coffee and take a breath.'

'I don't want a coffee, Frank.' Ryan was pacing up and down.

'Why don't you go for a walk and kill some time? You don't want to be agitated when Wayne gets here; that won't help any of us. You can pick up some cigarettes for me if you don't mind.' Ryan took Frank's advice. His attempt to discover what had happened to Pete Higgs had failed. But he only got as far as the top of the stairs, where he met Wayne bounding up the stairs heading for the office.

'Where are you going, Ryan?' Wayne asked.

'I was going to get Frank some tabs; he'll have to wait now.'

'Get yourself back inside; I need to press on. I've got a busy day lined up.' Wayne said. Ryan turned about and re-entered the office, followed by Wayne.

'That was quick, Ryan, nervous energy?' Frank asked, chuckling, without looking up from his desk.

Ryan cut in quickly, realising that Frank hadn't noticed Wayne's arrival. 'No time for smokes, Frank, Wayne's here… time for some answers.' Ryan realised he was coming over a bit cocky as he spoke, which reflected how he felt. Frank prised himself out of the desk chair and went to the sofas, followed by Ryan and Wayne.

'I'm sensing you're unhappy, Ryan; you look stressed. What's the matter?' Wayne asked.

'I'll tell you what's the matter; since you decided to sort Pete Higgs out, I've been waiting for the cops to put my door in and bang me up as a suspect. Was it really necessary? I was managing Higgs; he wasn't a problem.' Ryan expected an aggressive tirade from Wayne about why he was wrong. He looked towards Frank for a reaction; Frank remained poker-faced and silent.

'Higgs is dead. I heard the pressure got too much for him; alcohol and drug addictions, gambling debts, criminality. I believe he hung himself after getting stoned out of his head on drugs and booze.' It was Wayne's turn to sound cocky, pissing Ryan off.

'There was no need to whack him; we had enough dirt on him anyway. He wasn't going to grass on us.'

'Well, he won't now, for sure,' Wayne gloated, 'he was pushing his luck; ripping me off was a direct challenge to my authority. He would have continued pushing the boundaries further if I'd let it go. I've just nipped the problem in the bud. And kept the cops at bay; he couldn't be trusted.' Wayne paused. Ryan looked towards Frank but got no response or support.

Ryan shook his head in disbelief. 'Are we still pressing ahead with the Irish deal?'

'Why not?' asked Wayne incredulously.

'Because, once they discover Higgs's body, the cops will be all over us like a rash, that's why.' Ryan raised his voice unintentionally before quieting down when he realised how he'd come across. It wasn't worth agitating Wayne; what was done was now history. He looked over to Frank again, seeing that Frank was keeping his powder dry, in listening mode.

'Ryan, it's a suicide. Why the fuck will the cops be all over us?'

Frank interjected, 'If they buy it, of course. I'm surprised they haven't burst in and found him yet. He must have missed a shift by now.'

'He might be on days off or sick. Anyway, you two can speculate as much as you like. As far as I'm concerned, I've eliminated a liability, its damage limitation. Onto business; the shipment has arrived, and we're ready to shift our biggest earner. So, switch on, fellas; this is the main event.'

Ryan looked over to Frank but thought better of asking for his opinion on the 'suicide'; Frank avoided eye contact once again.

'Briefing time; let's run through it again; we can't afford to make any mistakes,' Wayne said, sitting forward on the sofa's edge.

29

Pete Higgs found solace standing motionless in the shower, enjoying the feeling of the powerful water jet spaying down, massaging his head; it felt soothing. A rare moment of tranquillity amidst the chaos that had consumed his life. His legs began to ache, so he reluctantly stepped out, dried himself, and looked in the mirror. The ominous dark patches under his eyes made him wince, he looked rough, but the ligature mark around his neck wasn't as prominent now; he touched it gently, triggering his mind to flashback to when he woke up with a noose around his neck.

He shrugged off the memory and fumbled through the toiletries and aftershaves before him. He selected an aftershave balm and gently applied it to his neck. It was cool and soothing.

Wearing a towel wrapped around his waist, he walked into his temporary bedroom and sat on the edge of the bed. The small room was reminiscent of his bedroom when he was a kid. Pete felt safe here. He looked at the clock and realised he had been asleep for fourteen hours; he'd not even heard DC Steve Comstive getting up and leaving for work.

Pete was still struggling to fill in the blanks of that night; he guessed Hyena was involved, as he appeared in the partial flashbacks both visually and audibly. Pete was desperate to piece together what had happened; one thing was for sure, he'd been hanging before his weight had become too much, ripping the hook from the ceiling. A thought which made him shudder. Initially on coming around, lay on the floor with a rope around his neck, Pete believed he had attempted to take his own life. But now he was convinced that Wayne had given the order to have him killed and his death staged to look like a suicide. He lay on the bed and closed his eyes. His whole body was sore; he'd never felt so tired, effortlessly drifting into a peaceful sleep.

Pete opened his eyes with a start; the front door of the two-up-two-down terrace slammed shut with a loud bang causing the metal letterbox to rattle. His room was in darkness, but for a solitary slither of light cast across the room from the street light outside, the silence returned momentarily. For a moment, he felt a wave of panic and fear. He didn't have the strength to withstand another attempt on his life.

'You still in bed? You lazy bastard!' Steve shouted from the foot of the stairs.

'No, I'll be down in a minute,' Pete shouted back; he slipped into his jeans and a T-shirt and went gingerly downstairs. The stairs were creaky and steep; he trod slowly and carefully, keeping a firm grip on the handrail. At the bottom of the stairs, Steve handed him a burger and chips takeaway.

'You're looking much better... better than before anyway, get that down you.' Steve said with a smile.

'I don't feel much better, but thanks for this, mate,' Pete said, following Steve into the lounge and sitting opposite him. The aroma of the food flooded his senses, highlighting his hunger. He couldn't wait to tuck in. 'How was work today?' Pete asked, feeling obliged to show some interest in his host, whilst tucking into his burger, and spilling tomato sauce down the front his shirt.

'Same old, nothing new; I was deployed in the new surveillance van. It's a great bit of kit; the cameras are superb, with three hundred and sixty degrees coverage. The quality of the zoom is unbelievable, cutting-edge technology.'

176

'Did you speak to Dave Ferguson?' Pete said, sitting forward, wincing because of the pain.

'Yeah, I told him you were staying here on the pretext that you wanted to leave your flat to distance yourself from Wayne Davies and his cronies. Dave had no problem; he knows you are on your arse. He seemed pleased with the news. He told me to tell you; you can ring him anytime.'

Pete felt a cold shiver, 'You did tell him it was for his ears only, didn't you?' He felt disappointed in Steve, there was now a chance Statham would find out where he was living. He silently cursed Steve, what a naive gobshite, what was he thinking, the dickhead.

'Of course, he knows the score, and he wants to help you, remember.'

'Did he mention Andrea Statham?' Pete asked, feigning only a passing interest.

'Christ, yeah, she's well in the shit. Complaints and Discipline Branch found more coke in her car; forensics have confirmed it's all from the same batch. Dave Ferguson reckons the quantity is more than personal use, so it's unlikely command will let her resign and walk away quietly; she's got some explaining to do.' Steve's answer had been carefully formulated with his supervisors in case Pete asked this question.

Pete just about managed to suppress a smile of satisfaction, 'Well, she's only got herself to blame.' Pete felt relieved they'd finally found the drugs. He'd planted that bag a week before the stuff in her desk drawer. He'd reluctantly accepted failure that it hadn't been discovered by Lee McCann. The thought of Statham getting sacked, followed by serving some time at HMP Styal lifted his spirits. What a result that would be, he slowly eased back further into his seat.

'She reckons someone planted the drugs in her desk and car.' Steve said, breaking Pete away from enjoying the thought of Statham's demise.

'Well, she's bound to say that isn't she; who the fuck would want to set her up?' Pete observed Steve's reaction. Nothing concerned him; Steve didn't appear to suspect Pete in the slightest.

'No scrotes would have access to her office, and it's unlikely to be a cop. Maybe they could match the coke sample to other seized drugs to establish a lead on where she bought it from?' Steve suggested.

Pete experienced a hot flush of panic; he'd not thought of that. Was it from the same stash seized by the police from Declan Marsh? He felt gutted that he'd not checked. He needed to look into that later.

Pete had no sympathy for Andrea; she kicked him while he was down, and now it was payback time. Pete relaxed on the sofa and put his feet on the coffee table. The food had hit the spot. He closed his eyes and chuckled imagining Andrea protesting her innocence to a jury.

'What the fuck are you laughing at?' Steve smiled, curiously.

Pete thought quickly on his feet, 'This fucking shitstorm, mate, who could have predicted this?'

Steve took a sip of his coffee, 'So what the fuck happened to your neck, mate? You've still not told me.'

'Basically, I got too close to Wayne Davies and his boys,' Pete said, placing his drink on the coffee table. He sat back; this goes no further, Steve. We trust each other, right?'

Steve drank some more coffee and nodded, 'Of course, mate, I know the score.'

'We've been investigating them for ages but we were getting nowhere. So, I even set Jason Hamilton up to be arrested when he took Lee McCann hostage, but he managed to slip by the police on the containment cordon. God knows how they must have been asleep. I still can't believe they let him get away, I gave him to them on a plate. I put my life on the line to save Lee and get Jason Hamilton arrested. Only to be let down by the armed officers outside.' Pete linked his fingers on his lap and looked down, taking a moment.

'That must have taken some balls…' Steve said, quietly.

Pete over-talked Steve, 'Since then, I've been getting in amongst them. I almost persuaded Ryan Young to become an informant. It now appears that I was pushing him too hard. Wayne Davies decided that I was working undercover. They beat me and threatened to harm my wife and kids. What sort of husband would I be, if I couldn't protect them?' Pete stood up, shaking his head and began to pace the room, hobbling to avoid more pain in his legs. 'I couldn't trust the job to protect them, could I?

'Fuckin' Hell, mate, what a nightmare. Maybe I can help you out here, you know, two heads being better than one. What are they up to? Can we not go after them?'

Pete returned to his seat and put his head in his hands, 'Yep, a nightmare, not good, is it, mate.' He didn't look up. But was satisfied that he had convinced Steve of his brave and committed actions.

Steve began to clear up their takeaway wrappers, 'I take it you don't want the bosses at work to know?'

Pete picked at the last of the chips; he wiped his hand across his lips, 'Nope, what I've told you is to go no further, mate. I can sort it in time. And put them behind bars. It's pointless going after them at the moment; things are quiet, in the planning stages. It would just be a knee-jerk reaction to the beating.'

'You'll get criticised, even if you get a result,' Steve said.

'I already have, mate. Andrea Statham thinks that I helped Hamilton escape. What fucking planet is she living on?' Pete said, regretting mentioning Andrea again and highlighting their conflict.

'I'm aware of the drug dealing aspect. Have Davies's gang got their fingers in any other pies?' Steve asked, sounding like a keen rookie rather than an undercover infiltrator.

'Firearms. Serious shit, Steve, that's why I'm trying to nail them.' Pete was satisfied that he hadn't said too much but feigned an element of trusting bond with Steve.

'Where are they sourcing the weapons?' Steve asked.

'I'm working on it; I must have been getting somewhere, hence the assault. The problem is; that I need to continue. If I got in a scrape, could I call on your support, Steve?'

'It goes without saying, Pete, of course you can,' Steve answered convincingly; you don't need to get into a scrape for me to help. The least I could do would be to give you a lift. You've been good to me since I joined the unit.'

'I won't ask you to do anything that would drop you in the shit, but just to help me if I'm cornered.' Pete sat back and relaxed; he felt good, in a safe place, unknown to Wayne Davies and his cronies, convinced that Steve had his back.

'I'll grab us a beer,' Steve said, walking to the kitchen like a dutiful wingman, 'I think we need one.'

30

Ryan slipped into his car and tossed the sports holdall into the passenger footwell. It landed amongst the discarded takeaway wrappers and other debris. He pulled back a plastic panel on the dashboard and secreted his Baikal pistol.

In his haste to get away from the sinkhole estate, he over-revved the engine whilst steering away from the kerb and accelerated past the boarded-up retail units. The hoodies on the corner looked at the commotion, gesturing obscenities to him as the car sped away. It wasn't a place to hang around any longer than necessary.

Ryan smelled a rancid odour and grabbed the lapel of his coat; he pushed it towards his nose. It reeked of the shit-hole he'd just visited; dampness and burnt plastic chemicals. Instinctively he lowered the window for a welcome blast of fresh air.

There was no queue at the drive-through; he ordered a burger and fries and pulled up in a quiet corner of the car park. The parked cars on either side were empty, the owners probably entertaining their kids inside the restaurant.

Ryan shoved the last piece of burger into his mouth; it tasted great. He wished he'd bought two; one was never enough. He double-checked that there were no more fries in the brown paper bag, then picked up his phone.

'Ryan... what can I do for you?' Frank Burton asked. Ryan thought Frank sounded tired or maybe even disinterested. He always got the feeling he was calling Frank at an inconvenient time. It made him feel uneasy.

'Have you heard anything about Pete Higgs?' Ryan asked.

'No, should I have?'

'Me, neither. I just thought you might have had an update from your contacts in the cops.'

'I'm busy right now. Is there anything else I can help you with, Ryan?'

Ryan had decided not to raise the issue with Frank beforehand but couldn't help himself. 'Wayne's messed up, Frank. There was no need to kill Pete Higgs; he'd been getting paranoid like Jason did towards the end. I'm thinking of doing one; I'll probably head back to Spain again, well out of the way. I'm not living through another shitstorm. I was lucky to escape the last time they tried killing me.'

Frank's silence made Ryan regret his rant all the more. He feared Frank would report back to Wayne. Maybe Frank was sitting on Wayne's side of the fence these days, but he'd said it now. His views were out in the open, over emotional or not.

Ryan's mind filled the silence, recalling the memory of running for his life through the trees, in the dark, to escape from Jason Hamilton and Wayne Davies when they attempted to kill him by the Manchester Ship Canal. He could smell the undergrowth and soil as if he was back there. He didn't want to risk pissing Wayne off, knowing what he was capable of; he'd been there, done that.

'What's done is done, Ryan. I've got Wayne in charge now. That's how it is; I'm sure he covered his tracks. We've overcome worse than this before, as you know.' Frank's reassuring voice brought Ryan back from the woods.

'Don't you get it, Frank? Killing a cop is a big mistake. You must reign him in, Frank; he'll listen to you. You didn't say anything at the last meeting; you left it to me. Are you getting pissed off too, Frank?'

Frank didn't get the opportunity to answer; an incoming call appeared on Ryan's phone. 'Got to go, Frank.'

Ryan felt a cold shiver and hesitated. Should he accept the call or not? Was it a trap? Was it the cops? They might have found Pete Higgs's body hanging and taken his phone. Ryan felt a wave of panic; he'd fucked up. He must have been the last caller logged on to Pete's phone. Hesitantly he touched the red circle, his phone stopped buzzing, and Pete Higgs's name disappeared from the screen, giving Ryan some respite. His mind raced into overdrive, regretting he'd returned from Spain. No way was he taking the rap for Higgs's murder.

*

On his way home, Lee McCann had picked up a takeaway; it'd been a long day. Andrea was busy plating the beef in black bean and special fried rice whilst Lee got showered and changed. She was still finding her way around Lee's kitchen but just about managed. It was a typical bachelor's kitchen; the top oven was brand new, unused, and still contained the instruction leaflet.

Lee walked in just as she poured the merlot. He hugged her, and Andrea held tight to the bottle as they embraced. They kissed before Lee pulled away and grabbed their meals, heading to the dining table. Andrea followed, 'So, you'd prefer a Chinese meal over me, eh?'

'It was a close decision, so don't lose heart,' Lee laughed, 'I've not eaten all day; I'm ready for this. Sorry, I'm late; the meeting was never-ending. Dave Ferguson introduced me to Steve Comstive. I was hoping to get myself an undercover deployment, but he wants me to assist with operational support to Steve.'

'Makes life simpler for you, I suppose,' Andrea said, 'How's Steve doing?'

'He's making good progress; Pete appears to trust him and has opened up to him in confidence, of sorts. Pete's been a bit economical with the truth, but it's a start.'

Lee brought Andrea up to speed with the details of the undercover operation whilst they ate dinner. She was familiar with most of it, but her ears pricked up when Lee mentioned the circumstances leading to Pete moving into Steve's house.

Andrea laughed out loud, 'Samuel mentioned that at the briefing earlier… Pete's asked to move in with the undercover officer infiltrating him, priceless. It couldn't have happened to a nicer bloke. I can't wait to see his face when he's arrested and realises what he's done. Andrea's mood visibly lifted, 'I'm surprised, though. It's not like Pete to open up to a new guy. I'll get us another bottle. This news justifies one.' She walked to the kitchen, shaking her head, and chuckling.

'I know, you couldn't write it, could you? But what had he done to bring on a beating like that?'

'I don't know, but I'm surprised the snake hasn't come cap in hand to the cops looking for protection and a deal with the Crown Prosecution Service.'

'There's time yet,' Lee said.

'I wouldn't put it past him.'

They took their drinks to the lounge; Lee selected some music from his tablet and joined Andrea on the sofa. 'What more could a man want; a great woman for company, great wine, whilst listening to Pink Floyd.' He placed his glass on the table and leaned closer to Andrea, kissing her neck.

Andrea had other things on her mind. She engaged momentarily, then reached out for her drink, 'Will we be open to criticism in court for allowing Pete to move in with the undercover officer?'

'Dave Ferguson ran the circumstances by the CPS lawyer; they are fine with it as long as it's managed carefully. They just need to balance the intrusion with proportionality. They also discussed the scenario of Pete Higgs approaching us with evidence, in return for mitigation... turning Queen's evidence.'

Andrea's mood darkened, 'No way, should we cut him a deal. He deserves everything that he's got coming to him.

31

Ryan remained frozen in place since declining the incoming phone call. His eyes locked on the phone screen, his fingers drummed nervously against the steering wheel, leakage of his inner turmoil. As expected, the screen illuminated once again, indicating an incoming call. His heart raced as he shifted in his seat, mustering the courage to tap the green circle. His senses sharpened in anticipation, yet the line remained eerily silent. 'Who is this?' Ryan finally ventured; his voice tingled with uncertainty. His curiosity fighting the urge to hang up.

'It's me, you clown; who did you think it was… a fucking ghost?' Pete's voice was unmistakable and alive. Ryan felt confused; he'd not expected to hear the voice of a dead man. He rubbed his forehead and sat forward.

'What's up, Ryan? Cat got your tongue?... I think you've got some explaining to do.' Pete's words hung in the air, laden with unspoken questions and tensions.

Ryan focused on regaining his composure, raising his voice. 'Don't blame me; I gave you the heads-up to disappear, fast. You should have got away when I told you to. Anyway, more to the point, how the hell did you survive that? I heard they strung you up.' Ryan realised his voice was a higher pitch than usual and that he was talking too much when he should be listening. He shut up and waited for Pete to talk. But a menacing silence followed.

'I'm not having it, Ryan. Wayne's crossed the line. If you know what's good for you, you'll fill in the blanks for me. I guess it was an execution order from Wayne Davies, but I want you to tell me who the monkeys in the balaclavas were… Or, I'll be coming after you first. It's decision time; who are you siding with? Me or Wayne.'

Ryan found himself with no time to present his defence or make a decision; the phone abruptly fell silent. He sat motionless, his eyes staring into the dark clouds of an oncoming shitstorm. He was in no doubt of Pete's serious intent. Ryan felt aggrieved at being threatened; he was under no illusion of the threat being carried out by Pete, but he'd tried to help Pete and refused to participate in the hanging; what didn't Pete understand about that?'

A text pinged up on his phone screen, 'Usual car park – 1 hour.'

Ryan reluctantly replied with a thumbs up. He decided it was best not to burn any bridges for now; it was time to build them and consider his options. He locked his car up and headed inside the drive-in for another burger. He now had an hour to kill and time to mull things over.

*

DI Andrea Statham and DS Lee McCann arrived early at Rivington Services on the M61. Lee had driven a circuitous route to ensure they weren't followed. Content with his counter-surveillance, he selected a parking space that provided a clear view of all vehicles entering the services. Andrea scanned the car park, watching the comings and goings of visitors.

'Here he is, bang on time,' Andrea said after a short wait; she watched the black estate car reverse into a space nearby.

Steve Comstive walked the short distance to their car and dropped into the back seat, a routine he was clearly used to. 'I thought you'd have bought the coffees with you,' Steve said, 'These cutbacks are stretching too far now.' He leaned forward between the two front seats and introduced himself to Andrea.

'We've only just got here; give us a chance; we wouldn't have wanted to get you the wrong drink or lukewarm coffee, would we?' Lee replied with a hint of sarcasm. 'We know how high maintenance you undercovers are. I'll go and get them now; I suppose you'll also want food?' Lee laughed before taking their drink orders and leaving the car.

'I believe you've acquired a new housemate,' Andrea said enthusiastically, twisting uncomfortably to be able to face Steve, 'I bet that was a shocker. It's not often your target wants to make things that easy for you.'

'You're telling me, Christ, I would have been working twenty-four-seven if I didn't have my girlfriend's place to visit for some respite from Pete Higgs. He was in a bit of a state when he turned up. Davies's boys have certainly got under his skin.'

'I believe so. Any idea why they attacked him?'

'Not yet, but I'm getting there; it's early days. It was serious enough that Pete didn't want them to find him. So, it's not done and dusted by any stretch. No doubt there'll be more drama to come. Higgs's saying that they suspect he's operating undercover. I'm not convinced that is the reason. I'm not buying it. Maybe he's overstayed his welcome and isn't useful to them anymore?'

'Do you think he'll return to the police cap in hand for protection in return for grassing on Wayne Davies?'

'No, he's made it clear that he can handle it. He's still telling me he's treading the dangerous thin line to get them convicted.'

'Bullshit… we've already got him bang to rights on; being concerned in the supply of unlawful drugs and malfeasance in a public office. And that will just be for starters by the time we've finished. The National Crime Agency surveillance teams have been doing a cracking job. I'm sure they haven't given us the full picture yet; you know how

188

they love their secrecy and need-to-know policy. He's bent, a proper bad one. Keep your wits about you.'

'I'm sure he thinks I'm green-eyed, an eager-to-please ambitious newbie; he certainly doesn't see me as a threat to him,' Steve said with a wry smile, satisfied with the positive reflection on his infiltration performance.

Lee returned with the drinks and handed them out. Andrea smiled at Steve as she passed him a coffee, 'Be careful, it's not got a protective sleeve on it, it's red hot. He only had one job and blew it!' she said, winking at Lee.

Lee laughed, 'Well, you'd better go for them next time, Ma'am.' He mocked, looking over his shoulder at Steve. 'So, where's your welfare officer? I thought she was coming today.' Lee said.

'She's busy with a court case, just us three today,' Steve said; he leaned forward and delved into the brown paper bag that Lee had placed next to the handbrake. 'Doughnuts, nice one, Lee. I'm starving.' He said, rummaging through the bag.

'Only the best for the grafters. Fill your boots,' Lee said, watching with amusement.

Andrea also watched as Steve selected two doughnuts. 'You won't stay slim for much longer eating like that. I put a stone on if I even look at a doughnut,' Andrea said.

Steve laughed and wiped his hands on the tissue. 'I don't usually have doughnuts, only when Lee's buying.' Steve said whilst munching on the first one.

'I've printed off a report for you; it covers Pete Higgs entering Lee's address when Jason Hamilton took him hostage and Higgs planting the drugs in my office, plus a few more bits about the OCG from our previous investigation.' Andrea passed it over her shoulder, 'Read it here, and I'll keep it safe. It doesn't matter if you mention any of the facts to him; it's all stuff that you could have heard from Lee.'

No one spoke whilst Steve read the report; Andrea sipped her coffee whilst checking for new emails on her phone.

'Interesting stuff,' Steve said, breaking the silence. He handed the report back to Andrea. 'He is sticking to the story that he was the only one who knew how Hamilton ticked. And, therefore, was the only person capable of saving Lee. How on earth did the firearms officers let Hamilton slip through their cordon?'

'Because Pete created a distraction by letting Hamilton wear his clothes. The firearms team assumed it was Pete leaving the premises. By the time they realised what had happened, it was too late,' Andrea said. 'Is there anything else you need from us?'

'No, the report covered everything I needed to know. I'm fully up to speed. Let's see how tonight's deployment goes; I'm out with him for a few beers. I'll get off then.' Steve unfolded himself from the cramped back seat and headed for his car.

Andrea watched him walk away. 'He seems switched on; I can see why he's highly rated.'

'He's an experienced operator; Steve's been involved in some tasty jobs over the years. Nobody has a bad word to say about his ability. Pete Higgs won't know what's hit him until it's too late.'

Andrea couldn't resist a sadistic smile, 'Let's hope so.'

*

Pete steered his car carefully around the tight-angled ramps up to level four of the multi-storey car park; the myriad of colours of body spray etched onto the metal

190

barriers by passing cars focused his mind. He stopped the car at the opposite end of the pedestrian exit stairway. A strategic choice that could buy him valuable time in case any adversaries pursued him via that route. As usual, the car park wasn't well-lit and frequented by only a scattering of parked vehicles. People were either too lazy to venture this far up or maybe street-savvy about their personal safety.

Pete fumbled inside his jacket and pulled out his cocaine stash. He grabbed the vehicle instruction manual from the footwell and prepared his lines on the plastic surface. Job done, he tossed the manual back in the footwell and stretched both arms, pressing back from the steering wheel. He looked at the clock on the dashboard; ten minutes late, or had Ryan decided to run with Wayne? Or even worse, was he bringing Davies with him? Pete exited his car and started pacing around, looking for any tell-tale signs of an ambush. With each step, the nervous energy drained from him, enhancing his confidence.

He heard the pedestrian exit door slam shut behind him and instinctively spun around, almost losing his balance. 'Are you on your own?' he shouted at Ryan. His thoughts of an ambush had unsettled him; he was fearing the worst.

Ryan continued strolling across the deserted car park level towards Pete; he waited until he was a few yards away and replied, 'Yes, that's what we agreed.'

'Get in the car,' Pete said; he watched as Ryan walked around to the passenger side. He couldn't be sure, but he thought he saw Ryan smirking. Before getting into the car, Pete had a final scan around the car park; the coast looked clear. Once back inside, Pete relaxed but started the car engine as a precaution in case he needed to make a quick exit.

'Are you okay?' Ryan asked, 'You look a bit edgy.'

Pete felt irritated by Ryan's attempt at playing mind games. 'Of course I am. Besides your boys trying to fucking lynch me, I'm living the dream… Who was it? I know Hyena was one of them; he's got it coming to him.'

Ryan laughed at the name, 'I've never heard him called that before, but I get it. Yes, he was; I don't know who the others were. I made it clear to Wayne that I wanted no part in it. That's why I called to warn you. I tried to talk Wayne out of it.' Ryan said, sounding sincere.

Pete believed him but didn't want to indicate it yet. He needed to keep the pressure on to extract the other names of those responsible. He guessed Ryan had given Hyena up as a show of compliance but would offer no more names.

'Well, you need to find out. Will you do that?' Pete was carefully watching Ryan's hands for any sudden movements.

'I'll see what I can do. Look, at the moment, everyone still thinks you're dead. I reckon it's best for you to maintain that belief for the time being. It's better than going after them; they're more ruthless than you are, and you have more to lose. You might not be as lucky next time.'

Pete noticed Ryan staring at the rope marks on his neck and pulled his shirt collars higher to cover them. 'I've done everything that Wayne asked of me; I didn't deserve that. What the hell's wrong with him? Is he a psychopath?'

'You know the score; you gambled his money at the casino. What the fuck were you thinking? He would never let you get away with that, would he? Wayne has never trusted you. It's just the way it is, and you aren't going to change him. But taking him on isn't the answer. Believe me.'

'I want the names by eight o'clock tonight. Or I'm coming for you, Ryan. Nothing personal, but your body being washed up in the river Irwell will be the wake-up call Wayne needs.'

Ryan shook his head, 'You're making a big mistake; you don't scare me either, Pete,' Ryan said defiantly, holding Pete's stare.

'Eight o'clock,' Pete demanded.

Ryan got out of the car and made his way back to the exit stairs. The door slammed behind him, the noise echoing across the deserted parking level.

Pete locked the car doors and drove towards the exit. He remained highly vigilant; Ryan might have confirmed Pete's presence to his cronies to call them in, ready for an ambush. Pete had a contingency; if anyone got in his way, they would get mowed down. Stopping wasn't an option.

The way was clear; Pete turned right out of the car park and then right again around the block in time to see Ryan heading towards the city centre. He observed until Ryan was out of sight, content that he was alone.

Pete mulled over his options; Ryan had planted a seed of doubt in his mind.

32

Pete scanned through the menu on the wall behind the counter; it was much of a muchness, with fries. He then glanced at the donner meat, sizzling on the grill spit; it smelled good. The skinny donner chef finished trimming the cooked meat and placed his knife on the side. He looked over and gestured towards Pete for his order. Pete resisted the temptation of a donner kebab and opted for a snack.

He left the takeaway with a tray of cheesy fries. The adrenaline and anticipation of what was in store had diminished his appetite. The hoodie-clad gang hanging around outside were jostling with each other and exchanging rowdy banter, intimidating anyone brave enough to pass by them. A gangly teenager, wearing a hoodie tied tightly over his head, riding a BMX bike, swung within inches of Pete's feet, almost colliding with him.

'Get out of the fucking way, prick,' Pete shouted, suspecting the near miss was an act of intended intimidation or show of bravado to his buddies. Pete halted briefly, locking eyes with the hoodie, only to be met with sniggering and snide insults directed towards him. He continued walking slowly past the bus shelter. A torrent of abuse and mimicking continued to be aimed at him from the gang; Pete reluctantly accepted he was outnumbered and put some distance between them to avoid further conflict. He crossed the road and sat on the bench in the empty bus shelter. The fries tasted good, but there was enough to feed a family of four. After eating all he could manage, he threw the polystyrene container onto the overflowing pile of litter next to the bin. The pleasure of enjoying junk food didn't last long; it was replaced by the onset of painful heartburn.

He pulled his hoody over his head and checked his watch; it was almost eight o'clock. The gang opposite had lost interest in him and quietened down. He avoided their gaze; he had bigger fish to fry and didn't need the distraction of a brawl with a bunch of teenage hoodlums.

Pete rechecked his watch. He stood up and paced around, staying near the bus shelter. As expected, the car he was waiting on came into sight and parked a few yards away. Pete jogged over and grabbed the front passenger door. It opened, to his relief. He dropped into the seat and slammed the door behind him.

'The names, have you got me the names?' Pete asked, staring straight ahead without looking at Ryan.

'Get real, Pete, I'm not grassing on Wayne Davies and his boys. I've not got a death wish. But I'm also looking out for you; you didn't deserve that. I've told you, keep your head down; I'll see you right. Take him on, and you lose, seriously. I've been down that road before, and I'm not returning there. You need to listen to me, seriously.'

Pete grabbed the rucksack by his feet among the litter that he had been eyeing up; he had a good idea of what was inside. 'This will do for starters. I'll be in touch.' Pete opened the door and stepped out. He leaned back into the car. 'The names, Ryan. I want the names.'

Ryan raised his voice with a look of panic, 'What the fuck are you doing? Put it back, you dickhead.' Ryan reached across to grab Pete's arm but wasn't quick enough. The door slammed shut. Pete was on his toes.

Pete set off at a brisk pace, slipping his arms through the rucksack straps and securing it onto his back. He repeatedly checked over his shoulder, back towards the car. Ryan had thought better of it: he wasn't in pursuit to retrieve his rucksack. Pete felt relieved and focused in front, upping his pace.

He was immediately startled by the hoodies suddenly running away in all directions from the bus shelter opposite. He clenched his fists, ready to defend himself against those heading directly towards him. He knew he couldn't outrun them but devised his plan quickly. He would drop the first one to reach him and go ballistic like a madman. He watched with surprise as they continued running past him and beyond. He wasn't their target. Why were they running? Something wasn't right. A panic washed through him; he feared that Ryan had armed himself and was now in pursuit.

Pete looked back towards Ryan's car; he couldn't believe his eyes. A police van was heading his way. A fight with the hoodies now seemed preferable to any police attention he was about to receive. He focused on maintaining a calm disposition, slowed his pace, and looked toward the fleeing hoodies like a concerned resident, shaking his head with disapproval, pointing in their direction.

The police didn't continue as he had expected but stopped alongside him, and a female officer alighted from the passenger door. She approached him in a manner he recognised well, getting close to him as quickly as possible; under her watch, Pete was going nowhere. She looked young in service; Pete didn't recognise her. Pete smiled and portrayed a concerned law-abiding citizen, 'Good to see you about; these hoodies are scaring the life out of the residents around here, especially the older folk.' Pete observed her reaction and felt confident that she'd not recognised him as a colleague from the job. All good so far.

'We've received intelligence of drug dealing in this vicinity. So, we're clamping down on it. What's in your rucksack?'

Pete was taken aback by her purposeful demeanour; he guessed she was on a mission. He also realised he was now flanked by two more officers. 'Are you having a laugh? It's those morons running away that you should be after.' Pete was beginning to fear the worst.

'Pass me the bag, sir. If there's nothing illegal in it, you've nothing to worry about, have you?'

'Give me a break; I'm in the job. You're going to blow an operation if you look in the bag. I need to get going before I lose the hoodies. You recognise me, don't you, fellas?' Pete pleaded, looking over to the male officers who looked senior in service. Pete knew he sounded desperate. He played his last roll of the dice. 'I'm DS Pete Higgs from the serious crime division. I'm deployed undercover and have just seized a stash of drugs from those targets, who are now escaping. You need to back off.'

'We know who you are. Just pass her the bag,' the officer closest to him said haughtily. Pete sensed he'd been targeted; this was no chance 'stop and search'; the officer looked familiar. They'd got their man. He reluctantly accepted he wasn't walking away from this situation and handed over the rucksack. The two male officers edged closer to him whilst the female officer looked inside, 'Before I place my hands inside, is there anything that could harm me? Needles or other sharp objects?' Pete felt the urge to run but accepted that the officers were much fitter than him. He felt sick in the pit of his stomach and immediately suspected that Andrea Statham was probably behind this. Why else would they have targeted him?

'No, just the drugs that I took from the gang who've just made off,' Pete said with an air of resignation.

'I suspect the packages in the bag are controlled drugs. You're under arrest on suspicion of unlawful possession of controlled drugs with intent to supply.'

The caution that followed became white noise as he felt the officers grabbing his arms and placing the handcuffs on his wrists. He decided that further attempts to convince them to let him go were futile. He was led to the police van and helped into the cage. His mind started to race through the possibilities of how they'd got onto him... Statham, the bitch, it's got to be, he muttered with contempt.

Ryan couldn't believe his luck; his hand had been on the door lock, and he was poised to sprint after Pete just as he saw the police van. If it had arrived a few moments later, he would have been explaining himself to the cops too.

Curiosity had got the better of him; Ryan had hung back and watched the cops talking to Pete before driving away. He felt relieved; if Pete hadn't nicked the rucksack and run, the cops might have searched the car.

Ryan drove to a secluded country park and ditched the car. He tossed the empty petrol container into the back seat, then set the vehicle alight. The pitch-black parking area was instantly illuminated. Ryan stepped back, sharpish, from the whoosh of heat, covering his face with his hands for protection. The flames from the car created dancing shadows in the surrounding trees and shrubbery.

The cops must have seen Pete leave the car; it wasn't worth keeping it. They'd be looking for it, for sure.

Ryan decided it was time to make some calls and bring Wayne Davies up to speed. He couldn't risk Wayne finding out from elsewhere.

Frank Burton answered the call, 'Ryan, to what do I owe the pleasure of this call?'

'You won't be so blasé when you hear what I've got to say, Frank,' Ryan said quickly, still high on adrenaline. 'Pete Higgs has just stolen a stash of brown and crack from my car. But guess what? The cops showed up, searched him and arrested him. He'll be sitting in a cell as we speak.'

'Is this some kind of joke, Ryan? Because I'm not getting it.' Frank's voice sounded tired.

'Pete Higgs isn't dead, he's sitting in a cell, and he's out for revenge against the lynch party,' Ryan spelt the situation out for Frank. 'Now, do you suspect I'm joking, Frank?'

'Get yourself over to my office, now. We need to consider this carefully. What did Pete say, exactly?'

'He's angry enough for Wayne to be seriously worried. I'll make my way over now.'

Frank placed his mobile on the desk, leant forward on his elbows and rubbed his temples. After a demanding long day at Magistrates Court, this unfolding drama was the last thing he needed. He took a moment, then lit a cigarette, took a deep inhalation, and placed it on the edge of the ashtray. He scrolled through his contacts slowly and selected Wayne; the voicemail kicked in. Frank took another drag whilst waiting for the beep. 'Wayne, I need you to come to my office; we have an urgent situation developing and need to talk.'

33

Ryan handed the taxi driver a twenty and told him to keep the change. He headed up to Frank Burton's office with a skip in his step. He ascended the stairs taking two at a time, eager to see Wayne's reaction to the revelation that not only was Pete Higgs still alive but currently sitting in a police cell, having stolen a stash of Wayne's drugs. Pausing briefly outside, he listened at the door, pleased that couldn't hear any voices from inside the office. That was good news; it would allow him to discuss the situation with Frank rationally before Wayne's arrival.

He pushed the office door open and was hit by the smell of cigarette smoke; Frank was sitting at his desk, cigarette in hand, leaning back into his chair. Wayne was perched on the edge of the Chesterfield sofa, busy whispering into his mobile phone. Ryan was disappointed; he'd missed Frank's conversation with Wayne in relation to Pete Higgs being alive and well. Ryan knew he would get his moment of glory in sharing the details with Wayne. He'd only given Frank the scantest of details over the phone.

'I think he's seeking some explanations,' Frank whispered, nodding towards Wayne, 'he's not happy.' Frank said before yawning and rubbing his eyes.

Ryan raised his eyebrows, 'No surprises there. Is he ever happy these days? Poor bastards' I wouldn't want to be in the shoes of the lynch party right now. What have you told him?'

'Just what you told me.'

Wayne finished his call and walked over to the desk, joining Ryan and Frank, who dutifully fell silent. 'So, take us through it from the start, Ryan,' Wayne instructed.

Ryan felt relieved that Wayne appeared calm but feared it could be the lull before the storm. 'Apparently, the boys lynched him from the punch bag ceiling hook, which evidently couldn't take Pete's weight. He must have dropped to the floor pretty quickly to survive that. Pete's got all of those full English fry-ups to thank for saving his life,' Ryan laughed, chuffed with his witty take on the situation.

'He must have dropped as they left the flat. I've read somewhere that the brain can only be starved of oxygen for around two to three minutes,' Frank interjected.

Wayne ambled back towards the sofa, rubbing his forehead. He turned around and slowly walked a few paces back. 'Thank you for the medical lesson, Frank, that's really useful,' Wayne said sarcastically. Ryan remained silent and looked at the floor, awaiting the inevitable tirade.

'So, why haven't we been arrested for attempted murder yet?' Wayne said.

'He's not reported it to the cops…yet,' Ryan said, seeing an opportunity to fight Pete's corner and prevent further knee-jerk retributions while keeping Wayne on tenterhooks over what Pete might do next. 'I think if we pay him off, he'll go quietly. But we'd have to let him walk away,' Ryan said, satisfied that the seed was planted with Wayne and a win-win conclusion for all concerned.

'But will he do that?' Frank said, extinguishing his cigarette.

'I think so. Pete's not happy, for sure. But he's wanted out of the firm for a while now,' Ryan said, content with his pitch as mediator.

Wayne returned to the sofa. 'Any thoughts, Frank?'

Frank gave a long sigh, 'For me, there's only one other option, and that's to whack him. I don't think we should go down that road. Too much risk; he'd be ready for you this time.'

'Ryan?' Wayne asked.

'I agree with Frank. He's angry and wants revenge; obviously, I mean, who wouldn't if someone tried to kill them? But I think I'll be able to manage him.' Ryan purposefully didn't remind them of the stash of coke that Pete had just had away and then lost to the cops. Wayne returned to the sofa and edged forward, tapping his fingers on the coffee table. 'What about the arrest? What the hell happened there? Wayne asked, clearly sounding overwhelmed by the unexpected update.

'When Pete called me, I insisted we met up; I knew you'd want to know the crack. Once he'd explained everything, I gave him the rucksack to deliver so that I could phone you and let you know the score,' Ryan said.

Frank looked up from his desk, having clocked the discrepancy in Ryan's account. Ryan continued, 'Out of nowhere, a police van appeared, heading straight for me. All the smackheads made a run for it, leaving me sitting there like easy prey for the cops. But the police drove straight past me and collared Pete Higgs. I didn't want to hang about, so once they started searching the bag, I did one.'

'So, that's another stash of drugs he's lost us,' Wayne said, 'What is it with this dickhead?'

'Give him a break, Wayne. I'd just sent him to deliver the stuff; he didn't have a clue I'd have any gear with me. Let alone hand it over to him. A stroke of luck, really; better him getting arrested than me,' Ryan said, working hard on an alternative version of events for damage limitation whilst looking over to Frank for support.

Wayne stood up and stretched off some tension in his shoulders. 'I see two issues here; did he set it up? Or if he didn't, is he going to start grassing on us to the cops to save his own skin whilst he's in custody?'

'I've got to agree with Ryan, Wayne; I think we can safely rule him out of having set it up. But the issue of him grassing is a different kettle of fish,' Frank said, to Ryan's relief. No one answered; the thought of Pete grassing conjured up a nightmare.

The silence was broken by Frank's mobile ringing. Ryan and Wayne looked his way; Frank shrugged his shoulders whilst checking out the display 'Unknown caller,' he announced, shrugging his shoulders, before taking the call.

'Frank Burton speaking.'

Ryan was surprised that Frank took the call and looked at Wayne, expecting him to be pissed off with Frank. But Wayne appeared to be deep in thought, his mind elsewhere, considering his options.

'Okay, can you run me through the circumstances of the arrest?' Frank asked.

Wayne stood up and returned to the desk, standing by Ryan, watching and listening intently to Frank.

'I'll set off straight away.' Frank concluded the call with the custody sergeant.

'Higgs wants you to represent him?' Wayne guessed, from what he had heard.

'He does indeed,' Frank said, leaning back against his chair.

'Excellent, let's see how the land lies; call me with a heads-up soon as, Frank,' Wayne said. 'If he's going to grass on us, we need to disappear for a while. I might take off to Wales as a precaution; we've still got the caravan in Rhyl.'

'Hang fire on that for now. Why don't you and Ryan wait here? My office is probably the safest place right now. I don't think he will grass; it's more likely that he will make some demands of recompense for your failed assassination attempt,' Frank said, raising his eyebrows at Wayne.

Frank took his coat from the back of the chair, picked up his cigarettes and dropped them into his briefcase. 'Do you want me to pass any messages or proposals for a mutually beneficial deal, Wayne?'

'Let's see what he's got to say first. I will wait here with Ryan just in case he grasses us to the cops. They won't come looking for us here. Keep me updated, Frank.'

Ryan's head dropped at the thought of spending the next few hours alone with Wayne and getting dragged into his plans for revenge. 'I'll nip out and get us some food, Wayne,' Ryan said, grabbing his jacket.

*

DI Andrea Statham listened intently whilst DI Dave Ferguson updated her about Pete Higgs's arrest. She sensed a sadness in Dave's voice; he didn't appear to be relishing Pete's demise. A sombre silence followed his briefing.

'Where is he being detained?' Andrea asked.

'The crime agency requested that he was taken to Preston, a different force area; it provides total impartiality, as to be expected in these situations.'

'The surveillance team did well to call in the uniformed patrol and catch him in possession of the drugs,' Andrea said.

'They did; it was a big call, though; who knows where he would have gone if they had held back and followed him. He may have implicated some of the others.

'Fair point, but if he's charged and looking at a custodial sentence, which is likely, he may be tempted to inform against Wayne Davies and his cronies to lessen his sentence,' Andrea said.

'And if we don't oppose bail, it might just put the cat amongst the pigeons. I imagine there will be some activity if Pete's released on bail.'

'Is that the plan?' Andrea asked.

'It's being considered. I'm on call tonight, so I will stay here until the interviews are concluded. If Pete is released, the NCA may ask for surveillance support. I'll give our on-call team leader the heads up.'

'Let me know what happens. I'll keep my phone on.' Andrea walked to her car, mulling over what she suspected Pete would do if given bail. Her gut feeling led her to decide she'd be safer staying at Lee's house for the night. Pete's behaviour had been unpredictable and reckless; rocking up at her address for a row couldn't be ruled out. Andrea knew only too well that he had an axe to grind.

34

Pete Higgs endured the bitter humiliation of being processed into custody. He was sitting on the wooden bench in a cell, minus his shoelaces, belt, and valuables which had all been confiscated by the Custody Sergeant, leaving him stripped of his personal effects. The rank smell of stale sweat laced with desperation was familiar, albeit this time from the wrong side of the cell door. He'd tried his best to ignore the loathing glances from the police officers working in the custody office, which they feebly struggled to disguise with insincere courtesy. He was now an outcast, a corrupt cop, not to be trusted. The lowest of the low.

He closed his eyes and let his head fall back, gutted that he'd snatched the rucksack from Ryan. An impulsive act; what was he thinking? He had nothing to prove to Wayne Davies and his cronies; going into battle with them was pointless.

He heard a familiar voice from outside the cell; Peter opened his eyes and looked towards the cell door, listening carefully as the key turned in the lock, with the rest of them rattling louder against the door. The door swung open, 'Your brief's here,' the civilian detention officer announced. Before stepping back to allow Frank Burton into the cell, the door slammed shut behind Frank.

Frank raised his eyebrows sympathetically, sitting beside Pete and placing his briefcase on the floor at his feet. 'What were you thinking?' Frank whispered, only just loud enough for Pete to hear.

Pete shook his head and looked to the floor, 'I wasn't thinking straight, obviously. But it's hardly surprising, is it?

Wayne tried to kill me. What am I supposed to do, Frank; wait patiently until he makes a second attempt or hit back?'

Frank shifted on the bench and coughed, 'Well, it's time to think straight now. Take the rap. Keep your mouth shut, and you'll walk away fully compensated. We're talking about a life-changing amount of money here, Peter. You could relocate abroad and start again. I've talked some sense into Wayne. Both of you should draw a line in the sand and move on,' Frank said, satisfied with his damage limitation pitch.

Pete craned his neck to help him hear Frank's almost inaudible voice. 'That's great; you're supposed to be my lawyer, defending me, and you want me to throw the towel in before the fight has started. Who are you here to represent, Frank; Me or Wayne?' On second thought, don't answer that; I can guess the answer.'

'There's a bigger picture at play here, and in fairness, you shouldn't have taken the rucksack. I will do my best, but I need to satisfy myself that you will keep quiet. It's for the best; you'll be looked after. You have my word on that.'

'I'll need to be looked after; I won't have a job for much longer.'

Frank leant forward and took his legal notepad from his briefcase. He clicked his pen and started to write, 'Let's get a prepared statement on paper ready for the interview.'

'No need, Frank, I'm going to be interviewed alone. I don't need you in there with me.'

Frank looked perplexed, placing his pen down on the pad. 'Why on earth would you want to do that?'

'Because I don't want to be charged with unlawful possession of controlled drugs. You want me to plead guilty. That ain't happening without a fight.' Pete stood and stretched his arms into the air. He looked at Frank and started to laugh. 'Don't panic; you're safe. I am not going to go Queen's evidence.'

'You need me in there, Peter; you know it makes sense.' Pete sensed a tone of desperation in Frank's voice. 'And think this through carefully; you'd still receive jail time, even if you decided to inform against the firm. You don't need me to remind you that life on the prison wing can be a dangerous place.'

'Spare me the veiled threats, Frank; we both know why you want to represent me. So, you can report back to Wayne Davies with your tail wagging. I thought you ran the firm these days; you need to grow a pair, Frank and let him know who's the boss. Keep your phone on; if I need you, I'll call. You've done your bit; you can report to Wayne and tell him he's nothing to worry about. But also tell him I want a golden handshake if I'm going to walk away quietly. He owes me.'

Frank shook his head, picked his briefcase up and got to his feet, 'I'll leave you with it then, be careful.' Frank pressed the buzzer, the detention officer opened the door and escorted him out of the cell area.

Pete returned to the bench and lay down; he closed his eyes and focused on his plan, only to be disturbed by a prisoner shouting and kicking off whilst being escorted to a cell. Pete imagined the local cops pointing to his cell door, letting colleagues know where the bent cop was being held.

A short time later, he was led to the interview room by the same detention officer who avoided eye contact and kept conversation to the bare minimum. This amused Pete; he guessed he had been the talk of the custody office, the bad apple, the corrupt cop from the big city. Now persona non grata, to be treated with contempt.

Pete took a seat on the secure chair bolted to the floor to prevent him from launching it at the interviewing officers. He looked across the interview room desk at the two National Crime Agency detectives: forty-something males wearing smart dark suits. Pete sensed an air of nervousness and wondered whether they considered him a worthy adversary or if it was just the pressure of expectation created by their bosses.

Pete had expected local CID to be conducting the interviews. He was perturbed that the crime agency was involved in the investigation and guessed they were investigating the Irish connection, which would explain their involvement.

The tape machine started to buzz loudly once the tapes had been inserted into the recording machine. The grey-haired detective led the introductions and began the interview, 'Peter, you were arrested in possession of a rucksack containing controlled drugs and a substantial amount of cash. Can you tell us why you were in possession of these items?' The detective took his elbows off the desk and sat back in his chair, maintaining eye contact.

'I have a prepared statement to make. I will not be answering any further questions during this interview. I have been investigating a local organised crime group for some time now, years in fact. Recently I have gained the trust of one of the drug dealers. He has agreed to work for me as a covert human intelligence source, an informant in old money. As you are aware, this is a high-risk policing strategy and sensitive practice. Getting the trust of these people does not come easy; it has been a long, arduous process.' Pete paused, satisfied with his professional and concise delivery.

'On this occasion, I got into the car, and once inside, I realised it was not the person I was expecting, there was a short altercation, and I took the bag. I wanted the dealer to think he'd been turned over by a rival gang member rather than approached by a cop. My actions were focused on protecting my informant and getting the drugs off the street. I obviously would have booked the stuff into the police property system had I not been arrested. I tried to explain this to the arresting officers, but they did not want to listen. They'd already made their minds up about me.'

'Why didn't you arrest the male in the car?'

'No comment.'

The two detectives continued firing questions, and Pete Higgs continued to make no reply. The interview was concluded. Pete was led back to his cell. He walked to the wooden bed at the far side and turned to face the detectives. Pete sensed the two detectives were disappointed with the outcome of the interview.

'I'm agreeable to participating in an intelligence interview if you're interested in knowing what I have discovered about the OCG so far. But I have one condition. I will only talk to DI Andrea Statham. No one else,' Pete said. The younger of the two detectives looked enthusiastic and very interested; it would be something positive he could report to his boss. It amused Pete; he'd met a potentially worse poker player than himself.

'Leave it with us; we'll see if the boss is interested, can't see it myself,' the older detective replied, disinterested, checking out his fingernails.

Pete lay down on the wooden bed. He felt confident he could convince Andrea Statham to delay charges and release him on bail in return for grassing on Wayne Davies. Whether he would grass was yet to be decided; all options remained on the table.

35

DI Andrea Statham had ignored her gut feeling and drove to the police station. She didn't hold out much hope of gathering any significant intelligence from Pete Higgs. The request from Pete had surprised her. Still, on reflection, she recognised he was a desperate man. She suspected he would attempt to draw on their relationship to pull a favour, for old times' sake. Curiosity fuelled her decision to agree to the meeting; what if he held more critical information than she had initially presumed?

She arrived at the police station, having rung ahead of her arrival. A practice she had developed over the years, minimising the risk of sitting around in a busy reception area, waiting in line.

Andrea strolled up towards the public entrance, where the paving was decorated with discarded cigarette butts. The automatic glass doors of the reception entrance slid open. The waiting area looked tired and grubby, uninviting even. At least it was still open, Andrea lamented. Too many enquiry counters throughout the country were closed. Alienating the public further from the police, making any other contact more impersonal.

A young woman wearing a pink onesie was standing at the enquiry counter explaining that she hadn't signed on at the police station, a requirement of her bail conditions, for two days because of childcare issues. She struggled to convince the weary counter clerk to allow her to sign the form retrospectively. Having realised, she was getting nowhere, the woman commenced a tirade of abuse at the counter clerk before storming out. The counter clerk returned to her sanctuary in the back office for a moment of respite while completing the necessary breach of bail paperwork.

A woman in a pristine black trouser suit approached Andrea from the door, labelled 'No Entry-Staff Only.' She introduced herself as DI Smith and shook Andrea's hand. 'Would you like tea or coffee before you start?' she asked, leading Andrea along a corridor.

'No thanks, I'll crack on with the interview. It's been a long day already.' Andrea replied with a polite smile.

'If you change your mind, come to the CID office. The pre-prepared coffee in the custody office is disgusting.' Andrea followed her, and they entered the custody suite, where two uniformed officers hovered near the custody suite counter, chewing the fat with the custody sergeant. They tagged along with DI Smith and Andrea as they headed towards the interview room, all pausing at the door. Andrea guessed they had been handpicked for the task. Both would complement any rugby team as formidable props. The officer with slightly wider shoulders and cauliflower ears stepped forward. 'Just press the panic button if you need us, Ma'am; we'll be straight in if needed.'

Up until now, safety hadn't crossed her mind. The thought of Pete Higgs attempting to take her hostage inside the interview room flashed across her mind. Even though she believed he was unhinged at the moment, she dismissed the thought as a non-starter immediately. He'd be a brave man if he tried that on with her. The Superintendent had insisted on the uniform back-up… just in case.

The door clicked open, and Andrea entered the room. Her gaze locked onto Pete Higgs's eyes, and something about his demeanour struck her as unsettling. His eyes seemed shrouded in darkness, almost sinister-looking. Andrea couldn't help but notice that his usually well-groomed hair

212

was now dishevelled, hanging longer than his usual smart cut. He was sitting in the 'suspects chair' screwed securely to the floor. Andrea took the seat opposite and placed her notepad and pen on the desk. The atmosphere hung heavy with surreal tension; Pete's smile, though disconcerting, appeared almost routine, as if it was just another day in the office. Two colleagues getting their heads together before interviewing a suspect. But this time, Pete was the suspect. How starkly things had changed. Andrea continued to return his stare, but not the smile. The person sat opposite wasn't the Pete Higgs she once knew.

'Thanks for coming, Andrea. Hopefully, we can get this sorted,' Pete said. Andrea suppressed an urge of cynical laughter at Pete, sounding more like a condescending bank manager than a corrupt cop trapped in the cross hairs.

'No thanks needed. The only reason I agreed was to help to get me reinstated. I'm still suspended as a consequence of the drugs discovered in my office… the drugs that you planted.' Andrea glared at Pete, hoping the accusation would put him on the back foot. She maintained a concerted effort to relax and not let him get under her skin.

Pete clasped his hands on the desk and looked down at them. Andrea anticipated he was about to say something profound but then changed his mind.

'Are you going to have the decency to admit to planting the drugs? Then I can get this suspension lifted and get back to work?' She snapped at him, leaning across the desk.

'Hang on a minute, I'm not the bad guy here. If we're pointing fingers at each other, you abandoned me when I needed you after Rachel kicked me out. Then you accused me of working with Jason Hamilton and helping him escape the siege. Then to top it all, you executed a firearms warrant at my flat. Let's get some realistic perspective on this. What the hell have I done to deserve this shit?'

Andrea didn't know whether to laugh at Pete's outburst or shoot back in retaliation. But she kept her composure and provided silence, anticipating Pete to continue talking.

Pete lowered his voice, 'Look, I need some help here. You must know I was trying to bring Wayne Davies's gang down, just as I did when Hamilton was the boss. Do you really believe I'd go corrupt? If you can help me to get out of this mess, I'll admit to putting the drugs in your office as a prank gone wrong. Albeit, I haven't got a clue how they got there. We go back way too far together. We need to work together on this; you've just got the wrong end of the stick, that's all.'

'Okay, let's work together. You requested an intelligence interview, not to sit here chatting about old times. What have you got to tell me?' Andrea picked her pen up, ready to start writing. She watched as Pete shifted nervously in his chair; she didn't lose eye contact, pen poised, ready.

'How do you want to pull it together? I've got a lot of information; Hamilton's dead, and I have more than enough evidence to take Wayne Davies, Ryan Young, and even Frank Burton down.'

'Just start talking, Pete. You know the routine,' Andrea said, tapping her pen on the notepad.

Pete leant forward into the desk, 'I need some assurances first. These aren't back-street gangsters. If I spill my guts now and the bosses decide not to do a deal with me, I'm fucked, a dead man.'

'You know how this works. The bosses will want to hear what you have to say before they can make a decision. What have you got?' Andrea sounded impatient.

'I know what you're doing. You're trying to stitch me up. Get what you need from me, then fuck me off. Well, it ain't happening. I want an initial memorandum of understanding; on paper signed by the senior investigating officer and the crown prosecution lead. Then we'll start talking. Pete sat back in his chair and shook his head.

'Andrea rose from her chair and headed for the door. 'You're wasting my time here. See you in court,' she said calmly, not giving Pete the courtesy of eye contact.

Pete jumped up, 'You'll fucking regret this, you bitch,' he shouted, 'That's it run away from the trouble like you've always done, leaving your pals to deal with the crap.' Pete banged both hands on the desk. The door burst open, and the officers entered.

'Whatever, Pete.' Andrea rolled her eyes and stood aside whilst the two uniformed officers flanked him, ready to escort him back to his cell.

'Go easy, guys, it's just a tantrum. He does this when he doesn't get his own way.'

The six-foot-plus officers nudged Pete into his cell and slammed the door shut. 'You've rattled his cage, Ma'am. He's not a happy teddy. I thought he would kick off for a moment back there.'

'He's got a lot to worry about,' Andrea replied.

Andrea didn't hang about at the police station; the heavens had opened, and rain was bouncing off the pavement. She cursed not having not taken her brolly and ran to the car, quickly taking shelter inside. She set off, heading to the M6 for the short journey to her next meeting. The windscreen wipers struggled to keep the screen clear of the heavy rain; she slowed down and moved into the inside lane amidst the spray from the heavy goods vehicles. The car radio was just white noise; Andrea was deep in thought, mulling over what was happening in Pete Higgs's head. He'd not even given her an idea of the intelligence he could provide. Maybe Pete had no intention of grassing? Perhaps he'd just wanted to see Andrea suffer and was curious to find how she was coping with the discipline suspension for the drug possession that he'd fabricated. One thing was for sure, he wasn't the Pete Higgs she used to know. He was losing the plot. He looked like a desperate man on the edge, cornered, not knowing which way to turn.

Andrea arrived at the Counter Corruption Unit and was shown to Detective Superintendent Samuels's office. Mr Samuel was sitting at his desk, in conversation on the telephone. He beckoned her to take a seat. Andrea opted for the sofa rather than the office chair adjacent to his desk. She took the notepad from her handbag and looked at the blank pages from the so-called intelligence meeting. Andrea heard a soft tap on the door, and Alison entered with the tea and biscuits tray. She placed them down, smiled at Andrea and left quietly.

'Sorry about that; phone calls have been toing and froing with the Chief's office all morning. I won't bore you with the details.'

Andrea remained silent for a beat; usually, he followed that phrase with a few juicy snippets, and she liked to keep abreast of current affairs within the Force. However, nothing materialised on this occasion. 'Well, the meeting went as expected. Pete claims he can blow the gang out of the water but wants to see our cards first: a deal heavily weighted in his favour.'

'He knows it doesn't work like that. He's trying it on,' Samuel said with a hint of tiredness.

'And he wants a memorandum of understanding on paper with signatures.'

'Did he have Frank Burton representing him?'

'Burton represents him, but Pete didn't want him present at the interview.'

'What's your gut feeling having spoken with him?' Superintendent Samuel removed his spectacles and placed them on the table.

'I think his number one objective is staying out of prison. He probably does have enough evidence on the gang for convictions in court, which would justify a lenient sentence for him. But I can't see him avoiding spending time inside, and I think he knows that. I reckon he was dipping his toe in the water. He'll probably request another meeting at some stage.' Andrea paused, gently tapping her pen on the notepad.

'I agree. Let's not be hasty; we can play the waiting game. The ball is in his court. He needs to give us an indication of what evidence he can provide. He has more to lose than we do,' Samuel said.

'I think we can do better than an intelligence interview.'

'How so?' Samuel grimaced.

'He's a desperate man, expecting jail time, being remanded at least. We could give him bail: with conditions and continue with the surveillance operation. He won't expect that; he'll expect us to refuse bail. So will the OCG.'

Samuel scratched the back of his head, then sat forward, 'Desperate men do desperate things; it certainly could stir things up a bit.'

'Wayne Davies knows how these things work; he will be suspicious about Pete not getting remanded into custody. It might just unsettle them enough to make some mistakes. Then we convict all of them, and Pete Higgs doesn't get to walk away with a reduced sentence.'

I like it, leave it with me. I'm meeting with the Crime Agency team later; I'll see what they think. It sounds like a good plan to me.'

36

It was late evening when Frank Burton arrived home, feeling tired, from the police station. He had been surprised to receive the call for assistance from Pete Higgs at the custody suite. Their relationship having somewhat chilled recently. Frank assumed this was down to Wayne's continuing feud with Pete. He considered declining the request, but the opportunity to keep abreast of developments was too great a pull for him.

He unlocked the front door; the house was silent and dark; Mrs Burton had obviously become tired of waiting and retired to bed, probably for the best. Frank felt worn out and just wanted to be left alone. He dropped his keys onto the study desk and lifted the whisky bottle from the drawer. He poured a generous tot and cradled the heavy crystal glass before taking a drink and heading to his leather recliner. He enjoyed the smooth Irish whisky with a peaty aftertaste. A gift from the Irish associates, passed on to him by Wayne.

He felt uneasy; his gut feeling told him something may be wrong. Why had Pete Higgs not wanted him present at the interview? He didn't want to believe the obvious answer, but there was a strong possibility that Pete may have started passing information to the police to save his own skin. Or at least negotiating a deal with them. Just what Frank had feared happening in response to the hard-line Wayne had taken to him.

Frank picked up his phone, knowing Wayne would be expecting an update.

It was answered on the first ring, 'What took you so long, Frank? I was beginning to think you'd been locked up too.'

Frank sensed anxiety in Wayne's voice. It worried Frank that Wayne believed it was a reasonable possibility for him to have been locked up. Did Wayne know something that Frank didn't? Frank suddenly felt unsettled; he'd always gone to great lengths to cover his tracks. If the firm collapsed, he counted on being the last man standing.

Frank sighed, 'It's been a long evening, Wayne, with a few surprises along the way. He didn't want me to represent him at the interview; stranger still, he was granted bail with conditions. He's also been suspended from duty, with a caveat not to visit police premises. That will obviously impact on his usefulness to us.' Frank took another sip of whisky; its warmth spread from his mouth to his chest, comforting and soothing. "I don't like it. What do you make of it?'

'It sounds like we need to be worried; do you think he's done a deal with them?'

'I can't rule it out, I'm afraid, but I don't think so. It's not Pete's style. I'd be more inclined to believe he's now hedging his bets. Bail was probably the outcome he was seeking.' Frank placed the glass on his desk, feeling much more relaxed and lit a cigarette.

'Maybe not his style, but he'll do anything to avoid time. I had this eventuality covered with the plan to kill him. If the boys had done a proper job, we wouldn't have this problem.'

Frank took another sip of whiskey, deciding not to mention his observation that Wayne's behaviour may have led to Pete considering making a deal with the police. 'Are you tempted to postpone the arms deal?' Frank asked instead.

'I can't afford to, Frank; The Irishman won't stand for it, plus the longer we sit on the merchandise, the greater the chance of it being found by the cops. Where is Higgs staying?'

The question gave Frank a sudden rush of blood, 'I don't think going after him again will be a good move; there is too much police activity.'

'Just asking.' Wayne's answer caused Frank a feeling of bewilderment; he rubbed his temples.

'I don't know, and it's probably best we don't know. The police surveillance teams are probably watching him, hoping to lure you in. Pete may even be in on it.' Frank said, taking a drag of his cigarette, confident his last comment would pour cold water on any plans Wayne was formulating to hit Pete Higgs.

'Okay, Frank, fair enough. Get into your police contacts. Let's get the inside track on this; we can't afford to fuck-up at this late stage. Keep in touch with him, keep digging, and maybe take him out for a pint. If necessary, you can always explain it away to the cops at a legal representation meeting. The focus has to be on the arms deal. We can't afford to be side-tracked. I will decide what to do with Plod later. Catch up soon.'

The call ended, and Frank refilled his glass, glancing at the label on the bottle; it was a new favourite. He shook his head, unconvinced that Wayne wouldn't have another shot at Pete Higgs. Frank reluctantly anticipated that tough times were ahead.

*

About the same time as Frank was arriving home, Pete Higgs exited the taxi a few blocks away from Steve Comstive's house. He wasn't worried about the taxi driver but preferred to be cautious; he didn't want to compromise the location of his bolt hole. He began walking a convoluted route back, watching and listening. He took out his mobile phone and selected the recipient. The call went straight to voice mail, 'So, you've got what you wanted, you fucking bitch, well done. Well, let me tell you, I'll clear my name and walk away from all this shit. But I'm not being stitched up; I'd rather kill myself. If you force me to do that, you'll have to live with it. If you have a conscience, that is.' Pete paused and decided it was probably best to end the voicemail before it turned into a rant.

He turned his key in the front door lock and entered Steve's address; the house was silent, just the landing light indicating any sign of life.

Pete tapped lightly on the bedroom door and entered the pitch-black room, whispering Steve's name. The bedside light was switched on by Steve, sitting up with a start, scrunching his eyes in response to the unexpected interruption. 'What the hell are you doing, Pete? It's 2 a.m., for fucks sake. I'm on an early shift tomorrow.'

'Get dressed and come downstairs; I need to talk,' Pete instructed, leaving the room.

'This had better be good. I'm going to be knackered tomorrow.'

Pete headed for the kitchen and grabbed a beer. He took a seat on the sofa and took a drink. He heard Steve walking down the stairs and put the can on the coffee table.

Steve sat to his left on a chair and yawned, still looking half asleep; his hair was all over the place.

'It's all come on top for me, mate. I'm in serious shit. I was locked up for possession of a bag full of Class A drugs earlier. I had it away from a dealer; for intelligence development and ran into a uniform patrol, who wouldn't listen to me.' Pete leaned forward and grabbed his can, creating a dramatic pause by having a drink. The lager spilt down his chin and onto his top. He wiped it away with his forearm.

'Shit, what are you going to do now?' Steve said, looking more alert on the back of the shock disclosure.

'I don't know. I've been suspended from duty. It's all coming on top, mate. I'll have to move out because it puts you in a compromising position.' Pete said, placing his head in his hands. I've given the flat as my bail address; it will be on the intelligence system following the execution of the warrant there.'

'But nobody knows you're here, so it's fine. Where can you go anyway?'

'Not sure, mate. I'll have to sort something out.'

'It's okay with me; you can stay here. Let's just keep it under the radar for now.'

Pete drained the can and stood up, 'This is down to Andrea Statham, mate. She won't be satisfied until I'm locked up. She's got it into her head that I'm bent. I asked her to attend an intelligence interview with me while I was in custody. The only thing she cared about was accusing me of planting drugs in her office. It's as if she couldn't give a toss about convicting Davies and his boys. She's lost the plot, mate.'

'I know, you keep saying that, Pete; you're obsessed with her. But why would she want to do your legs? What has she got to gain? Did you plant the drugs?'

'Did I fuck as like plant the drugs. We've been through all that before, Steve; you know the score.'

'So, what next?'

'I need to carry on and finish the job. I'm close to Wayne Davies and Ryan Young; they're there for the taking. If I can get the evidence to put them away, it will justify my actions and put me in the clear.'

'You'll need to move fast, mate; they'll be looking to get you banged up. I'm surprised you got bail?'

'They talked about doing a deal… maybe they're giving me some time to roll over before they charge me. So, you're right. I need to move quickly.'

'You're good pals with Lee McCann; why don't you speak with him? He's the closest to Andrea Statham. She might even listen to him.'

'I might just do that. But if everything goes tits-up, I might need you further down the line. You could write a statement that I was seeking to bring down the gang, having been presented with the opportunity of getting close to them.'

'I could do that, but I don't think it would work. At the end of the day, you have gone on an unauthorised investigation, a one-man crusade. Using questionable techniques, to say the least.'

'I need to finish the job, Steve; I'll get the evidence and take them down. They have a big arms deal coming soon, and that's my opportunity.'

Steve moved to the edge of his seat. 'Well, if they've got a decent caper coming up, that's your opportunity. What sort of firearms are they dealing with?'

Pete paused and looked Steve in the eyes; he didn't want to tell him too much but wanted to keep him onside. 'Firearms, mate, that's all I know at this stage.' Pete edged forward in his seat, maintaining eye contact. 'Serious shit, If I can nail them on it, it will be the best result the Force has achieved in years. And prevent a shit load of guns from hitting the streets.'

'That is serious shit, mate. Do you not think it's best to let the Serious Crime Squad know? Is it military-grade stuff or bikals and the like?' Steve pressed.

Pete felt uncomfortable with Steve's questions. 'I will tell you when I find out more about it. This is why it's imperative that I keep going after them.'

Steve eased back into his chair and exhaled, 'Christ, mate, I know they were moving shit loads of drugs, but not firearms, too. How can I help you, mate?'

'You're helping me with keeping a roof over my head and keeping it quiet. If I need anything more, I'll let you know.'

'Fair enough, mate.' Steve got up out of the chair, 'Right then, I'll go and try to get a few more hours kip.' As he walked up the stairs, Pete watched, feeling gratified that he had a naïve, clueless wingman in the palm of his hand. He grabbed another can from the fridge. Relieved to see there was a shelf full to drink.

37

Pete slowly opened his eyes and immediately noticed the light seeping into the room through a crack in the curtains. He squinted at his watch, struggling to shake off the remnants of sleep; it read ten to eight. It seemed like he'd enjoyed a quality, restful night of sleep. He rolled out of bed and set about making a coffee. The house was empty, eerily quiet; Steve must have left quietly, being careful not to awaken him.

He took a seat in the peaceful quietness of the kitchen, cradling the mug. The initial hit of the caffeine felt good, invigorating him from his slumber. He felt confident about achieving what he needed to do, but he knew he had to move fast and avoid any attempt by the police to re-arrest him. He suspected they bailed him in the hope that he'd do something rash and not let him run for too long before re-arresting him.

His planning was interrupted by his mobile phone vibrating on the table, still in silent mode. He answered the call even though he expected it to be aggravation from Ryan.

'If you want your drugs back, it's a no-can-do, mate. The cops took them,' Pete said, striking first before Ryan had time to speak.

'I know, I was watching; what were you thinking, you dickhead?' Ryan said as if goading a reaction. Pete was surprised at Ryan's nonchalant attitude to the actual loss of the drugs. He was prepared for a tirade of threats and abuse.

Pete sidestepped Ryan's question, 'We need to work together, Ryan. The cops are all over me, and they're moving in on Wayne's firm; it's only a matter of time. We can both come out of this well and be long gone before Wayne realises we've turned him over. Jason and Wayne have tried to screw you over before, and they won't think twice about doing it again. You need to strike first this time.'

'You sound like a broken record, Pete or an eighties double-glazing salesman; give it a rest. Wayne's not happy; he thinks you are doing a deal with the cops to take us down, to save your own skin; he wants to know why you were interviewed without Frank and how you managed to get bail?'

'That's an easy one. Because I can't trust the fuckers. Wayne wants me dead, and Frank reports back to him. I got bail because I dangled them a carrot, but I was just buying time. I won't be grassing on anyone. Not that Wayne doesn't deserve it.'

'I get it, and I believe you, but you need to trust me. If you behave yourself, I'll see you get paid off and can walk away from Wayne into the sunset.'

'Now, who's sounding like a broken record? Are you not listening to me, Ryan? What part of; the cops are closing in on us, do you not understand? The firm's going to be taken down. Me and you need to get what we can out of this and head off into the sunset before it's too late.'

'Just a minor detail; what are you suggesting we head into the sunset with?'

'Don't be a gobshite, Ryan; you must have access to drugs and cash we can steal from Wayne. And what about the firearms? They've not been shifted yet. We've got enough there to set up our own operation and keep us going for a while.'

Ryan didn't answer. Pete hoped his suggestion was gnawing away at him, tempting him to join forces.

Pete took the silence as a positive, 'Well, what do you say?'

'I say, you stick close to me and don't do anything stupid. Let me sort out the plan, and I'll ensure we come out on top. I'm meeting with Wayne later to discuss the Irish deal. I will need you to work closely with me on that one, but it's probably for the best that Wayne doesn't find that out. Where are you staying?'

Pete laughed cynically, 'That remains a secret. I'm not fucking stupid. I don't want another visit from Hyena and his friends, dumb and dumber. Nor the cops, for that matter. Better you don't know for now.'

'If you're happy that it's safe, fair enough. I've got Jason's old apartment; if you need somewhere else or things turn nasty for you.'

'It's safer than staying anywhere Wayne knows about. And I've got a naïve young cop looking out for me here, who doesn't have a clue about what's really going on,' Pete said, before pausing, wary of giving Ryan too much information. 'I'll be in touch,' Pete ended the call.

He made his way to the kitchen, feeling the relentless need for alcohol clawing at him. He took a can of lager from the fridge. He'd used all his cocaine, so lager was his only other option for now. He fought the strong urge to neck it; he knew he needed a clear head to think straight, looked at the can and then put it back in the fridge.

Pete felt spooked; he'd felt safe at Steve's house until Ryan planted the seed about having somewhere safer to stay. What if Steve felt duty-bound under pressure to give his location away? He'd already told Dave Ferguson about the arrangement. For now, he'd keep moving. Pete locked up the house and headed for his car. It was time for a fry-up and then to score cocaine.

*

The National Crime Agency detectives had left the meeting looking satisfied with the overall plan. Detective Superintendent Samuel, DI Dave Ferguson, DS Lee McCann, DC Steve Comstive, and his cover officer remained behind with DI Andrea Statham to run through the finer details of their involvement in relation to Pete Higgs.

'I know Pete Higgs is small fry from the perspective of the Agency, but we can't miss this opportunity to get him convicted. He's been lucky up to now, but his luck won't last forever. He's had me over as a mug. I should have gone with my gut instincts months ago and nailed him,' Andrea said.

'It's not an issue, Andrea; we were onto him anyway. There's nothing more you could have done. He's been very calculated and cunning, but hopefully, now more complacent. The Irish targets have arrived in Liverpool, so we know the deal is imminent, and we have a good idea of where it will be taking place. Let's introduce the misinformation and see what happens,' Samuel said.

Ryan was sitting on the sofa, watching Wayne pace up and down alongside the floor-to-ceiling windows of the apartment, convinced the pressure was getting to him. He'd seen it all before when Jason Hamilton was running the firm. Ryan was surprised at his restlessness. In contrast, Frank was seated on a stool at the breakfast bar, looking very laid back, flicking through the pages of a broadsheet. Frank tipped his ash onto a saucer in the absence of an ashtray.

'One thing is for sure, Jason had good taste. I wouldn't mind this apartment for myself. The view of the city is idyllic,' Frank said, breaking the tension of the silence.

Wayne stopped pacing and looked out of the windows as if he hadn't noticed the view before. 'I'm sure I can do a deal, Frank,' he said without turning around.

Ryan coughed, 'You'll have to get me out of here first. If we pull this job off, this is mine. I'm nicely settled here, thank you.'

Wayne glanced at Ryan with furrowed eyebrows, 'Well, let's see if you can walk the walk first, Ryan. Don't be getting ideas of grandeur just yet.'

Ryan shook his head, disapproving of Wayne's sly dig but didn't bite back. He took satisfaction in the possibility of running with Pete Higgs's suggestion, leaving Wayne to pick up the pieces, which was still a viable option.

Wayne continued, 'So you've switched to the new burner phone, Ryan?'

'Yes, just for the Irishman, you still use my 899 phone,' Ryan said.

'Are you happy with the decoy plan?'

'Yes, it's all set.'

'Who have you chosen for the decoy run?'

'I'm using Pete Higgs,' Ryan said, with steely deliberation, as if it was the obvious choice, sitting forward in his chair. He waited for a backlash from Wayne. Frank looked up from his newspaper with a quizzical look on his face.

'Like fuck you are,' Wayne shouted, turning back from the view of the city.

'Here me out, Wayne; I'm guessing he will be under surveillance, so he'll take the cops with him. He trusts me, and it allows me to keep tabs on him. Meanwhile, we have less heat on us.'

'Any thoughts, Frank?' Wayne asked.

Frank folded his newspaper, placed it back on the breakfast bar, and nodded his head, 'It sounds like a good plan to me. The bonus is that we can keep an eye on him during this critical time. One less worry for you, Wayne, as you don't trust him. Personally, I think he'll behave himself. I like it, Ryan.' Frank concluded as if declaring the matter was now closed. Ryan nodded to him, then looked over at Wayne feeling more confident and grateful for the support.

'Right, you set the timings for the deal via text and arrive at the plot early. Once you have eyes on the Irishman, call me in. The two vans, one with the merchandise and one with the backup, can be waiting in the layby nearby; they'll blend in well with all the other vans parked up near the burger van. If the cops come sniffing, the backup lads need to create a distraction to allow the merchandise van to disappear.' Wayne said, starting to pace up and down again.

'I'll work from here, the Wi-Fi is excellent, and I have less chance of being disturbed,' Frank said. Ryan was amused at Frank's expertise of never getting his hands dirty and was in no doubt that Frank wouldn't be seen for dust if things went tits up. Rumour had it that Frank had dual nationality, holding a passport for some Eastern European country.

Wayne took a mobile phone from his jacket pocket and handed it to Frank, 'I've put the new burner numbers into the contacts. That phone is only to be used for the banking transaction.'

Frank took the phone and checked the contacts, 'Have you done a test call?'

'Sure have, Frank,' Wayne replied sardonically.

Frank placed the phone into his briefcase and smiled at Wayne, who didn't respond.

'I think that's about it then, fellas. Let's communicate by phone from now until the job is going down. If you have any concerns or last-minute jitters, tell me now, don't risk a fuck up,' Wayne's stare was focused solely on Ryan while he spoke.

38

DC Steve Comstive left the Undercover Policing Unit and got into his car. The drive home wasn't a long one, and traffic was light on the roads. He entered his house, which was rented as part of his cover story for the duration of the operation and deactivated the security alarm. He checked around the place, but there was no sign of Pete Higgs. Albeit he needed to get whatever information he could from Pete Higgs, he was thankful to spend some time on his own. He decided to call Pete after he had had something to eat and drink. Cheese on toast was the best he could muster, simple but delicious. It was a simple snack that rarely failed to hit the spot.

Refreshed, Steve went upstairs to shower and change. He passed Pete's room and couldn't help but notice his bag and other belongings were gone. Steve was surprised and wondered why Pete hadn't told him he was leaving. Maybe Pete had been called to action? Could the deal be unfolding sooner than he had expected? With a surge of urgency, Steve grabbed his phone and made a call. He didn't want to be caught napping. The pressure of failing his objective kicked in; it was time to act.

'Steve, good timing, mate. You seem to have a sixth sense whenever I get the beers in. Do you fancy a few?' Steve felt the tension ease, instant relief. The deal wasn't going down just yet, and he'd located Pete Higgs.

'Good shout, I'll be there in half an hour.' Steve didn't fancy a beer but didn't want to miss an opportunity to gather intelligence and discover if Pete had moved on. He took his work seriously and was committed to the deployment; home life came second.

He pulled the loft ladder down from the hatch and climbed up into the roof space. To the uninitiated, it was a right mess up there, full of boxes and other stuff. Steve made his way to an old television and removed the back panel, accessing the voice-activated recorder. He pressed play and listened to Pete's phone call with Ryan, picked up by the covert microphones discreetly positioned inside the house. Any further information could assist his deployment strategy at the pub. Afterwards, Steve replaced the panel and climbed down onto the landing. He chuckled to himself, *'Naive cop who doesn't have a clue what's actually going on.'* Well, I've been called worse, I suppose,' Steve reflected, taking the comment as a backhanded compliment. He had obviously portrayed his undercover persona just right.

Pete put his phone away and carried the two pints back to the table. Lee McCann was also busy talking on his phone, so Pete placed his pint before him and took a drink.

'That was Steve Comstive on the phone; he's joining us,' Pete announced.

'For fucks sake, Pete, I'm risking my neck meeting you whilst you're suspended. Word will get out if you invite every Tom, Dick and Harry,' Lee said, sounding sufficiently peeved but not too affronted to make Pete consider cancelling Steve.

'Relax, mate, we can trust Steve; he's sound, he's my boy,' Pete said confidently.

'Sound or not, mate, it's against my better judgement being here; but you had my back, so I'll do what I can for you,' Lee said, sure that his bond of loyalty had registered with Pete.

'And I appreciate that, mate; you know I do. But you'll struggle to help me with this; it's a witch hunt, and your girlfriend is trying to convince anyone who will listen that I'm bent and up to no good.'

'To be fair, you're not helping yourself; you've handed her all the ammunition she needs. Uniform stopped you, in possession of coke and heroin, for fucks sake.'

'Lee, you've got to fight fire with fire. We aren't going to take this gang down if we don't push the boundaries. They know every trick in the book to avoid detection. What do we do? Give up because it's too hard to do? I stole the drugs from them for a reaction to rustle their feathers. I was going to the station to book the stash into the evidence store, and the uniform plods fucked it up for me. Andrea and the rest of them don't believe me. I need to finish the job and serve the gang up on a plate with sufficient evidence.' Pete was confident that he sounded genuine and that Lee had been taken in with his latest bullshit version of events.

'So, what's next?' Lee asked.

'Me putting my neck on the line as usual.' Pete knew his answer was evasive but couldn't risk telling Lee too much. His gut feeling was that Lee still wasn't convinced that he was bent but wasn't comfortable with his risky tactics. Probably skewed by Pete having saved him from Jason Hamilton's clutches: a misguided sense of loyalty.

Pete looked along the empty bar towards the doors; Steve Comstive was walking towards them. Steve took a seat at the table, 'I'm ready for a beer, fellas. What are you having? It's my shout.'

'It's my round; I'll get them,' Lee took the orders and made his way to the bar. Leaving Steve to get to work on Pete.

'I've been doing some digging, mate. Apparently, the Informant Unit has a good snout into Wayne Davies's gang.

I reckon you need to talk to Andrea Statham soonest, share your evidence and get some mitigation for the drug possession charge before it's too late. If there's a grass in the gang, you're fucked. Otherwise, they'll just send you down with the rest of the gang,' Steve said, hoping the misinformation tactic requested by Det. Supt. Samuel might unsettle Pete into making a rash decision.

'That's good advice, Pete, he's right.' Lee said, appearing from Pete's blind side with two beers, 'Sorry Steve, did you say lager?'

'Please, mate.'

Pete stood up, 'Easy for you guys to say. You've not got a crazy bitch obsessed that you're bent and trying to get you sacked. Anyway, how do they know it's not me feeding the intelligence from the gang? I do feed the intelligence into Crimestoppers Online, you know.' Pete headed for the toilet. He needed a line to help him to up his game.

Pete entered a cubicle; the door lock was busted as usual. He placed his wallet on the cistern. He felt lightheaded and anxious at the thought of a grass in the firm. He'd never considered there may be an informant operating against the OCG. He cursed himself for making such a schoolboy error. Could it be Ryan? The police may have recruited him at the same time as Carl Smith when they were both in custody, on the last occasion that members of the firm were arrested. Or could it be Hyena? He certainly looked capable of being a police informant. But then again, he probably wouldn't have taken part in his attempted murder. Pete's mind was unsettled and racing with what-if questions flying back and forth. The fact was, he didn't have a clue who the informant could be. Could it be Frank? He set up two lines of coke but caught the side of his wallet, sending it crashing to the floor. White powder spread everywhere. 'Fucking hell,' Pete cursed. That was the last of his batch. His irritability rocketed alongside the paranoia of his ruminating mind. He closed his eyes and took in some deep breaths.

Steve returned from the bar with more beer; he winked at Lee as he sat down. Neither spoke whilst they waited for Pete to return.

Pete returned to the table and took a long drink, conscious that he probably appeared troubled. 'Fucking hell, just what I didn't need. Rachel has just rung me and cancelled my time with the kids this weekend.' It was the best lie he could develop in the time available to cover his rattled disposition. 'Cheers, Steve. I hear what you're saying, fellas, but spilling my guts out to Andrea Statham doesn't guarantee me anything. I need to finish what I've started,' Pete said, picking up on their earlier conversation.

'So, what's their next move?' Steve asked, careful not to sound too keen.

'It's a while off yet, so don't get excited. I've got lots to do before then.' Pete changed the subject to work matters. Since he'd been suspended, he'd lost touch with the comings and goings of the Serious Crime Units and the latest gossip. Having covered workplace gossip and the latest football debates, a silence followed.

Pete didn't want to get pissed; he had work to do. But the lager made up for his wasted coke. 'Right, that's me done, fellas. I've got a hot date tonight,' he necked the remainder of his pint and grabbed his jacket from the back of the chair, 'I'd appreciate a call if there are any developments, fellas,' Pete said; he turned and headed for the doors.

Once outside, he turned right but doubled back once out of sight of the pub and used the cover of a parked van to watch Lee and Steve in the pub. They'd not attempted to follow him or made any phone calls after his exit. Satisfied that they weren't double-crossing him, Pete headed off down an alleyway carrying out his counter-surveillance checks. He couldn't afford to be arrested again: being given bail for a second time would be extremely unlikely. He needed to score some coke. His head was mashed, and regaining his focus was his priority.

39

The lift doors glided open, unveiling a spacious landing area decorated in shades of grey. Pete stepped out and immediately saw the entrance to the apartment. For a moment, he felt vulnerable; images of the flat interior covered in protective clear polythene sheeting flashed before his eyes, just like in the movie scenes. The kind of setup that preceded the victim's grisly demise. Pete feared he may have made a mistake in accepting Ryan's invitation. Was he walking into an ambush, giving Hyena and his cronies a second attempt to kill him? The deadly silence exacerbated his disturbing thoughts; he feared he was walking into the lair of his enemy.

He pressed the buzzer, gripping the concealed knife tightly in his pocket with his other hand. If there was a welcoming committee, he wasn't going down without a fight. The bolt of the lock clicked, and he grabbed the handle pushing the door open. He was presented with a vast open-plan area, a luxury apartment. Ryan was standing at the far side by the floor-to-ceiling windows looking out over the city, dressed in shorts and a T-shirt, not appearing to present a threat. The fears of being tortured vanished instantly as Pete established that no welcoming committee was waiting for him. He was in awe of the decadence before him. This is what he wanted, what he deserved, and what he could still achieve if he played his cards right.

'Not bad, is it?' Ryan said.

Pete continued walking towards Ryan, taking in the view, 'Stunning, mate.' He stopped at the windows, looking out over the city.

Ryan started laughing, 'That view has that effect on everyone.' He walked over to the kitchen and returned to the windows with two beers, handing one to Pete.

'So, this was Hamilton's bolt-hole back in the day; he should have quit whilst he was winning and enjoyed the spoils,' Pete said, walking away from the windows, taking in the surroundings.

Pete followed Ryan to the black leather sofas and relaxed, confident that he was safe.

'Have you thought about what I said? If we pull it off, maybe we could have something like this in Bristol?' Pete suggested, feeling inspired by the luxurious surroundings.

'We don't need to rip Wayne off to make some serious money; we need to work with him. You need to trust me, Pete.'

'I'm talking longer term, Ryan; we should take as much as possible with us and generate more business elsewhere.' Pete took a drink of beer, then rubbed the back of his neck, releasing the stress and tension and feeling more relaxed.

'Trust me, Pete, work with me, and you'll do well out of this caper. If we take Wayne on, it makes us all weaker at a time when we need to be strong and one step ahead of the cops. You don't need to get on with him; it's just business.'

The entrance door opened, and Pete looked over to see Wayne Davies walking towards him. Pete looked back towards Ryan for an explanation, but Ryan showed no reaction. Pete stood from his vulnerable position on the sofa. He swiftly placed his hand into his pocket, gripping the knife's handle. Weighing up escape options as the fear swelled within him. He positioned himself defensively, putting equal distance between himself and the other two, wishing he had stayed at Steve's place.

'This looks cosy,' Wayne said, dropping into one of the seats. He looked over towards Pete and stared at him, 'It obviously wasn't your time, was it? You lucky bastard. Let it be a lesson, don't fuck with me.'

Pete was frantically trying to make sense of the situation and establish whether or not there was an imminent threat; he didn't reply to Wayne. He concluded from the non-verbal behaviour and lack of tension that he was going to be okay. As a precaution, he strolled over to the windows, putting further distance between himself and Wayne, trusting that Ryan was not a threat.

Wayne continued, 'Lesson learned? You don't fucking steal from the hand that feeds you.'

Pete felt the urge to fight back but lacked the appetite for a row, or was it a fear of escalating the chance of conflict?

'Ryan wants me to give you another chance. But I'm wondering whether or not you're of any use to us now that you've been ditched by the cops. I gather you can't access any databases, for starters,' Wayne said.

'I know I fucked up. My head's not been straight. But staging my suicide was a bit over the top, for fucks sake. Let's draw a line in the sand and move on. I've still got the contacts and know how the police operate. I won't fuck up again,' Pete said, not making eye contact with Wayne. Offering the olive branch wasn't easy, but he was in survival mode, focusing on the bigger picture, and swallowing his pride.

'That sounds like a plan,' Ryan intercepted.

'Well, it needs to be because if he fucks up again, you're carrying the can for him, Ryan,' Wayne said as if Pete wasn't present.

Pete was conscious that Wayne was staring at him, attempting to intimidate him or maybe assessing whether he could be trusted. Either way, Pete was no longer feeling threatened. He would work closely with Ryan and tolerate Wayne, for now, knowing at some stage soon he would exact revenge. His hand slid from the knife, and he returned to his seat feeling relieved but remaining on high alert.

'Are we still good to go?' Ryan asked.

Wayne switched his attention from staring at Pete and looked over to Ryan, 'We're cooking on gas, mate, no change from our last discussion.'

'Am I being brought into the loop or what?' Pete asked Ryan, mirroring Wayne's behaviour, knowing it would piss him off. Pete was regaining his confidence by the minute. 'I can be of more help if I know what's going on.'

Ryan didn't answer; he looked towards Wayne for the answer. 'It makes sense, Wayne.'

'You'll be told what you need to know at the time,' Wayne said without giving Pete the courtesy of at least a glance. 'You need to keep a low profile, as discussed, Ryan. Let's keep the police surveillance teams guessing. Be ready to go; it will be short notice when you get the call.'

'No worries, we're ready,' Ryan responded.

'Right, I'm out of here, things to do; people to see.' Wayne left the apartment, Pete instantly felt at ease again, and his confidence returned. 'I'll get us another beer,' he said. To get more information from Ryan, he knew he would need to ply him with alcohol and loosen him up.

*

The following day Pete Higgs gently lifted his head from the pillow; he felt the instant recognition of having had one beer too many, his head was thumping. He could hear movement from the kitchen and smelled the welcome aroma of fried bacon. He got dressed and strolled to the kitchen.

'Have you got any paracetamol?' Pete asked, leaning on the breakfast bar.

'Look at the state of you,' Ryan laughed, 'What a session; you went for it last night. Do you remember searching the kitchen cupboards and hitting the sherry when we ran out of beer?'

Ryan showed no signs of a hangover, which made Pete feel angry with himself once again. The night was a blur. What the hell had he talked about? Ryan slid the tablets across to him.

'I needed a good drink; it will do me a world of good,' he lied to justify the amount he drank as an intentional act, to appear in control of his drinking, which he clearly wasn't. He felt relieved that Ryan hadn't made any gloating references to any drunken disclosures, inadvertently shared in drink.

Ryan slid a pint of water his way and a plated bacon sandwich before him. 'Get that down you. I think it's going to be a long day. Wayne has got a few jobs lined up for us.'

Pete knocked back the water and poured another before helping himself to more bacon. 'What are we actually doing?'

'I'm not sure yet; I don't ask too many questions. And neither should you,' Ryan said.

'Whatever, but it makes us weaker and more liable to fuck ups. I'm getting a shower,' Pete left the kitchen none the wiser.

When Pete returned from his shower, Ryan was chatting on his mobile. Pete tuned into the conversation to get an angle on what was happening. He guessed Wayne was on the other end, as Ryan's participation mainly consisted of 'yes, will do' answers.

Call finished, Ryan turned around, 'Good timing, we've got work to do. Let's go.'

242

Pete hadn't gained any worthwhile information from their conversation and thought it better not to ask any questions. They made their way to the car, carefully checking the vicinity for unwanted police attention.

'The coast looks clear. You drive, take us on one of your anti-surveillance routes for twenty minutes. Let's make sure we're not being followed,' Ryan said, passing Pete the car keys.

After half an hour of meticulous counter-surveillance driving, Pete felt a surge of confidence, gradually replacing his earlier apprehensions. He was in his comfort zone, showcasing his talents to Ryan. The roads they navigated were a confusing rat run, a deliberate choice aimed at shaking off anyone trying to follow. He had utilized every trick in the book; abrupt U-turns, dipping into small alleys, and randomly changing lanes. Each manoeuvre was executed with a meticulous precision that only came from experience.

Finally, as they found themselves heading through a quieter residential area, the surroundings felt devoid of any danger. Pete's sharp eyes continuously scanned the rear-view and side mirrors, assessing and reassessing their surroundings before he looked over to Ryan, 'Will that do you?

'Metro link station, Stretford, we should be just in time,' Ryan said, not mentioning Pete's efforts.

Pete didn't bother asking what they'd be just in time for. He performed a last U-turn and headed for Stretford.

Pete parked the car close enough to see the Metro Link entrance but maintained a reasonable distance from any CCTV cameras. He felt wary of being so close to Stretford police station. The cops often used the metro link to head into town. He put his baseball cap on and slumped back into his seat. He didn't want to be seen.

After a few minutes, Ryan announced, 'They're here now.' He sounded relieved and buckled his seatbelt, ready to go.

Pete looked ahead and saw two wannabe gangsters walking towards the car. 'You're having a fucking laugh, aren't you?' He'd recognised Hyena straight away, 'If he comes anywhere near me, I'll tear him up,' Pete said, glaring at Ryan.

'Not now, Pete, I get it, but not now, stay focused. Save it for later. Your time will come. We've got work to do,' Ryan pleaded.

The back doors of the car opened simultaneously, and the two males dropped into the back seat. Pete couldn't hold back no matter how hard he tried. 'You've got a fucking nerve. I could have you banged up for attempted murder,' he seethed through gritted teeth, glaring at Hyena through his rear-view mirror.

'I just did as I was told,' Hyena said, not sounding as confident as when they last met, 'It was nothing personal.' Pete took some satisfaction in Hyena's discomfort. He looked and sounded fearful. He looked over his shoulder and caught sight of Hyena nervously grinning at him.

Pete felt a sudden rage; he unclipped his belt and dived between the front two seats launching himself at Hyena, landing several well-connected punches to his head. Hyena raised his arms in a futile attempt to deflect the blows while trying to climb over the seat and onto the parcel shelf. Ryan grabbed Pete by his collar and yanked him back into the driver's seat. 'For fucks sake, Pete, leave it out,' He sounded rattled.

Pete gripped the steering wheel hard with both hands. 'When we've finished, I will break your fucking legs. And that's just for starters,' Pete shouted over his shoulder.

'That's enough. We've got work to do. Calm down the pair of you,' Ryan shouted.

'It's not me. It's that crazy bastard,' Hyena mumbled whilst attending to his cut lip, feeling sorry for himself, his mocking grin having disappeared.

Pete continued to glare into the mirror at the other fella sitting in the back. 'Were you one of the lynch party as well,' Pete hissed at him.

'Leave me out of this shit; it's got fuck all to do with me,' he said, avoiding eye contact by staring through the car window. 'I thought we were meeting to brief you about the packages, Ryan, not partaking in a fucking bitch fight.' Pete switched his glare back to Hyena; the colour had drained from his face, and the tension in the car was palpable.

Ryan coughed, 'If you've all forgotten, let me remind you, we've got some graft to do today.' There was no explosion into round two; Ryan was met with silence. He took the opportunity to continue, 'First off, the distraction. Have you two planted the rucksacks as planned?'

'Yeah, all done; the bins had only just been emptied, so they've probably not been found yet,' Hyena said, in between tending to his lip with his tongue.

'Nice one. Pete, a word outside,' Ryan instructed.

Pete joined Ryan at the back of the car, instinctively pulling his baseball cap lower. He felt better for administering some pain to Hyena but knew the job was only half finished.

'Look, mate, I don't blame you for giving him a crack. He did try to whack you, after all. But remember, he was only acting on Wayne's orders,' Ryan said, taking on the role of mediator.

'Don't pretend you wouldn't have done the same,' Pete said, glaring into the car at Hyena.

'Are we done then, for now? Can we get on with business?'

'Of course, let's make some money,' Pete replied.

'They've planted four rucksacks containing dummy bombs around Manchester city centre. We've even added traces of Semtex to keep the sniffer dogs happy. That should keep the cops busy whilst we get on with the proper business.'

'Christ, Ryan, you don't do things by half; that's some distraction,' Pete couldn't hide the surprise in his voice, 'If the cops pin that on you, you won't see the light of day for a long time.' Pete wondered how he could distance himself from the over-the-top distraction plan.

'We need to get this deal done with no fuck ups. It's a proper earner with a guarantee of more to come; their network is massive,' Ryan said. 'The drugs will become small fry, the money is in gun running these days, and Wayne has the contacts.'

'Does he fancy himself as a Bond villain?' Pete scoffed.

'I don't give a shit as long as he pays well. Are you good to carry on?'

'Where to?' Pete said, walking back to the driver's door. His mind was ruminating around the new information. Was it time to jump ship? Maybe put a call in to let them know the bombs were fake? Or was the money too good? He slipped the car into gear and headed for Trafford Park. He needed a big pay day.

40

DI Andrea Statham was trawling through intelligence logs whilst DS Lee McCann was studying CCTV footage. 'Something's bubbling,' Andrea said, hoping to find a golden nugget of information before her.

'I know, they've gone too quiet. Pete Higgs and Ryan Young have disappeared off-grid,' Lee replied. 'Pete didn't give Steve an explanation as to why he moved out of his house. And Steve didn't get a chance to ask; Pete mentioned he was going on a date but wouldn't have needed to take all his worldly goods with him. The last time we saw him at the pub, he looked stressed out of his head. Having said all that, maybe he has just moved in with his new woman, who knows?'

'The surveillance teams had eyes on Wayne Davies yesterday, so at least one of them is still under observation. He met with Frank Burton at their favourite café. After that, he gave the surveillance teams the run-around, almost baiting them,' Andrea said. 'There doesn't seem to be anything relevant in these intelligence logs. Even the logs we thought were misinformation have dried up. I wonder whether the Crime Agency is sharing their intelligence with us or holding stuff back on a need-to-know basis?'

'Is it worth bringing Frank Burton into custody?' Lee mused.

'As a last resort, maybe, we've no concrete evidence on him. It would be a wing and a prayer move. Why would he talk?' Andrea asked.

*

Samuel walked back into the main office, his pace slower than usual. Andrea sensed he was mulling over something important. The atmosphere in the room seemed to thicken, his serious demeanour injecting a dose of tension into the air.

He settled into the chair at the adjacent desk, his movements uncharacteristically slow, as if every action was being measured twice before being carried out. He stared at the desk, lost in deep thought, before the sound of Andrea's concerned voice pulled him back to the present.

'What's up, boss?' Andrea asked.

Samuel cleared his throat, his voice grating slightly as he started to relay the unfolding crisis, 'A Force command gold meeting is being convened urgently in response to a bomb warning we have received at the Force Headquarters.' He paused, taking a breath as though gearing up to continue, 'The caller didn't offer a valid code word, but a patrol has stumbled upon a suspicious device inside a litter bin in the city centre.' The area's being cordoned off, and the bomb disposal teams are attending. It doesn't feel right to me.

Andrea could feel her heart accelerating, and she shared a rapid glance with Lee, whose face mirrored her own. Lee paused the CCTV footage, drawn into the conversation.

'Anyone claiming responsibility for the bombs?' Lee asked.

'Not yet, but they've indicated there are secondary devices,' Samuel replied.

'I smell a rat here; there is no credible intelligence, no codeword, and a mysterious absence of anyone stepping forward to claim responsibility. Adding to this the claim of other hidden devices—it sounds like a distraction tactic.

'Surely, you're not suspecting it's down to Wayne Davies and his cronies?' Lee asked.

'Well, they know we're onto them, and if they are gearing up for a big job like we suspect they are, why not? It wouldn't be difficult to set up.'

As she spoke, Samuel nodded in agreement, 'We can't discard that possibility. We are potentially looking at a strategy to tie up our resources. We'll know soon enough, though, when the Bomb Disposal guys examine the device.'

Andrea nodded. 'You can see what's going to happen here; we'll be losing resources just when we need them,' Andrea said. She selected the incident log for the bomb warning on her computer and began to read through the developments, which consisted of twenty pages already. Half of the bleeding Force is being placed on stand-by already,' Andrea exaggerated. She caught Lee's eye and nodded towards the screen. 'Right, come on, Lee, let's get back to work and find some new leads.' Andrea said, 'Luckily, we still have the crime agency resources.'

'I've finished the CCTV viewing; it's a negative. I'll take a drive and check Pete's usual haunts while you finish the intelligence logs,' Lee reported with a hint of frustration at being office-bound.

Samuel stretched his legs, feeling the tension of the day in his body as he stood up. He rubbed his temples, trying to shake off the headache that was beginning to form as he gathered his thoughts. 'All right,' he said, 'I'll touch base with the Crime Agency. They must have unearthed something useful by now. It's about time we got lucky.'

'While you do that, I will take a drive around and check Pete's usual spots. Sometimes good old-fashioned coppering gets the results,'

Andrea re-focused on her screen, hunting for any further helpful material. 'What's Steve Comstive up to today?' Andrea asked.

'He suspects something's about to happen too after Pete moved out of his house without saying anything about where he was going. Steve's visiting their usual haunts, hoping to bump into him. Pete isn't taking his calls. Steve suspects that Pete has changed phones.'

'That makes sense; he's probably switched to a burner phone. Go and find him. I know just the place for you to start,' Andrea said.

*

Frank Burton was sitting at his desk waiting for Wayne Davies to call. He was fidgeting with an empty cigarette packet. It wasn't like him to run out of cigarettes; coffee would have to suffice for now. His mobile vibrated on the desk, and Frank felt instant relief. He could replenish his stock once the call was done and dusted. It wasn't a call he wanted to take in a public place. His phone continued to vibrate. 'Hello, Wayne.'

'Are you at the apartment, Frank?'

'No, a last-minute change of mind. We can't be certain that the police don't know about it. I'll be safer here.' Frank was a creature of habit and preferred familiar surroundings. Once he'd been left alone at the apartment, an uncomfortable feeling of unfamiliarity swept over him, causing him to head for the safety of his office.

'No worries, are you all set?'

'Yes. How are you doing?' Frank was confident in delivering his part successfully; it was the ability of the others that concerned him.

'Good to go, mate. I gave the surveillance teams the run-around, and I'm pretty confident we have identified most of their vehicles. I'll have plenty of spotters on the ground to distract them if they get in our way. I'm with the truck, the merchandise has been loaded, and we're all set.'

Frank had an itch that he needed to scratch. 'Are you sure Pete Higgs won't be a problem? I'm not sure you've placed him in the best company. Will it not push him over the edge? He would have been of better use on the plot.'

Wayne laughed, 'I knew you'd say that: don't worry, Ryan's there to keep an eye on things, and I've taken some other precautions too. I'm confident he'll do as he's told.'

Frank shook his head; it sounded like a needless bit of sport for Wayne to revel in, maybe a distraction. He couldn't help but fear what the other precautions were but knew better than to ask. 'Okay, I've got a quick errand to run. I'll await your call.' He hurriedly pulled his coat on and headed to the mini-mart for supplies, ready for a long day.

41

'Take a left down there,' Ryan said, pointing down a rough gravelled road. Pete's eyes darted from mirror to mirror, watching for any tell-tale signs of police activity or surveillance before turning. He slowed the vehicle right down, carefully dodging the pot-holes. 'Head for the lock-up at the far end,' Ryan instructed. Pete headed to the far end and stabbed the brake heavily outside the derelict-looking building. He felt a bump as Hyena was thrown forward into the back of his seat. Ryan's seat belt activated; he stared at a smirking Pete and shook his head, 'Knob-head,' he said before reaching across and blasting the horn.

The rusted roller shutters of the lock-up began to creak open, lifting slowly. Pete drove the car forward cautiously into the lock-up. The place was empty, apart from a hire truck and several gang members milling around. Pete scanned their faces; none of them looked familiar. He stopped the car, and the four of them got out. Hyena followed Ryan as if seeking to distance himself from Pete. They approached the group of males standing around at the other side of the unit and joined in the banter and chatter.

Pete stood at a distance, leaning nonchalantly against the car, his arms outstretched on the roof. His posture might have suggested relaxation to an outsider, but inside, a storm was brewing, a knot of apprehension slowly tightening in his stomach. He cast occasional glances at Hyena, who seemed to be feeding off the group's energy, his confidence swelling visibly with every raucous laughter and energetic exchange.

The roller shutter door erupted into action again, breaking the rhythm of the scene. The metallic rattle shook him from his internal turmoil as his eyes found the wiry figure operating the control panel, hidden partly in the shadow of his hoodie.

A pickup truck accelerated into the building towards Ryan's group, engine roaring and declaring its presence with a deafening echo that bounced off the walls. The vehicle made an elaborate entrance, the driver attempting a handbrake turn that was more ostentatious than skilled. The room was quickly filled with a pungent odour of burning rubber, which hit the back of Pete's throat.

Pete watched, almost in slow motion, as a bulky figure with a skinhead wearing a filthy Hi-Vis jacket emerged from the driver's seat, sauntering with an exaggerated swagger towards the group. The man was greeted with a response of derisive banter and taunts about his grand entrance, yet the mocking was friendly, almost endearing. It was followed by a round of fist pumps and man hugs.

As the group's laughter reached a culmination, Pete felt an increasing disconnection from the mirth around him. A quiet yet conspicuous outsider, he was like a shadow lingering on the fringes of their light. The recognition, the acknowledgement he deserved, remained elusive, enhancing his isolation in the firm.

A tight feeling began to constrict his chest as he instinctively pulled out his phone in an attempt to mask his growing discomfort. As he flicked through the posts and images on social media, it served a dual purpose: to shield him from the vivid reminders of his isolation and to grant him a semblance of being engaged and preoccupied.

But no amount of scrolling could drown out the laughter that echoed in his ears, the camaraderie that eluded him. It was a stark reminder that he was on the periphery, not a member of the group before him. It gnawed at him, this unsettling show of a lack of acknowledgement and respect. The time spent waiting, and hanging around, wasn't good, either. Pete's mind ruminated with paranoid fears; could these gangsters be the ones who tried to kill him? He scanned around the vast unit; it would be a perfect place for a second attempt. He became aware of a figure approaching in his peripheral vision.

'Is that your burner phone?' Ryan asked, walking towards him. Unknowingly rescuing Pete from his inner turmoil.

'No, It's mine. I was just switching it off,' Pete lied, covering his mistake.

'Fucking hell, Pete, what part of no personal phones do you not understand? Give it here.' Pete sensed Ryan's irritation and wasn't in the mood to argue. 'No way, it stays with me.' He replied firmly.

'What's the pick-up truck doing here?' Pete asked to change the subject.

'Protection. The pick-up will be following the truck. If needed, the driver can create a distraction or collide with any surveillance cars to prevent them from following. Take a look at this list: check if we have missed anything?' Pete took the piece of paper and looked at the details of the surveillance vehicles listed. Most of them were National Crime Agency cars, but several from his old unit were on the list too. He was begrudgingly impressed at the research carried out on the police surveillance teams.

'Impressive, you've added quite a few to the list I gave you.' Pete added a further two vehicles to the list. 'I got these from my last recce; they've just been delivered,' Pete said loud enough for some of the others to hear and bear witness to his expertise and usefulness.

'Hopefully, they'll be busy with the bomb scare in the city centre. Do you think they'll be reassigned today?'

'Maybe, but I suspect they'll keep a skeleton team on us, minimum staffing to ensure they don't miss a trick. I guess they'll struggle to establish a starting point to pick us up from, so we should be okay.'

'Sounds good.'

'As long as you're not using vehicles known to them: they could pick them up on the ANPR cameras. Have you scanned the vehicles for tracking devices?'

'Done.'

'Who's driving: you or me?' Pete asked, getting impatient.

Ryan shifted uncomfortably on his feet and looked towards the group, chatting by the truck. 'Change of plan. He's driving,' Ryan said, nodding towards Hyena, 'and you're riding shotgun with him. I want you to focus on your counter-surveillance skills. Wayne needs me elsewhere.' Ryan held his stare as if daring Pete to protest.

'You're having a laugh. No way.'

Ryan held his hands up in surrender. 'Wayne suspected that you wouldn't be happy; he's taken a precaution to ensure you stay onside with the plan.'

'What the fuck has he done?' Pete stepped into Ryan's personal space.

'He's got some boys watching your wife and kids, but don't go off on one; it's only an insurance policy. Behave yourself, and they'll be fine, none the wiser. You have my word.' Pete detected a waver in Ryan's voice.

He placed his hands on his hips and looked at the floor, shaking his head. 'You bastards.' Riding shotgun with Hyena was now the least of his problems. Pete turned around, walked a few steps away from Ryan, and returned. 'I thought we had an understanding?' Pete raged, continuing to pace alongside the vehicle, his jaw clenched with tension;

he then punched the side of the vehicle. Ryan reacted by jumping back, out of harm's way. 'You're playing with fucking fire now. You don't fuck with my family. I'll fucking kill you both if anything happens to them,' Pete shouted, his voice echoing around the unit. The group of males stopped in their tracks, quietly watching Ryan and Pete.

'Nothing will happen. I've got your back. You know what Wayne's like. Just don't do anything stupid, and everything will be fine. Seriously. I couldn't tell Wayne not to do it, could I? For fuck's sake, Pete, when will you start to trust me.'

'I hope so, Ryan, for your sake. If anything happens to them, you'll wish you'd never met me.' Pete approached the truck and climbed into the passenger seat, slamming the door behind him. He busied himself adjusting the mirrors, then sat back into the passenger seat and closed his eyes; he needed to compose himself. He should have seen this coming. He cursed himself for being so naive. The thought of his family being harmed was a game-changer.

The driver's door opened, and Hyena climbed into the driver's seat and started the ignition without acknowledging Pete's presence; Pete responded in kind. Both looked ahead as the roller shutter door opened. Pete felt enraged, but he understood the situation. He was between a rock and a hard place, with no way out...for now.

*

DI Andrea Statham drummed her fingers on the desk while waiting for DS Lee McCann to answer his phone. It irritated her that he never seemed to answer his phone, but his laid-back approach to life was one of the things that attracted her to him. She decided she couldn't hang around and went to the car park. Just as she'd plugged the phone on charge, it rang. She quickly unplugged it; hands-free might be too loud, allowing passers-by to eavesdrop. 'Hi Lee, thanks for getting back so quickly,' she said, failing to hide the sardonic tone.

'Sorry about that, I was on the other phone; what's happening?'

'We might have had a bit of luck at last. Pete Higgs's phone has been triangulated; I've done some research, and we might be able to identify a location for him, or at least where he's been, as a starting point.

'Do we still have a signal?'

'No, it's gone dead. I've got a team undertaking a CCTV trawl in the area; let's see who appears on the security cameras.'

'Anyway, I'm just getting into the car at Samuel's office; I'll pick you up in fifteen minutes. We need boots on the ground. We've lost a lot of staff to the bomb threats in the city. Where will you be?'

'I'm just checking outside Pete's old flat to see if his car is outside. It's the last location on my list. Pick me up at the garden centre; I'll ditch my car there.

*

Wayne Davies placed his phone on the table and closed his eyes, focusing on the plan; he ran through it again. Stage one had been easy; he'd sourced the weaponry from trusted contacts, most of whom dated back to his military days and were now involved in the armed security network in the Middle East. Wayne looked at his watch: the shipment would be moving, and the truck would have been on the road for ten minutes by now. He leaned forward and placed the three mobile phones in a line. There was nothing else to do for now; just wait.

The middle phone started to vibrate; a caller ID was not required. 'How's it going?' he asked.

'The truck is heading for the holding area. No sign of a follow, looking good.'

'Okay,' Wayne said and ended the call. He smiled; Ryan had not mentioned Pete Higgs's reaction to the insurance policy; it must have gone well. Ryan had proved himself an effective operator since returning to the fold. Wayne was impressed with him. Not that he would tell him; Ryan worked better when he was trying to impress, under pressure.

Wayne looked at his watch before picking up the third phone. He sent a text, 'No change.' Knowing that the Irishman would probably accept nothing less. Wayne had made a good impression and didn't want to mess it up. He knew there was the possibility of many more deals after this one and the opportunity to enter more criminal markets. Trust was everything, and once word of his effectiveness got around, business would flourish. Wayne had big plans. He sat back and rested his eyes.

42

Andrea watched as Lee McCann approached the passenger door and entered the car. He handed one of the coffees to her and took a sip of his own. Andrea took off the plastic lid and gave it a stir, 'That needs to cool down a bit,' she said, watching the steam rise off the coffee and placing it in the cup holder. 'Have you heard anything from Steve Comstive?' Andrea asked expectantly.

'Not yet, he's visited everywhere he can think of where Higgs might be, but there's no trace of him yet.'

'And it's the same story with Wayne Davies and Ryan Young; this is no coincidence, Lee.'

'I know; they certainly don't want us to find them.'

'Or rumble their next drugs shipment, to be more specific.'

'This distraction in the city centre is no coincidence. It's got their signature written all over it. No terrorist organisation has claimed responsibility,' Lee said.

'There's time yet; some crank will want their hour of fame.'

The hands-free ringtone interrupted them. Andrea reached out and knocked down the volume before answering. Lee instinctively closed his window, shutting out any potential eavesdroppers whilst carrying out a 360-degree recce of the immediate vicinity. 'Hi, boss, you're on hands-free speaker. I'm out in the car with Lee.' Andrea always warned the caller when using hands-free to avoid embarrassing disclosures to unintended parties; she'd been there before.

'We've had a great result with the local authority CCTV footage trawl. Working outwards from the location where we traced Pete Higgs's mobile phone, we kept the time and location perimeters tight, and it's paid off. The CCTV viewing team are still working on the footage, but we have identifications of Pete Higgs, Ryan Young and others. The activity is around an old warehouse off the A56. We have footage of them leaving the area in a rental truck and a positive identification on the registration plate.'

'That's a great result, Excellent.' Andrea gave a thumbs-up to Lee and continued, 'Where's the last sighting?'

Samuel gave the location and the truck's details, which Andrea scribbled down on the back of the tatty police vehicle mileage logbook. Samuel continued, 'We've already got covert ANPR camera markers in place to locate the truck, and the surveillance teams are in position, ready to react.'

'I'll get my team to commence inquiries into the warehouse and truck rental company. In the meantime, I'll touch base with the Video Imaging Evidence Unit and get the fast-track lines of enquiry moving.'

'I'll make my way to the Crime Agency major incident room. Meet me there when you've sorted your stuff out. It's essential that we have a presence there and can have our say. I'm sure this will be a fast-moving operation once we're onto them. We need to be involved in the decision-making process,' Samuel said before ending the call.

Lee was busy talking on his mobile as Andrea finished her call. He was tasking their team members with inquiries concerning the warehouse and truck. All lines of investigation at this stage had to be covert so the OCG weren't alerted that the police were onto them, a point which Lee drove home to the team. The last thing he wanted to do was tread on the toes of the National Crime Agency, but at this time, no one had eyes on the suspects, so all lines of enquiry were worth pursuing.

Andrea checked out the location on the A56 on her phone. 'Samuel has just clipped my wings. He wants me back at the Crime agency major incident room. That's maybe a good thing; I'll be aware of updates as they happen and keep you informed.'

'Unlucky, the privilege of rank, I suppose,' Lee mocked, 'I'll hook up with Steve Comstive. Maybe we can locate Higgs and get the Agency back on track. You can drop me off outside Old Trafford on your way if you don't mind.'

Andrea gave Lee a sideways glance of mock disdain, 'Anything else, sir? Before I return to the office.'

*

Pete Higgs found himself studying Hyena as he manoeuvred the truck from the track onto the A56. He looked comfortable behind the wheel in his jeans and black hoodie and handled the vehicle with ease. Pete guessed this wasn't his first time in the role. His ability suggested that he had experience; Pete guessed he'd probably been nicking cars since he was a teenager and was now a trusted getaway driver. In his jeans and hoodie, Hyena looked like any other delivery driver speeding around Manchester, trying to meet ridiculous delivery time expectations. He was satisfied that Hyena's quiet disposition was a sign of subservience or fear even. Suspecting he did not want to goad Pete into a reaction he would live to regret. Pete was content with that for now.

Pete's mind flicked back to his family, he wondered whether Ryan was bluffing about having Rachel and his kids watched. He aired on the side of caution that it probably wasn't a bluff. Wayne had tried to have him killed once already, the motive was there, and he was more than capable of carrying out his threat. But he felt confident that

Wayne would also be aware of the severe ramifications that would follow if anyone laid a finger on them.

Pete looked over at Hyena again; he knew he could overpower him if needed and give him some more payback; he was extremely tempted. But the risk to his family was more important. He still held the hope of a reconciliation with Rachel at some stage, even though the chance was extremely slim. Surely, she'd understand when she learned of the immense pressure he'd been working under to crack this case.

Another thought entered his head. Should he telephone Rachel and warn her of the threat? No… An option but a course of action that could get messy; Rachel would naturally panic and call the cops or do something unexpected. He quickly made a decision to go with the flow and keep his options open. He convinced himself they were safe, for now, so long as he acquiesced with the plan. His attention returned to the job. Hyena was still focused on his driving along the A6, paying no attention towards his passenger, which suited Pete.

'What's in the back of the truck?' Pete asked.

'Shooters,' came the reply; Pete began to process the information with trepidation. 'Kid's shooters, you know, water pistols,' Hyena said, grinning for the first time since they had set off. 'They look realistic. The cops will think they've hit the jackpot when they first clap their eyes on them.'

A memory of the police busting into his flat and finding water pistols flashed across Pete's mind. He tried to ignore it. 'Where are we going?' Pete asked. Hyena's grin and joviality disappeared instantly. He suddenly looked uncomfortable. 'Ryan said you don't need to know… Are you sure the police aren't following us?' Pete found it comical that Hyena was trying to play the tough gangster. He was more tempted than ever to give him a good kicking.

'You've been on the A56 for too long. Turn off and drive around a few blocks. If you told me where we're going, I could do the job properly, you fucking idiot,' Pete goaded, unable to refrain from including a dig at Hyena. Pete sat back, satisfied that he'd re-addressed the balance. He intended this to be his last job with this firm. He would walk away with a big payday and take time out, maybe abroad, to get things back on track, whether Ryan came on board with him or not. He wasn't bothered either way. Pete placed his hands behind his head. Good times were on the horizon.

*

Lee opened the passenger door and stepped into Steve's car. The music grabbed his attention. He glanced at the media display, 'I never had you down as a Seventies fan. Thought you'd be an eighties new romantic kind of guy, you know, big hair and mascara.' Lee said with a smirk.

'No way, Saturday Night Fever all the way, for me, mate,' Steve replied, tapping the steering wheel over-enthusiastically.

Lee turned the volume down, 'That's better; I can hear myself think now.' Lee updated Steve on the rental truck's sighting and discussed possibilities of where it could be heading.

'Well, it's not a bad lead. The truck is going to ping an ANPR camera at some stage, surely.'

'Maybe, but not if Higgsy has anything to do with it; he's familiar with the camera locations and knows all the rat runs to help avoid them.'

'Well, it explains why I haven't been able to locate him. I even looked at his home address. We can't rule out that the split with his wife could have been a ruse. I couldn't hang around for too long, though; a couple of scrotes were parked around the corner, watching his address.'

'Maybe Higgs's bitten off more than he can chew and pissed them off. It sounds like an act of intimidation to me.'

'Or looking after them for him, I've submitted an intelligence log for limited dissemination. It was a gang pool car; lots of intelligence linking it to Wayne Davies's boys. I couldn't get close enough to identify the occupants. Anyway, the Incident room staff will be aware now. It's worth putting a surveillance team on them if they have any teams available.'

Lee's phone started to ring; he glanced at the screen, hoping Andrea was informing him of a positive update.

'Girlfriend checking up on you, eh?' Steve asked with a smirk. Lee gave him a disdainful look from the corner of his eyes.

'We've got eyes on the rental truck. The surveillance team are on its tail. It looks like they're heading to Trafford Park to me. I'll keep you updated,' Andrea said.

'Nice one, Andrea, looking good. We'll head over in that direction in case we're needed.' Lee ended the call and looked towards Steve. 'We're on; let's make our way over there,' he said, ignoring Steve's mocking grin.

43

'I think they're onto us,' Pete said with anguish, edging forward in his seat to get a better view through the wing mirror. 'That white van is following us, definitely. Pullover outside those shops on the left.' Pete had clocked the tell-tale signs of a surveillance unit operation; he'd hoped he was wrong whilst studying the manoeuvres of the van. But now he was in no doubt.

'We're nearly there; shall I not just carry on?' Hyena replied, not taking his eyes from the road ahead of him.

'What, and lead the police straight to the meeting place? Are you completely fucking stupid?' Pete asked, feeling a wave of irritation building.

Hyena burst out laughing, 'I'm fucking with you,' he said and drove the truck to the side of the road. Pete felt perturbed by his attitude. Considering the cops were probably onto them, Hyena didn't appear bothered by it.

'Wait here.' Pete climbed down from the cab and walked into a sandwich shop. There was a queue, which worked in his favour; it bought him time to stand and watch for surveillance vehicles. He stood by the window, looking out at the traffic. The white van had continued along the A56; no surprises there. It would stop ahead and park up, awaiting to continue the surveillance once the target vehicle had passed by. In the meantime, another vehicle would replace it and take pole position as the lead surveillance vehicle; in a rotation system. Pete suddenly felt a wave of nausea when he saw a motorcycle speed by; he'd definitely noticed it travelling behind them earlier. He was now in no doubt; the police were onto them.

Pete left the shop and stood by an old telephone box, which provided sufficient distance and cover from the road. He was scanning around the vicinity for any foot surveillance operatives. A strong urge to flee and leave the fallout for Hyena to deal with flowed through him. He felt physically sick. He grabbed his burner phone from his pocket.

'Ryan, the cops are onto us.' As Pete said it, he understood there was little Ryan could do to assist him other than change the plan or abandon the truck.

'Are you sure? I thought you were keeping a watch out?'

'Of course, I'm fucking sure. I was keeping a watch out, Einstein; that's how I know we're being followed,' Pete barked back, gnarled at Ryan's glib comeback.

'You need to go to the alternative location and ditch the truck,' Ryan said. Pete was about to answer when he saw a police patrol car park up behind the rental truck. 'Shit, it's coming on top here, a cop car has stopped behind the truck. They're moving in on us, to strike.' Pete experienced a severe dose of flight or fight; every bone in his body was seeking an escape from this mess, and his legs felt like jelly.

'Get out of there, Pete,' Ryan said, 'there's nothing more you can do now.'

Pete looked around; it would be easy to slip away. The terraced streets and alleyways provided a network of escape routes. He could climb into a backyard and lie low if he needed to hide. Pete fought the urge to run just yet; he continued to watch the scene playing out before him. Hyena would probably be the fall guy if the cops pounced, which wouldn't cause him to lose any sleep. His mind was in overdrive, assessing options, too busy to reply to Ryan.

Ryan ended the call after Pete didn't answer his question; he knew Wayne wouldn't like what he was about to hear. 'The cops are following the decoy van. Higgs reckons he has spotted the surveillance vehicles.' Ryan kept it short, awaiting the flak that was likely to follow.

'Do you think he's grassed us up?' Wayne asked deadpan; he was like a dog with a bone where Pete's loyalty was concerned.

'No way. He was in a bit of a state, probably shitting himself. He knows the score,' Ryan said, hopefully quelling Wayne's paranoia and preventing a knee-jerk reaction in relation to Pete's wife and kids.

'You need to tell him that if I find out he has been double-crossing us, telling the cops everything, he's a dead man walking.' Wayne clenched his jaw, locking eyes with Ryan. Ryan squirmed in his seat; he knew what Wayne was insinuating, questioning whether he could still trust Ryan due to his misguided loyalty and belief in the bent cop.

'He knows that. And he knows you're having his family watched. He's onside. Let's not lose focus here, Wayne. Let's get the deal done with no fuck ups.'

'Tell them to keep driving. Delay their arrival by half an hour. We'll be done and dusted by then,' Wayne said. Ryan got straight onto his phone to pass the instructions, relieved that Wayne hadn't wanted to escalate matters with Higgs's family, bringing on Armageddon.

Wayne walked a few steps away and made a phone call too. 'How's it going down there?' he asked.

'No change. We've had to park around the corner. We would have attracted too much attention at the front,' came the reply from the watcher outside Pete Higgs's house.

'I want to make sure the bent cop knows we're serious. One of you knock on the door; I want a photo of you talking to his wife. And keep your back to the camera, for fucks sake.'

'No worries. I'll text it to you, Wayne.'

Wayne returned to Ryan and stood by the car. Ryan looked around the disused railway yard, satisfied that his lookout boys had all angles covered. The corroded tin roof of the platform canopy gave them sufficient cover from above. The old carriages created convenient obstacles for concealment and protection from being ambushed unexpectedly.

Wayne shifted on his feet. He reached to his waistline and touched the pistol stock tucked behind his belt. Ryan watched and instinctively felt for his pistol too. Its presence reassured him. But it was a last resort that he hoped wouldn't be needed.

*

DI Andrea Statham left the major incident room. She needed fresh air and, more importantly, to be out on the ground. Andrea wanted to be involved if Pete Higgs and his cronies were being arrested today. She felt the urge to have a cigarette for the first time in a good while but fought off the cravings, deciding a caffeine hit would suffice. She headed out of the building for the nearby drive-through.

She activated the hands-free, 'Hi Lee, are you free to speak?'

'Yes, you sound like you're in your car.'

'I am; the briefings are finished for now. Mr Samuel is staying in the incident room, so he will keep us updated.

'Any news?'

'The suspicious packages in the city centre have been confirmed as fake improvised explosives. All police resources have resumed normal duties. The surveillance is progressing; it looks like Higgs is running some counter-surveillance to catch us out, so it's still not clear where they're heading, but my guess is still Trafford Park. I'm concerned that we've not seen Davies and Young yet.'

'Maybe they're already at the rendezvous point. They clearly don't want to be caught with their hands on the gear. They've got mugs like Pete and his accomplice to risk doing that.'

'Where are you heading now?' Andrea asked.

'Well, if your hunch is right, they're probably heading for the premises where they were followed to the other night, the place that Samuel briefed us on. I'll head towards there and lie low; if the surveillance and strike teams appear, I'll be ready to tuck in behind them.

44

Pete retreated further from the telephone box; he stepped cautiously towards the storage bins containing brushes, spades, and other household tools on display outside the hardware store. They provided cover from the truck. He expected the vehicle door to swing open and Hyena to do a runner, but the driver door remained closed. Maybe Hyena hadn't seen the uniformed cops? A uniformed policewoman exited the patrol car and walked towards the sandwich shop. Pete watched her every move; she joined the queue and appeared to be studying the menu board. Not showing any obvious interest in the truck. Pete felt a wave of relief. His legs felt drained of energy; it was time to get away. He pulled on the peak of his baseball cap, covering his eyes and headed for the truck. Panic over, for now. He quickly glanced around one last time, then climbed back into the cab.

'How far away from the destination are we?' Pete asked, trying hard not to sound ruffled.

'Almost there, less than a mile,' Hyena replied, his expression blank, 'Well, are they following us?'

'It feels like a game of cat and mouse. They have probably realised we are onto them, so they'll probably change tactics,' Pete said, studying the wing mirrors.

'What now then?' Hyena asked.

'Right then, one final detour, drive around the next block; let's see if we can lose the cops for good.' Pete studied the vicinity, his heartbeat thundering in his ears, bringing every ounce of concentration to bear as he peered out of the car windows. He knew the area well and felt up to the challenge. He couldn't see the white van with the sinister-looking, blacked-out windows or the motorcycle. Pete felt like he was back to square one, looking to identify any surveillance vehicles. He focused hard whilst Hyena resumed the journey, swinging the vehicle into a sharp left turn. Pete watched carefully for the reactions of the drivers behind them. He continued to order a series of instructions on directions, which Hyena dutifully followed. The streets of terraced houses were a perfect environment to lose the surveillance teams.

A vibration from Pete's phone interrupted his concentration. He cursed, not wanting to take his eyes off the traffic behind them. Pulling his phone out, he saw he'd received a photograph: Rachel and his kids were outside their house with the puppy on its lead. Rachel appeared to be talking to two hoodies. His heart began to pound, and anger instantly overtook him. He studied Rachel's face. To his dismay, she looked concerned. It didn't look like a pleasant situation. His mind started to race; had the bastards threatened them, or even worse, taken them hostage? He needed to get to them now, to look after them. Or should he call the cops? Pete noticed a line of text under the photograph. 'Behave yourself, and they will be fine.'

The truck stopped suddenly outside an industrial premises close to the Manchester Ship Canal. His focus flashed back to the present. In a panic, Pete hastily checked the mirrors, realising he'd not been watching out for the police surveillance teams. His head had been elsewhere, in a dark place. He couldn't see any vehicles, but they wouldn't allow themselves to be close enough to be seen anyway. Pete felt helpless and out of his depth; he'd have to go with the flow from here. There was nothing else he could do now. It was too late.

Hyena waited for the door to open, then drove the truck inside. To Pete's surprise, there was a scene of normality before him, a busy operational warehouse, workers going about their usual routine. A forklift truck was driven across their path, causing Hyena to stop the wagon.

'That's us done,' Hyena said whilst grinning, 'I'm out of here.' His voice irritated Pete to distraction.

'What the fuck's going on?'

'We were just a decoy, mate,' Hyena said before dropping from the cab and walking towards the exit door. Pete watched in disbelief as a guy in a hard hat and high visibility vest shouted, 'You can't park the truck there, mate.' Pete knew he needed to get on his toes; it was time to leave. He headed for an exit sign marked 'stairwell'. It looked like the quickest option to leave the main warehouse.

As he opened the door, he heard the sound of tyres screeching. He saw two covert police vehicles skidding to a halt behind the truck, blue lights flashing from behind the radiator grills. He felt confident they'd not seen him as they approached Hyena and the wagon, weapons drawn, yelling 'Police, get on the floor,' and other instructions. He watched in disbelief as Hyena made a run for it towards the main entrance. Pete winced, expecting to see him dropped by a bullet. The dog handler had released an Alsatian. Pete watched as it jumped and clamped its jaw around his arm. Hyena released a piercing scream followed by a torrent of expletives as he fell to the floor, struggling in a futile attempt to escape.

Pete was just about to escape through the doorway when he noticed Lee McCann. He cursed when he realised Lee had seen him; they held eye contact for a moment before he let the door go and headed up the stairs at full pelt.

45

Wayne's mobile phone began to ring. Ryan watched with eyes widened in a concoction of exhilaration and anticipation as Wayne answered the call. Ryan felt a buzz of excitement, certain that the call was from the Irishman and that the deal was imminent, at long last. The firm's biggest deal was about to happen.

'We're here; where are you?' The demanding voice that emanated from the phone carried a hardness; the edges of the Irish accent sounded menacing, maybe a throwback to Wayne's time in the army.

'Just hang fire there for a minute. My boys will check that the cops have not followed you and then direct you to us.' There was a clinical precision to his words, betraying no hint of a pounding heart that Ryan expected mirrored his own. Wayne ended the call and immediately made another. 'Can you see them?' He asked, his focused voice breaking through the tension.

'Yes, they're next to the coal bunker, as requested.' The response came back quickly.

'How many vehicles?'

'Just the transit van. I can see three in the front. I don't know if anyone is in the back.'

'Any sign of backup or cops?'

'No.'

'Okay, mate. Show them through.' Wayne ended the call and placed the mobile in his back pocket. Wayne looked at Ryan, 'This is it, mate. Let's get on our game. No fuck ups.' Wayne initiated a fist pump as the tension grew.

'I'll send the text,' Ryan said. He took out his phone and texted the group, '*It's on.*' Ryan's attention was immediately taken by a diesel engine approaching from between the disused railway carriages lined up on a siding and the decrepit buildings. A silver van came into view and headed towards them. It stopped ten metres away, and a bald man stepped out of the vehicle, six feet plus tall, with a heavy build. Dressed all in black, he portrayed an intimidating presence.

'That's Pat, the guy I met last time,' Ryan said, as if to fill the gap, as the male approached them.

'No shit Sherlock,' Wayne replied with raised eyebrows. Ryan laughed and put his comment down to excessive nervous energy.

'Good to see you, Pat. I hope the ferry ride over wasn't too choppy.'

'Good afternoon, gentleman. Let's have a look at the merchandise then,' Pat replied in his familiar strong Irish accent. Ryan sensed a hint of impatience in his manner and observed that he certainly wasn't as laid back as he was at the previous meeting; he felt the growing tension hanging heavy in the air.

'I'll call them in. They're not far away,' Wayne said.

'For fucks sake, we haven't got all day, boys. Let's get the deal done, eh?' Pat said. He turned about and headed back towards his van, shaking his head. 'They're not fucking ready, fellas,' he shouted towards his accomplices whilst raising his arms into the air.

'Who's rattled his cage?' Ryan asked, surprised at the Irishman's reaction, watching him walk back to the van.

'He's just flexing his muscles; he probably wants a discount on the price,' Wayne laughed and called for the merchandise to be brought to them.

*

Lee sprinted after Pete, ignoring the developing scene by the rental truck, satisfied the armed officers had the situation under control. He swung the door back and ran through, narrowly avoiding it hitting him as it rebounded back. His heart was pumping fast from the sprint. There was only one way to go; he headed up the stairs, his thighs were burning, but he was determined to catch Pete Higgs. He passed the third floor, wondering how many more steps there were, surprised at how fast Pete Higgs had ascended them. His lungs were on fire. Surely Pete couldn't be too far ahead of him. Lee suddenly feared that Pete had somehow exited the stairwell and feared he'd overlooked an exit, but he was now committed. Reassuring banging noises came from above, confirming he was still heading towards his target.

He reached the top of the stairs and saw the roof access door ajar. Nothing but blue sky beyond it. Thankful for the chance to get his breath back, he cautiously stepped through the doorway, prepared to defend himself against an attack by Pete Higgs.

Lee stepped out onto the flat roof of the building, and he immediately saw Pete Higgs ahead of him. Pete looked knackered; he wasn't the fittest. Lee placed his hands on his hips to help get his breath back and slowly walked towards Pete, who continued walking ahead, albeit with nowhere to go. There was a surreal peacefulness in the slight breeze and blue sky surrounding them.

'It's over, Pete. Let's go back down. There's nowhere for you to go,' Lee shouted, relieved to be getting his breath back.

Pete continued walking until he reached the low brick wall at the roof's edge. He glanced over the edge, peering down at the parked cars below. A blanket of dizziness overwhelmed him, not helped by the exhaustion he was suffering from following his sprint. The drop induced a rush of blood through his veins and fear that gravity was about to pull him over the edge. He turned around and wiped the sweat from his forehead and stinging eyes. Lee continued walking towards him.

'Don't come any closer, Lee, that's enough; stay back,' Pete shouted breathlessly and stepped onto the wall of the building edge. He watched as Lee stopped and bent over, resting his hands on his knees.

Pete frantically looked around for an escape route, feeling gutted there was only one access point from where he had entered. There were no adjacent buildings to jump across to either, like the action scenes in the movies. This is it, he accepted. Nowhere to go.

'Christ mate, be careful,' Lee shouted, 'come away from the edge; you're making me feel jittery.'

'I'm fucked, Lee. I might as well take a jump and end this mess now. The best result for everyone,' Pete said, becoming aware that his hands and legs were trembling.

'Just step away from the wall for now; I'll stay back here and get my breath back,' Lee said.

'I need you to arrange for a patrol to attend my house. These fuckers have threatened my family.'

'Okay, you step down, and I'll make the call,' Lee said. Pete stepped off the wall and sat down on it, his head in his hands.

Lee telephoned Andrea and asked her to task a patrol, purposely loud enough for Pete to overhear the conversation. He gestured towards the armed police officers, slowly advancing towards them, to stay back. 'It's sorted. A patrol is on its way to your house. They'll get back to us ASAP with an update. Your family need you, Pete, especially your kids; you need to be here for them. Rachel knows the pressure you've been under; we all do. Just come away from the edge, mate. We can sort this out.'

Pete looked up, 'I'm fine here.' He felt trapped, and his mind began ruminating through his fears; prison was a certainty, and he couldn't contemplate life behind bars.

'Where are the others, Pete?'

'They've used me as a decoy. I don't know where they are. I've been blackmailed for some time now. I've had to comply with their requests; otherwise, they would have harmed my family,' Pete said, facing the floor, mitigating his actions the best he could. He didn't want his kids to be ashamed of him.

'Is there someone you can call and find out where the deal is going down? Help us to find them, Pete, do the right thing. It's what Rachel and the kids would want you to do; put away the bad guys.' Lee paused, letting his words sink in.

'I suppose I've got fuck all to lose,' Pete said. 'But what do I get in return, Lee? I'm the victim here, just trying to protect my family.'

'I'll do all I can for you, Lee, you know that. But I can't make false promises. You have to trust me,' Lee said, discreetly glancing at his watch.

'I know the score, pal,' Pete said, sounding broken and defeated.

'You need to help me so I can help you, Pete. Can you ring anyone to find out where the deal is happening? You need to help me nail these bastards. We don't have much time.'

'I'll give it a try,' Pete mumbled. He grabbed his phone and made the call. Lee took the opportunity to give a

278

thumbs up to the firearms officers, indicating he was in control.

'Is it urgent, Pete?' Ryan answered.

'Did Wayne set us up, Ryan? The cops are all over us. We're surrounded here.'

'Did he fuck, mate, I promised you that I'd look after you, and I will. Keep your mouth shut, and I'll make it worth your while.' Pete laughed cynically, 'Yeah, of course you will.' Pete heard the familiar distinctive noise of scrapyard breaking machinery in the background. He'd heard it before; it was next to the disused railway sidings, a location used regularly by the firm.

'I've got to go. The Irish lads have just turned up, Pete. Trust me, mate. No one has set you up.'

'Where are you?' Pete asked, albeit he already had a good idea of their location.

'It's better you don't know.' The phone went dead.

Pete looked towards Lee, who was in the process of sitting on the floor a few feet away from him. 'I take it he wouldn't tell you?' Lee asked, sounding disappointed.

'No.' Pete paused, deciding whether or not to tell Lee where he thought they were. He felt tired and burnt out. Pete knew that if he let himself go, he'd fall over the edge, gravity would do the rest, and it would all be over; the option appealed to him; he just wanted out. He'd had enough.

Lee's phone interrupted them, bringing Pete back to the present.

'Fantastic, great news, I'll tell him,' Lee said. He looked at Pete, a pathetic version of his former self; Pete looked dejected and desperate. It took Lee back in time to when they were both being held hostage by Jason Hamilton, tied up, bloodied and bruised. 'Rachel and the kids are fine, mate. They are safe at your house.'

'Cheers, Lee, you're a top fella and a great cop. I'll miss you, pal. You'll find Wayne Davies and Ryan Young at the disused railway sidings next to the breakers yard. They're about to sell some firearms to an Irish cartel. You'll catch them if you're quick; get over there, mate.' Pete pulled himself up, stepping back onto the wall. 'Tell the family I love them, and I'm sorry.'

Lee lunged forward. Pete had manoeuvred himself into a position where his legs dangled over the edge. Lee managed to get Pete's head in an arm lock restraint and pressed his back into the wall for leverage. Lee was struggling to take Pete's weight. Pete started to lash out at Lee's head, shouting, 'Let me go, Lee.'

Lee didn't have the breath to shout back. Pete heaved with all of his might; he felt himself slowly sliding over the edge. There was a jolt; Lee had released the headlock and grabbed Pete's arms. Pete was now fully hanging over the side. He looked up to see the determination in Lee's contorted face but could feel Lee's grip slipping along his arms towards his hands. He was confident that Pete could not hold on for much longer; Pete began to swing his legs to gain momentum and make Lee's grip loosen.

The firearms officer grabbed Lee's legs shouting, 'Let go, he's going to take you with him.'

Lee didn't have the chance to let go; he no longer had the strength to hold on; he screamed out with the realisation that he had lost his grip.

Pete felt a wave of relief as he slipped from Lee's grasp and fell away from the building, falling towards the ground.

A thud, followed by the wailing of a car alarm from below, prompted a flood of activity. One of the firearms officers immediately grabbed his radio, requesting medical assistance and police uniform response to attend at the scene, outlining the circumstances to control.

Lee slumped down by the wall, for a moment, before pulling himself together. As difficult as it was, he couldn't let Pete's demise incapacitate him. He had to act on the information Pete had given him and informed control of the suspected location of the arms deal.

He stood up and began walking towards the stairs; a firearms officer shouted after him, 'You need to wait here for the debrief. You're not in a fit state to carry on. Come back, mate.'

Lee continued walking, the operation wasn't finished, and there was nothing more he could do for Pete Higgs. He felt a mixture of numbness and tiredness spread through his body. But he knew he had no option but to dig in and keep going.

46

Lee headed for the staircase, His head swilling with mixed emotions; could he have done more to save Pete? Was it right to just carry on? How would Pete's kids feel when they found out about their dad? He took no satisfaction whatsoever from seeing Pete's demise. Lee was shocked that Pete had decided to kill himself. Albeit he'd made choices which resulted in this mess, a shitstorm of his own making, he was a desperate man. A sober realisation hit home that it could easily have gone wrong during the attempted rescue, and both of them could have tumbled over the edge to their deaths.

Lee headed down the stairs and attempted to regain his focus; he still had work to do. Pete had brought it on himself; he'd decided to go down the path of corruption. But Lee still couldn't understand it being a reason for suicide. As Lee walked down the stairs, he felt physically sick; he needed to get busy and to occupy his mind.

DI Andrea Statham answered her phone, 'Are you okay, Lee? I've just received the update. Is he dead?'

'Yes, I don't want to talk about it right now; I'll tell you about it later. I'm fine, but things might be getting even better. I've just texted you a What Three Words location: the disused railway sidings beside the dodgy scrapyard. That's where Wayne Davies and Ryan Young are doing the arms deal right now. I've informed control, and they are dispatching patrols right away. I'm heading over there. I'm only ten minutes away.'

'I'll see you there. I'll let the major incident room know I'm making my way to the railyard,' Andrea said, her voice subdued.

Lee entered the main warehouse from the bottom of the stairs. The scene before him was now under control. All police vehicles, but for a van, had left, most likely on their way to the railway sidings.

Lee could hear someone shouting from the prisoner cage in the van's hold. 'I'm going to sue you for these dog bites. There was no need to let the dog loose. It's police brutality. Where's Higgs? Have you let him get away, you bent bastards? You're all the same. He put me up to this. I've done nothing wrong.' One of the officers slammed the van's rear doors closed, and the shouting became muffled. The officer threw the first aid kit onto the front passenger seat and shook his head.

Lee ran over to his car. He couldn't see Steve Comstive and didn't have the time to find him. Lee guessed Steve had probably grabbed a lift with a patrol and was also on his way to the railway yard. Andrea needed backup, and he had to get there fast. Now he wanted to round up Davies and his cronies and finish the job.

*

The box van pulled alongside Ryan's car. The two couriers stayed seated in the cab, with the engine still running, as instructed by Wayne. The box van was followed into the yard by a white people carrier. Wayne got the driver's attention and pointed to where he wanted the people carrier to be parked. The driver gave him the thumbs up and positioned the van between Ryan's car and the Irish contingent. Wayne needed his backup close by in case things went pear-shaped.

Wayne and Ryan walked to the rear of the box van; Wayne flipped the roller shutter open. As expected, the back was full of rough timber wooden boxes with rope handles at each end stacked high.

Pat and his two associates joined them at the van's rear, 'Better late than never, eh, fellas?' Pat said, staring at Ryan. 'Get into the back, Liam. Check four different crates.'

Ryan felt convinced that Pat had an edge on him today. Gone was the jovial, laid-back attitude he displayed at their last meeting. Maybe, Wayne was right, and this was his game face. He also had to look the part in front of his boys. Reputation was important.

'If there are any issues with items, now is the time to tell us, fellas. We wouldn't like to get back over the water and find any problems, would we, Liam,' Pat said, looking into the back of the van. Liam was sweating; he'd been moving the boxes about to gain access to those lower in the stack. 'These boys wouldn't turn us over, Pat. The last thing they want is for us to feed them to the pigs. Eh, boys?' Liam answered without looking up from his inspection.

He was now holding a Kalashnikov, with the butt tucked into his shoulder whilst he looked through the sights. He then cocked the weapon, looked into the chamber, and then released the action by pressing the trigger. He continued to carry out a general inspection of the firearm. Ryan watched carefully. This guy was no stranger to weapons. He handled them like a pro. Ryan guessed he looked old enough to have been involved in the troubles, not someone he wanted to upset.   After the long wait, Liam placed the firearm back into the wooden grooves in the box and replaced the lid. Liam continued, having left everyone hanging on his comments about feeding the pigs, 'For sure, Pat, that would cause unnecessary difficulties for everyone. No need for it, Pat.' Liam's voice was quiet, with a strong accent. Ryan could only just make out what he was saying; his accent was stronger than Pat's. But he understood the general gist.

'Well, what do you think?' Pat asked, 'Don't keep the boys waiting, Liam.'

'I need to check a few more, but they're okay up to now, I suppose. I've seen worse,' Liam said, opening another crate and taking out a Glock pistol for a similar once over.

'Okay, boys, so far, so good,' Pat said. 'Do you need to tell me anything before we do the deal?' Pat's tone was menacing. Ryan was starting to feel anxious; he couldn't put his finger on it, but something didn't feel right.

'It's all there, as per the agreement, and it's all good quality stuff,' Wayne said, matter-of-fact, taking control, 'I only deal with military contacts who are known to me personally, people who I have visited several times. Trusted people.' Ryan couldn't help but be impressed with Wayne's words and his delivery style. He was more than holding his own in the face of the implied intimidation. Ryan just hoped Wayne was right; he feared upsetting these guys.

'Pass me the Glock, Liam.' Liam leaned down from the back of the van, supporting himself on a hanging rope, and handed Pat the pistol. Pat pulled back the working parts and inspected the chamber. His movements were slick. He moved towards the van's edge and stripped the pistol down into its component parts, placing them on the van floor in a line. His speed and familiarity were impressive; Ryan watched, taken aback by his skills.

'Okay, how much can you knock off the price as a gesture of goodwill?' Pat asked, staring Wayne in the eyes intensely. Deadly serious.

'No discount, we have agreed on the price. Goodwill will come further down the line when we have established a good business relationship,' Wayne replied. He held Pat's stare and looked totally unfazed. Ryan felt uncomfortable. He feared there could be trouble ahead.

Pat laughed, 'Fair play to you. I'll get onto our banker to transfer the money.' Pat walked back towards his van, speaking on his mobile phone.

*

DI Andrea Statham had managed to get alongside an old signal box building. She didn't want to risk getting any closer until uniformed and firearms backup arrived. She had spotted several lookouts in positions around the railway yard.

Andrea could identify Wayne Davies and Ryan Young from this distance. She sent a confirmation of the sighting to the Incident Room and requested that the armed response units put their foot down. For now, Andrea would watch and wait from a safe distance. Her phone started to vibrate in her pocket; she checked the caller ID and saw it was Lee.

'I've got eyes on them. There's a white box van containing the weapons and four other cars. Young and Davies are both here together with the buyers.'

'How many people?'

'It's not easy to see, but I'd say around eight, excluding the look-outs.'

'Okay, sit tight until the cavalry arrives. These lot won't fuck about. They'd shoot you rather than look at you. See you in five minutes.'

Andrea was conscious that she'd made an error. She wasn't wearing a protective vest, but it was too late. She didn't want to risk being seen going back to her car to get it.

Det. Supt. Samuel spoke to Andrea on the telephone and confirmed that the teams were almost at the scene. He, too, emphasised the need for her to keep her head down. Andrea slid behind an old rusted metal tank full of water.

*

Pat walked back to the rear of the box van. Liam had climbed down and was wiping his hands on a cloth rag. 'The money should be in your account by now. Tell your boys to get out of the van; we'll take it from here,' Pat said. He was gesturing to Liam to drive the van.

'Hold your horses, Pat. I need to confirm we have the money before that truck goes anywhere.'

'Fuck me, boys, did you hear that? The man doesn't trust us,' Pat said, looking over his shoulder to Liam and their accomplice.

'Liam grumbled something, but Ryan couldn't understand what he said.

Wayne walked back to the car and got into the driver's seat. He put his mobile to his ear, 'Frank, have we received the funds?'

'No, nothing yet,' Frank replied.

'Okay, stay on the line until we have confirmation.' Wayne watched Pat walk to the box van cab and try the door. The handle flipped, but the door didn't open. Pat looked towards Ryan, 'What the fuck's going on? Do you not trust us, seriously? We need to shift this stuff; we're like sitting ducks here, waiting for the cops to arrive. Are you setting us up, Ryan?'

'You know the score, Pat, it's cash on delivery. We weren't born yesterday,' Ryan said, trying hard to put on a professional front.

Pat scowled at him, 'No, but you're still fucking amateurs.'

Wayne watched as the situation appeared to be getting more heated. He was feeling more concerned, 'Frank, any sign of the money?' Wayne asked impatiently, the tension clearly apparent in his voice.

'No, they've not sent it. It would have registered by now as it did on the practice runs. You need to get out of there, Wayne,' Frank said. Wayne hung up and was about to get out of the car, but stopped in his tracks when he saw what was unfolding by the box van.

Liam walked casually towards Ryan, his hand simultaneously moving to the small of his back. Ryan sensed what was about to happen but was too slow to react. Liam produced a pistol from his belt and grabbed Ryan around his neck in a headlock, yanking him backwards, off balance, and pushing the pistol to the side of his head.

Pat simultaneously started to bang on the cab window, yelling, 'Open the fucking door, or we'll shoot him.'

Ryan was overcome by panic; he had no doubt that Liam wouldn't hesitate to pull the trigger to show he meant business. He slid his hand to his waist to feel for his pistol and released it from his belt. He positioned the pistol behind him, holding it tight, pointing in the direction of Liam's gut and pulled the trigger. Instantly Liam's arms slipped from around his neck, and he fell to the floor, dropping his pistol, clutching the gunshot wound. Ryan bent down and picked up Liam's pistol before backing away from him.

Wayne had drawn his pistol and thrust his arms straight ahead, pointing the weapon at Pat, who raised his arms into the air, looking over his shoulder at Liam on the floor. 'Let's not get excited, boys; it's a misunderstanding, that's all. He's always been a fiery fucker, he just gets nervous, that's all. You must have spooked him, boys.'

Wayne didn't answer. He signalled to the driver of the box van to leave the yard. As the vehicle set off, they were interrupted by the sound of screeching tyres and over-revving engines, along with flashing blue lights reflecting on the box van and other nearby vehicles.

47

Andrea instinctively ducked down further behind the water tank when she heard the unmistakable sound of a gunshot. When no more shots followed, she slowly peeped over the top, expecting Ryan Young to have fallen to the floor. Andrea was shocked at witnessing an assassination and felt helpless to do anything about it. But, surprised, she saw it was the man holding the pistol to Ryan's head, who had fallen to the floor clutching his abdomen. Confused, Andrea noticed a pistol in Ryan Young's hand and suddenly felt vulnerable without her protective vest and helmet.

While she tried to understand what the gangs were shouting at each other, their voices were suddenly drowned out by the arrival of several armed response police cars, black tactical SUVs with blue lights and headlights flashing. Armed officers began decamping from the vehicles, taking defensive positions and shouting commands for all present to drop weapons and get down on the floor.

Andrea continued to watch the situation as it unfolded before her. A car suddenly accelerated away from the approaching police officers. She spotted Wayne Davies behind the wheel. He sped past the box van, away from the police officers, in an obvious attempt to evade capture.

Ryan Young sprinted towards the car, waving his arms in the air at the Wayne Davies. Andrea knew she was too far away to intervene and stop Ryan Young from getting into the car. But surely, they wouldn't get far. The area was swarming with police patrols. To her surprise, Wayne Davies didn't slow down to pick him up; he continued accelerating, driving at speed away from the scene. Ryan Young looked astonished; once the car had sped past him, he turned about and started sprinting towards the rail carriages before disappearing out of sight behind them. Two armed officers gave chase, but Young had at least a one-hundred-metre start and took full advantage of it.

Andrea felt a wave of adrenaline and panic surge through her veins. Ryan Young was heading straight towards her position. She sat tight, considering her next move.

Several armed officers surrounded the box van. The two occupants slowly exited the cab with their hands in the air and lay on the floor, placing their hands behind their heads in response to the commands of a firearms officer. An officer, covered by his colleagues, cautiously crept forward and fastened plastic ties around their wrists. More officers began to advance and detain the rest of the gang members.

*

DS Lee McCann had followed the convoy of vehicles into the rail yard. He watched as the armed officers quickly took control of the scene, grabbing his protective vest from the car's boot at the first opportunity. Scanning the area, trying to locate Andrea, he couldn't see her and was becoming anxious. He telephoned her mobile, but it went straight to voicemail. Where the hell was she? He guessed she had arrived already. Had Davies taken her hostage?

Lee decided to make his way to the signal box building. Hopefully, she was still tucked away in a position of safety. He sprinted across the yard and climbed over the coupling mechanisms between two rail carriages. He cursed as he nearly slipped off because of the thick black grease and oil which now covered his hands and clothing. Using the cover of the carriages, he ran alongside them, heading towards the signal box, listening to the updates from the armed officers on his radio.

*

Ryan was fuming; he'd never experienced anger like it before now. Why hadn't Wayne stopped to pick him up? Wayne must have thought he had a better chance of escaping if it was every man for himself. But Ryan knew he had to channel his anger into focusing on getting away from the rail yard. It was now a matter of survival, every man for himself, whilst the cops were busy at the van.

He approached the end of a line of carriages and slowly looked around. He couldn't see any cops nearby and evaluated that his best chance was to head towards the building in front of him and then into the adjacent scrap yard. He knew some of the lads who worked there; maybe they would help him to get away concealed in the boot of a car. He knew he had to be quick because, from experience, the police dogs and helicopter wouldn't be far away.

He was just about to step off when he heard something. He paused and stood perfectly still, listening, straining his ears. His worst fears engulfed him; it was a police radio. They were following him and weren't far behind. He scanned the area, fear swelling within him of being gunned down by the police. The fear almost made him instinctively walk out from the cover with his hands on his head. He didn't want to die.

From his position, he saw Lee running in the same direction as he was heading; relieved that it wasn't the armed officers, he raised his pistol and fired a shot. He watched as Lee fell to the ground, amazed that he'd managed to hit him.

There was no other option. Ryan had to go for it; the sound of the gunshot would draw the attention of the cops towards him. Murdering a cop would attract a life sentence if they caught him. His next challenge was a ten-metre dash across open ground to reach the cover of the building. It would give him a short respite, time to consider his next move, the quickest way into the scrapyard. It was his best chance to get away.

On reaching the building, Ryan jumped to the floor, taking cover behind a pile of wooden railway sleepers and overgrown vegetation. He lay still, his heart pounding from the sprint from the carriage. He scanned the area, no sign of any cops. Maybe the cops were following a thorough, time-consuming systematic search. It was an opportunity for him to use the time well.

*

DI Andrea Statham felt focused and prepared. She had steadied her breathing and was ready to prevent Ryan Young from escaping. Fighting with the odds stacked against her was nothing new. She had experienced and survived a tough apprenticeship as a uniform cop on London's streets and deprived housing estates.

Having watched Young sprint to the signal box, she expected him to continue his escape using it as cover. She guessed he would approach along the left side; the other side would be difficult underfoot because of all the debris dumped there. The confrontation was inevitable; it wasn't in her DNA to take the easy way out.

Andrea pressed her back flat against the wall, at the edge, as close to him as possible without being seen. She was motionless, listening for the sound of him approaching. Her knuckles were white, fists clenched tightly. Then she heard the footsteps on the loose stones, faint at first but getting louder as he approached where she stood. The next footstep would bring him into view; her heart was pounding. Andrea knew she had to make the most of her element of surprise.

At the first sight of movement in her peripheral vision, she jumped out, simultaneously screaming at the top of her voice like a banshee. The tactic worked; Andrea was relieved to see the shock on Ryan Young's face. He looked stunned, scared even. The reaction boosted Andrea's confidence.

Before he could compose himself, she connected a punch with her right fist into his nose. He staggered backwards and tripped over, falling back. Andrea followed him, her body dropping on top of him in an attempt to wind him. She saw the pistol fall to the floor, then landed another punch in his face. This time there was no element of surprise. He'd had time to regain his composure and punched her back, connecting with the side of her head. A blinding light flashed across her eyes, followed by intense pain, as if she'd received an electric shock. Reality dawned on her. She was now fighting for her life.

She managed to get an arm around his neck and engage a headlock, curling herself up into the foetal position to present a smaller target, squeezing his neck with all the strength she could muster, but cold fear began to spread over her.

'I'm going to fucking kill you, Statham,' Ryan shouted, his voice feral.

Andrea frantically scanned around. Stopping him from retrieving the pistol was now her priority. Too late, she saw the pistol in his hand. Andrea broke away, rolling away from the building. The fight had become flight; survival was now her priority.

'Fucking stand up, bitch. You couldn't leave us alone, could you? Well, I hope it was worth it.'

Andrea slowly got to her feet and staggered to the wall of the building for support. She prayed that her colleagues had heard her scream and were trying to locate her. Escape now was an impossibility. She had to buy time; it was the best she could do to save herself.

Ryan raised the pistol, pointing it directly at her head. Andrea maintained eye contact; any human bonding could buy her time. 'Why have you let it get to this, Ryan? Threatening to kill a police officer isn't the answer. Is this what you really want? You'd escaped it all once; Kirsty was proud of you. What would she think of you if she was here now? Give me the gun; you know you don't want to kill me.

'How the fuck do you know that Kirsty was proud of me?'

'She told me, Ryan.'

Ryan appeared agitated. 'Fuck off, I'm not stupid. I know you're trying to play mind games. Turn around, face the wall with your hands up.'

Andrea realised mentioning Kirsty hadn't had the desired effect; in fact, the opposite. She slowly turned around.

*

When he heard the gunshot, Lee McCann instinctively fell to the ground to take cover. Once satisfied that no other shots were being fired, he edged alongside the carriage for cover. Lee watched as Ryan Young sprinted towards the signal box. His body tensed with trepidation. He guessed Ryan was heading straight to Andrea; if she was still there. He felt a surge of fear, not for himself; he had to save her. The thought of Andrea suffering ripped into him.

Lee sprinted towards the signal box building; he decided it was shit or bust. He had to stop Young. There was a mighty scream; he recognised it was Andrea. Engulfed with horror, Lee found extra energy, hitting full pelt; he was almost there.

Lee tripped and fell to the floor; the jagged stones ripped into the skin on his hands. He looked up, expecting to see Young approaching him; he was that close to where he suspected they would be. But he wasn't there. Lee grabbed an iron rail joint, picked himself up and sprinted at full speed.

On reaching the signal box, he saw Andrea and Ryan Young only feet away. His confidence swelled, and he charged at Young with one intention, to grab the pistol. As if in slow motion, he saw Ryan Young look towards him, a look of shock and surprise spread across his face as he pointed the pistol towards Lee.

A survival thought ran through Lee's mind that he should run in zig zags to present a difficult target. But he reluctantly accepted in a heartbeat that he didn't have time; he was too close.

Ryan fired the pistol. Lee felt no pain; he was ecstatic at the realisation that Young had missed and launched himself at Ryan, smashing the piece of iron into the side of his head. Ryan went to the ground, with Lee landing on top of him. Ryan looked winded. Without hesitation, Lee welted him on the side of his head with the iron casting a second time. Ryan instantaneously went limp. Lee felt a mixture of elation and fear that he'd saved Andrea but may have killed Ryan.

He grabbed the pistol and swung around towards Andrea. 'Are you okay?'

Andrea sank onto her haunches. 'I am now… You took your time,' she laughed. As the adrenaline began to subside, her head started pounding following the blows inflicted by Ryan Young.

Two armed officers approached as Lee placed Young in a recovery position. He was breathing but unresponsive. The police medic crouched beside Ryan, 'Good effort, mate. I'll take it from here.'

Lee and Andrea hugged whilst the police officers tended to Ryan. 'I think we need to get you checked out at the hospital; a couple of nasty cuts there,' Lee said, checking her over.

'You were just in time.'

'Do you think he would have shot you?'

'Thanks to you, I didn't need to find out.

48

A few months had passed before Andrea and Lee met with the Crown Prosecution lawyer, Lynne Brand, and the Crime Agency Detective Inspector, Shaun Osgood. Their respective teams had been extremely busy since the armed strike at the derelict railway yard.

The Video Imaging Unit were probably the most active, trawling the significant scenes and routes to capture evidential footage. They located new evidence and further evidence to corroborate the existing case from CCTV.

The meeting lasted over three hours, and the prosecution file was handed over for the CPS to evaluate. The CPS would then assess the evidence and prepare for the prosecution in court. During this process, more work would be generated for the investigative team to ensure the case was watertight.

Shaun Osgood declined to join Andrea and Lee for a drink afterwards; he had another meeting to attend. They walked to Deansgate, mixing alongside commuters heading for home. Andrea slipped her hand into Lee's, 'The canal shooting that set this in motion seems a long time ago. Obviously, we'll never convict Jason Hamilton. Do you believe Ryan Young that a Colombian cartel was responsible for killing Hamilton?'

'I'm not convinced about who pulled the trigger, but I believe he's dead.'

'There's a lot of work to do to build a case against Wayne Davies to prove that he was the accomplice on the canal. We'll probably struggle to convict him of Smethurst's murder.'

'Maybe, at the end of the day, it hinges on the word of Ryan Young, but Davies is looking at twelve years anyway for the other offences, so it's not a bad result.' Lee reasoned as they turned into Bootle Street and headed for one of their favourite city centre pubs.

They found a table in the corner. It was buzzing with early-evening drinkers; the place had a good vibe, and they both had many happy memories of good times there.

'Shaun seemed impressed with the evidence; that's a good start,' Andrea said after savouring her first sip of prosecco.

'The evidence is solid, and we got them all remanded in custody. We're fine. We probably didn't need Ryan Young to turn Queen's evidence, but I suppose it may strengthen the case.'

'He'll have to make good use of any reduced time the Judge gives him to disappear. Once Davies gets out, he'll be after him; I can't see Davies letting him get away with that,' Andrea said.

'And that's if they don't get to him on the inside. He may have been remanded to a secret prison location. But the lags in prison can find out; he's up against it.'

Lee broached the subject they had both been avoiding. 'I'm gutted I didn't save Pete; I almost did. It was so close.'

'You did all you could, and there was nothing more you could have done. The firearms officer said you were lucky not to go down with him.'

'I suppose so; I was lucky he grabbed my legs and hung onto me,' Lee said quietly.

'Pete knew the risks, and he took them, but going to prison wasn't an option for him. If you had saved him, I'm in doubt he would've had another go at suicide.'

'It's his kids that I feel sorry for; let's hope they'll manage to live with it and move on as best they can.'

The barman approached their table carrying a pint of lager and a large prosecco. 'Compliments from the gentleman at the bar in the black suit.' They both looked towards the bar as the barman placed the drinks on the table. Frank Burton smiled back with a friendly wave from his bar stool.

He asked me to pass on a message, he said, *some you win, some you lose* and sent his best wishes. The barman said before continuing to collect empty glasses.

Frank turned away from them, conversing with the shady-looking guy standing beside him.

Printed in Great Britain
by Amazon